The Secret Letters From X to A

PRAISE FOR THE SECRET LETTERS FROM X TO A

"A deeply affecting work. Nasrin Parvaz succeeds in conveying the intense fear and claustrophobia of what it must be like to live under any intolerant, fundamentalist regime. Even reading the story felt like a subversive act in itself.

It raises challenging issues, especially for those of us who are lucky enough to live in more broad-minded societies. There is a warning too, not to take our own freedoms lightly. I came away thinking that no truly humane society can be built on a foundation of extremism, whether that be right-wing or left-wing. We should be genuinely fearful when any kind of politics is more concerned with adherence to strict ideologies than having empathy for individual human rights."

Rhiannon Lewis, author of *My Beautiful Imperial*
(Victorina Press, 2017)

"Stories are the frailest and most ephemeral of weapons, and yet they may be all we have to fight the multiple forms of power that oppress us. In a story about story-telling, resistance and love set in Tehran in 2002, *The Secret Letters from X to A* offers us a nail-biting account of a young historian who finds a secret cache of letters hidden in an interrogation centre he has been hired to transform into a museum. The letters from the past weave their way into the present, changing the life of the protagonist and putting his own hidden love at risk.

Written by an award-winning poet and former prisoner who lived some of the stories she recounts, this eloquent and thoughtful novel interrogates what it means to live under a regime where everyone can be considered "a prisoner who [hasn't] been arrested yet." In a time when democracy is increasingly under threat and when hidden truths are rising to the surface, this story resonates with universal significance far beyond its time and place.

Catherine Temma Davidson, author of
The Orchard and The Priest Fainted

The Secret Letters From X to A

Nasrin Parvaz

First published in Great Britain in 2018 by Victorina Press
Adderley Lodge Farm,
Adderley Road,
Market Drayton, TF9 3ST
England

Typesetting and Layout: Heidi Hurst
Cover painting © Nasrin Parvaz
Cover design © Fiona Zechmeister

British Library Cataloguing in Publication Data
A catalogue record for this book is available from the British Library.

ISBN: 978-0-9957547-7-5 (Hardback)
ISBN: 978-0-9957547-3-7 (Paperback)

Typeset in 11pt Minion Pro
Printed and bound in Great Britain by Charlesworth Press

In memory of all those who entered this so-called museum
as prisoners,
particularly those who were never able to leave.
May their stories survive within the walls of the museum-
behind-the-museum,
until I hope, one day, they can be told.

CONTENTS

FOREWORD

History is written by those in power. In Tehran you can visit a historic circular building once known as the Joint Committee Interrogation Centre, later renamed Towhid by the new regime. Closed down in 2000, Towhid opened again in 2003 with a new identity: the Ebrat Museum of Iran, exhibiting displays of torture that supporters of the Islamic Republic maintain were committed only under the Shah's regime and never under their own. 'Ebrat' means 'warning'. Children are frequently taken there on school trips.

Chapter One

A FAMILY VISIT, TEHRAN, 2002

One evening in June, Faraz was watering the garden when he heard the doorbell ring. His father called out, 'I'll get it.' Faraz's girlfriend Nasim, who was sitting reading, jumped up and went into the hall to peer through the window. On seeing who it was, she immediately ran upstairs. Faraz's Uncle Rohulah strode in like an intruder, though perhaps he realised that if he had called first, some of his brother's family would have stayed in their rooms, pretending not to be at home.

It was more than a year since Faraz had seen his uncle; he wasn't happy to see him. Every time they met, Faraz discovered something new about Uncle Rohulah that he didn't like. Now Rohulah seemed to take up all the space, making it difficult to breathe. Faraz even felt the scent of jasmine sucked out of the air.

'Faraz, I have a job for you. The money is good.'

They sat on the carpeted veranda floor where Ana, Faraz's mother, was painting a small watercolour. She quickly put it behind the wooden pillar, so Rohulah couldn't see it.

After greeting her brother-in-law and asking about his wife and children, Ana poured tea from the samovar. There were all kinds of fresh fruit in a large engraved copper tray, as well as dates and pastries.

'Have some of the cake. It's from yesterday, Faraz's twenty-seventh birthday.'

'Inshalah, we will one day be eating your wedding cake,' said Rohulah to Faraz.

Faraz did not respond. As ever, Uncle Rohulah reminded him of the night he learnt about his cousin Forood's death. He had been just seven years old when, late one evening, he was woken by the sound of missile defence and overheard his parents whispering.

Now, looking at his uncle, Faraz wondered what kind of human being he was and how strange that Forood could have been so different. How close the two families had been until Forood's arrest, while after his death they never saw each other. Nima and Rohulah, his father and uncle, were estranged. Normally once a year his uncle came to see them, but Nima didn't visit Rohulah's family at all. Sometimes they met at a wedding or funeral but greeted each other as strangers.

Until he grew up, Faraz always thought it was only teachers who treated children and women as equal to men. Although his father was a teacher, it was his love of Forood that had influenced Faraz to become a teacher, too. His older cousin had been his role model, his hero.

Faraz's mind jolted back to the present. His uncle and father were talking about the job offer and Nima was speaking through gritted teeth, 'Which interrogation centre is it?'

'The Joint Committee. We want to transform it into a museum.'

'What kind of museum?' asked Nima.

'Prison museum. They have one in London. The supreme leader and many of the ministers spent some time in this interrogation centre during the Shah's reign. We're going to show how the monarchy tortured prisoners.'

'What about its use for the last twenty years? Are you going to show that as well?' Nima enquired.

Rohulah avoided his gaze. He stared at the fountain pouring water endlessly back into the little pool. Faraz felt the tension in the air. He could hardly believe this was why his uncle had come.

'Well, we didn't use it as much as they did.'

Although his father was angry, Faraz was intrigued by the thought of getting inside the interrogation centre. He assumed that the only way to go in was as a prisoner or interrogator, or as someone else who worked there, like his uncle Rohulah. Faraz's heart beat faster as he remembered an ex-prisoner describing to him how they used to communicate with each other. He had laughed as he told Faraz that some of his letters were still there, because they had all been transferred without warning and his friend couldn't take them.

Faraz watched his uncle Rohulah dip a cube of sugar into his tea and put it in his mouth. He slurped noisily from the cup.

'What do you say? Would you like to work there during the summer?' asked Rohulah, biting into a baklava. 'It's very good money.'

'Why are you asking us?' Nima demanded, trying to control his anger.

'I have to recruit trustworthy people. I trust only my family.'

Faraz thought how ironic that his uncle, who didn't trust his son, was talking about his trust in his family.

'I'm sorry. I'm too old for such excitement,' Faraz's father said.

'What about you, Faraz?'

Although he was sorry for hurting his parents by accepting the job, Faraz didn't hesitate. The chance to get into that terrible place and see where Forood had been held, to understand something of what had happened to him, was too important to miss. 'Yes, okay then,' he said. 'When does the work start?' He was grateful his parents weren't going to humiliate him by challenging his decision in front of his uncle.

'Next week. Can you be at the front gate next Saturday morning at eight?'

'Yes, I'll be there.' Faraz saw the gleam of triumph in his uncle's eyes.

Rohulah left and Faraz looked at his parents. They were deeply upset.

'How can you bear to go there?' asked his mother.

'I want to see where they locked up Forood. Was he tortured there as well?'

'Of course he was. They wanted information about his friends.' Nima almost spat the words.

Faraz had never seen his father so angry. 'Did Uncle interrogate Forood?'

'He told the chief interrogator that he didn't want to see him or hear anything about him, and they could do whatever they wanted to convert him to Islam and make him collaborate with the "state of god",' Nima snapped.

'What did Uncle do when Forood was executed?'

'He said there should be no difference between the treatment of our sons and other people's sons. Infidels, spies and anyone who undermines national security or revolts against our holy leader should all pay with their lives,' growled his father.

'So, he believes in equality, then?'

'Yes, sure.' Nima paused for a second before asking, 'Why are you involving yourself in this?'

'I'm keen to see this prison for myself. They'll convert it into a museum anyway, whether I help or not. Someone else will do it if I don't,' Faraz argued.

'You can go and see it when they turn it into a museum,' shouted his father, his face wine red with anger.

'No. I want to see it now, while it's still the place where people went through the doors as prisoners, not as visitors. I want to see the place that Forood saw. I want to see it before it gets sanitised.'

Their raised voices brought Nasim out on to the veranda. Seeing her startled expression, Faraz stood up. He took her hand and led her away, upstairs to their room. He sat on the sofa and pulled her small body on to his lap. Their heads and faces were at the same level now.

'What's going on?'

'I accepted a job my uncle offered, and my father thinks I shouldn't take it.'

'What job?'

'It's to help convert a prison into a museum. A summer job.'

'And you accepted?' Nasim's jaw dropped and her eyes widened.

'Why shouldn't I?' He touched the back of her neck. It

was a year now since she had stopped shaving her head, yet her hair was still short.

'He must be paying a lot. Do you need money?'

'It's not for the money. Anyway, someone else would do it, if I don't.' Faraz shrugged. He needed to have her in his arms. He tightened his palms around her waist, not letting her move away. She froze.

'Think about it, Faraz. That someone else is ready to do it is the worst justification for accepting.'

'But I want to see it before it changes.' He kissed her. 'Please try to understand. I want to see what all those prisoners saw.'

'You're wrong if you think you'll see what they saw or experienced there.' She looked at the floor, stiff in his arms.

'You trust me, don't you?' Faraz kissed her head. He put his finger under her chin pulling her head up. Her brown eyes were clouded with disappointment.

'What's your uncle up to? Why you?'

'I'm not sure. It is very strange.'

Chapter Two

FALLING IN LOVE

One year earlier, on his way home after school, Faraz had called in at a garage near his house. A new young mechanic crawled out from under a car and said hello to him. Faraz felt there was something strange about this young man, who would be handsome if he changed his clothes. The young man walked towards him with an easy manner and asked what he could do, before suddenly looking at his feet whilst Faraz explained what the problem was with the car.

'It makes a funny noise. I think it needs looking at.'

'Sure. I'll look at it after I finish the one I'm working on. Are you in a rush? Do you need it for tomorrow?' By patting down his clothes and trying to shake off the dust he avoided making eye contact with Faraz.

'No, I can come and fetch it whenever it's ready. You're new here, aren't you? I always bring my car here and I've never seen you before. What's your name?'

'Nasim. I started here six months ago,' he said, still trying to avoid Faraz's gaze.

'I see. I think I brought my car here about seven months ago. How is Agha Morteza?'

'He's fine. He's not in today. He'll be here tomorrow.'

'Shall I call you to see when I can collect the car?'

'Yes. Or we can call you when it's ready. Agha Morteza must have your number.'

'He does.'

'Then we'll call you.'

'Thank you. Nice to meet you – and have a good evening.'

'You too.'

Faraz walked away, but before turning the corner, he looked back at the young man, who was watching him. Faraz pretended he was looking at something else and began to walk faster. He felt confused by his sudden feelings for Nasim, especially as he'd never felt anything for a man before. He wondered about the name Nasim, which was one of the rare names used for both boys and girls.

That evening he went to the Art Café to see his friend Bahram.

'Something's happened?' Bahram said immediately.

'No. Nothing.'

'Are you sure? You look lost. I could swear that something has happened to you. Your face is like a mirror to your mind. Some people can hide their emotions. You can't. At least, not from me.'

'Have you ever fancied a guy?' blurted out Faraz.

Bahram burst out laughing. 'What are you talking about? Anyone can be gay I suppose, but not you, surely.'

'I thought so, too, but I felt something for a young man I met today. I'm confused. I still feel confused. And I'm sure that he felt the same.'

'Really? You mean he is gay?'

'I don't know. But I could tell that he felt something for me.'

'Nowadays everyone is becoming gay or lesbian in this country. Perhaps I should suspect myself of the same,' Bahram said, laughing.

'I'm serious.'

'Where did you see him?'

'At the garage where I dropped off my car.'

'What's his job?'

'He's working there.'

Again, Bahram started to laugh, even harder than before and this time Faraz laughed too.

'Well, you can laugh but it's still pretty weird for me,' said Faraz.

'How long has it been since you had a girlfriend?'

'It's about four months.'

'Yes, I think it's time to find you a new girlfriend. I'll ask mine if she thinks any of her friends deserve you.'

'I don't need your help!'

'You're going for the mechanic, then?' Bahram teased.

'Oh, shut up.'

***

Two days later Faraz had a phone call informing him that his car was ready. He went to the garage and said hello to Nasim and Agha Morteza.

Nasim asked him, 'Would you like to check that the noise has stopped?'

'It's okay. If you say it's fine, then I trust you.'

'Yes. But if you don't mind, we could take it for a spin up the road, just to make sure you don't hear the same noise.'

'If you insist,' Faraz said, and they both walked towards the car. Nasim gave him the keys and sat in the passenger seat.

Faraz started the car, feeling awkward. 'It seems fine,' he said as he drove. They were now out of sight of the garage.

'Yes, it is fine. I just wanted to talk to you.'

'What about?' Faraz asked, feeling alarmed and uncomfortable.

'Well can we meet and talk? I can't talk right now. I have to go back to work.'

Faraz looked at him and said awkwardly, 'I'm sorry, but I'm not gay.'

'Nor am I.'

'Oh, then I'm sorry, I thought you wanted to see me because you felt something.'

'Listen, I can't talk now. The thing is that I'm not a guy,' Nasim stammered.

'What?' Faraz pressed the pedal hard and they both jolted forward. 'Sorry.'

'It's okay.'

'Does Agha Morteza know this?'

'No. No one knows. You're the first person I've said it to. I feel I can trust you.'

'You're joking, aren't you? If you're not male, then how come you're a mechanic?'

Nasim unbuttoned her shirt; her breasts were pushed down by a corset, 'I have to live as a man, otherwise I wouldn't survive.'

Faraz was shocked.

'I really have to go now. Can I see you?'

'Of course. When do you want to meet? Tonight?'

'Yes.'

Faraz didn't know how to spend the next few hours. Time seemed to stand still. He walked in the garden, looking at flowers and into the little pond as if in search of something. Then he looked at the space left by the big fig tree, which used to stand there in the middle of their garden until last year. The year before last, it had stopped breathing slowly and no matter how much he and his father tried, they could not revive it. They couldn't figure out what was the problem. It used to produce lots of fruit every year, but it was loved for more than its sweet figs. It took two years for it to die completely. Even last year part of it had been green and full of leaves and then fruit. But this spring it hadn't grown any green shoots; while other trees and flowers around it started to come to life, it stood dead. Nima said he couldn't bear to see it like that, dried up, day after day and he cut it down. Now Faraz looked at the empty place where the fig tree used to be, yet the garden was green. He wondered if other trees and flowers, especially the red rose which was nearest to it, missed it. In the past, when the sun was shining strongly, the fig tree provided shade for other plants, but now he could see that they were all baking in the afternoon sun. He thought even if only for the cool shade it provided for them, the red rose bush and other greenery must have been missing it.

He was excited. In society, as a result of so much pressure on women, they were trying to highlight the best of their womanhood; so much make up was applied, so many surgical enhancements undergone every day by women. Now he had a rendezvous with a woman who didn't care about gender and didn't want to prove she was equal to men, but lived freely.

In the evening he put on his best clothes, but then changed into his casual blue shirt. The contrast with his black hair emphasised his complexion. He went to the place Nasim had told him to wait. She soon arrived wearing a man's outfit.

'Would you like to go and sit somewhere?' asked Faraz.

'Yes. That would be nice. After work in the garage I need to put my feet up. I don't want to take you to my place. It's a small room and my landlady is right next door. She might hear us.'

'We can go to my house, if you like, and you can rest while we talk,' suggested Faraz.

'Yes, why not?'

They went to Faraz's house and into his room. Faraz brought food and a bottle of forbidden wine, and they sat talking and eating. The voice of Pavarotti filled the room.

'So, tell me how a girl like you ended up working in a garage?'

'Well, it was the only job that I could find as a man.'

'And did you have to look for a job as a man? Couldn't you find a job as a woman?'

'No. Everywhere I went and asked for a job, they were only interested in my body rather than my brain or my skills. I soon realised that if I looked for a job as a woman I would end up in the street, once men had turned me into a prostitute. There are thousands of them on the street right now.'

'What happened to your family?'

'I was forced to marry after I finished high school three years ago. For two years I stayed with him and tried to change him, to make him a human being. But I was defeated.'

'Did he beat you?'

'Yes, very badly. But I would retaliate, which made our situation worse. I hated him and one day when he was at work, I left him for good.'

'What about your parents? Couldn't you go home?'

'No. They wouldn't support me when I wanted to separate. I had tried a few times already. So this time I didn't go to them. I just disappeared out of all their lives. And now I can live with myself.'

'Haven't you seen your family since you left your husband?'

'No.'

'Don't you miss them?'

'Of course I miss them, but I'm better off without seeing them.'

'Do they know you're safe? They must be worried about you?'

'Well, a couple of days after I ran away I called home and talked to my mother. I wanted to tell her that they should not look for me or contact the police. She was upset, not for me but for her reputation, and said my father was very angry with me. She said my husband had reported me missing to the police after he had called my parents and made sure I wasn't with them. My mother was trying to convince me to go back, saying that they would make sure my husband wouldn't beat me again. I said I would not go back and that I must now assume I don't have a family.'

'I'm sorry.'

'Don't be. The only person I miss is my little sister. I miss her a lot. I call her when I'm sure she's alone at home. Twice I waited near her school to see her and we talked for a few minutes before I let her go. She won't tell my parents or anyone about seeing me.'

'You must have had a hard time, without any support.'

'Yes, until I found the job at the garage. But I wasn't alone. I was lucky that I could change my clothes and find a job as a man. There are so many young women sleeping rough on the streets because they've been victims of domestic abuse and now don't have any support.'

'It must be hard to live as a man. I mean, to conceal your sex.'

'Don't all women have to do that: hide inside a hijab or behind all those beauty products or cosmetic surgery?'

'I suppose you're right.'

'So, will you give us a chance to get to know each other, and perhaps become friends?'

'I thought we were friends already,' said Faraz, kissing her.

'How old are you?' asked Nasim.

'Twenty-six. What about you?'

'I'll be twenty-two next week.'

'Then we should have a proper birthday party for you,' said Faraz, looking into her eyes.

'What's your job?'

'I'm a teacher. My father is a teacher, too.'

'What about your mother?'

'She was a teacher, but she lost her job during the Cultural Revolution in 1980. Since then, she paints.'

'Does she sell them, or does she paint as a hobby?'

'Both. She sells them when she can. And one can say it's more than a hobby for her. She's obsessed with it. Now you have to sleep, you look tired.'

'I feel exhausted.'

'I'll change the sheets so you sleep in the bed and I'll sleep here on the sofa.'

'I'll be all right on the sofa. I just need a toothbrush.'

***

In the morning, Faraz lay in bed and watched Nasim across the room as she woke up and looked around. Her eyes shifted from one painting to another on the walls, and Faraz realised she was fixed on the large painting. It was of a demonstration, with people's fists above their heads as if flying away from their owners' bodies. The demonstrators' faces were the colour of rage, and the tableau exuded anger and hatred. It felt as if the fists were coming out of the canvas.

'Shall we join in?' Nasim said, smiling.

In another painting a scarf was dancing in the wind, pulling itself away from long hair, exposing the glimpse of a smile on a small girl's face, as her black hair seemed to be dancing in the blue sky. Nasim got up and went closer to the third painting. It was a large painting of a pomegranate tree, pregnant and heavy with big fruits, and you only had to look at it for more than a second to realise other things, such as that the fruit was bleeding.

It was as if it was raining, but it wasn't water, nor did it pour from the sky: it was blood that was pouring from the pomegranates. The ground under the tree was soaked in red; a puddle of blood.

'I've never seen such paintings. They take my breath away,' Nasim said. 'They must be expensive and illegal to buy or sell. Where did you buy them?'

'These are my mother's paintings. She calls that one The Tree of Humanity, and those pomegranates are our hearts bearing invisible spears.'

***

A few days later, Faraz went to the Art Café to see Bahram, who hadn't yet arrived. He waited in a corner and looked around. The young couple at the next table caught his attention. The girl was with the boy, but he was with himself. Sometimes she put her hand around his neck, but there was no reaction from him. He was busy with his notebook, sketching, and indifferent to her. There was no eye contact between them, nor did they talk. They were sitting beside each other, but the way he was sitting, with his back to her, made Faraz wonder why people stayed in such a relationship.

Close to them a second couple were sitting, drawn into each other, talking and gazing into each other's eyes, drinking in every minute of being together. They looked and acted so differently from the first two, as if the first man was taking his relationship for granted, while these two relished every second together. Faraz was thinking about how people differ and bring their differences into their relationship, when he heard his friend's voice.

'What's the matter this time, man? Your eyes are full of stars. Not one star – a whole galaxy!'

'Well, we're together.'

'You mean with the mechanic?'

'Yes.'

'I can't believe it. Not you.'

'I love Nasim.'

'Is that his name?

'*Her* name.'

'Oh sure, excuse me. Her. Anyway, congratulations. I'm happy if you're happy,' Bahram teased him.

'No, I mean it.'

'We'd better drop the subject. We've been friends for so long, and I don't care who you sleep with, but I do wonder why I never realised you were gay. When I look at my students, I usually know which ones are gay, or might come out later. I wonder how I got it so wrong with you for so many years.'

'Don't be daft. I'm telling you that Nasim is a girl!'

'You mean, physically, she is a girl, with breasts and everything? Ah, is she a transsexual?'

'No. She was born a girl.'

'But the other day you said she was a guy and a mechanic. If she's a girl, how come she ended up in a garage?'

'Simple. She couldn't find a job as a girl, and so pretends to be a guy.'

***

Faraz and Nasim could not marry, because according to her birth certificate she was already married and belonged to another man. She needed a divorce in order to marry again, and that was something she couldn't obtain without her husband's consent. So she stayed in Faraz's house as his fiancée in the eyes of his parents, who quickly took her to their hearts and loved her. But she continued to dress as a man when out and about in the neighbourhood and was introduced as a distant relative who had come to Tehran to work. She didn't want to lose the freedom she had as a man and was lucky that Faraz and his family didn't interfere with her decision. In fact, they all felt she would be safer as a man whilst living in their house with Faraz, who of course was a young man without a marriage certificate. Faraz's parents were happy to help a young woman who had been forced to live as an outcast and, through their trusted contacts, managed to enrol her on private courses in IT. She discovered a flair for web design and was soon able to work from home as a freelance designer.

She and Faraz often wished they could walk out together as a couple and not be harassed by the moral police. But it would have been dangerous for both of them, particularly for Nasim, so she went out alone when she had to; otherwise they all went out together, like parents with their two boys!

Chapter Three

GRANDMOTHER'S FOOTSTEPS

Early the next evening after his uncle's visit, Faraz went to see his grandmother. The scent of saffron and rice greeted him as she opened the door and they hugged each other.

'Happy birthday!'

'You shouldn't cook for me, Grandma.'

'I enjoy eating with you.'

He followed her to the dining room. The walls were covered with framed pictures of the family in the old days. The table was set.

She pointed to a beautifully wrapped box. 'Open your present. I'll bring the food.'

He examined the box, wondering why it was so much bigger than all the others his grandmother had ever given him before. He opened it carefully. He was taken aback to see a woman's elegant bracelet with two rings sitting on top of some money. His grandmother entered the room carrying a tray of food. He looked up at her with questioning eyes. Her smile was kind.

'You look surprised,' she said.

She served the rice in silence for a few moments.

'The bracelet and the ring are the ones I had for my marriage, seventy years ago. I was fourteen when I married. I was so happy.'

Her posture changed, her back bent by age. Faraz could tell from her eyes that she was thinking back to the distant past. He served himself quietly. She'd made his favourite soup with green lentils, aubergine and *kashk*.

'I'd like you to give them to Nasim. She is a lovely girl. The other ring belonged to your grandfather. I chose it for him. He loved it. He wore it till his last breath. I want you to keep it.' She pushed a stray white strand of hair under her hair clip. Her eyes shone.

'He was eighteen years old when we married. As he grew older and bigger, he had to swap the ring to another finger. We used to laugh about it. Years later, as he aged and lost weight, the ring changed fingers as well. When I took it from his hand the day he was killed, it was back on the same finger that I had put it on the very first time. I've kept it with his blood on it. Until yesterday. I washed away the blood before putting it in that box for you.'

Fighting back tears, Faraz took out his grandfather's ring. He put it on. He had only a faint memory of his grandfather, mixed in with sounds and cries of his family and his uncle's family, all talking at the same time.

'They shot him in Jaleh Square. So many people died. Grandpa was there… He was just watching. Some said he was shouting slogans… he…'

Faraz was only four years old when his grandfather lost his life. But he knew the date: Bloody Friday, 8th September 1978, the day the Shah massacred the protesters. Faraz wondered which of all the terrible events that occurred had wounded his grandmother the most: her husband's death; her son, Rohulah, joining the Islamic Guards; the loss of her grandson, Forood, when his own father turned him over to the authorities and stood by while he was executed? Or long afterwards, now, when she refused to see Rohulah because of Forood? The sadness lay heavy in the cool room, stifling Faraz. He longed for fresh air. His mother had told him that before Rohulah joined the Islamists, he'd been his own mother's favourite. But not any more. Now she only had Faraz's father. He wondered how Rohulah felt about her rejection.

When Nima became a teacher, Rohulah had an ironmonger's shop in the old bazaar. Though he was not among the richest, Rohulah and his family were much better off than Faraz's family. After the revolution, Rohulah employed a young man to work in his shop when he joined the Islamic Guards.

'Thank you for the delicious food and your presents, Grandma. I'm sure Nasim will love them. She sends you her love.'

'Give her my love, too. You two are discreet, aren't you? You know what will happen to you, if they find out.'

'We know, Grandma. We never go out together. There's no problem.'

'And no one else, other than your parents, knows the truth?'

'No one in the family, except you. The rest think we're married. Don't worry. We'll be fine.'

'Are you going to teach street children in that society, what's its name, during the summer?'

Every summer, during his three months' paid holiday, Faraz worked with NGOs such as the Street Children and Child Workers Supporters' Association. He wondered how she would react if she learned of Rohulah's job offer.

Faraz was relieved that his family would not tell her. Over the years, Rohulah had attempted to visit his mother several times, but she never let him in. The last time he had knocked, she had shouted at him and called him a murderer. Since then, he had given up trying.

'I don't know yet,' Faraz said evasively.

After some hours, he kissed his grandmother and left her house. She called after him quietly, 'Take care of yourself. You have reached Forood's age. He was twenty-seven when we lost him.'

He was touched that his grandmother saw Forood in him but felt sad at her years of suffering. She scarcely went out. Not even to the small gathering his parents organised for his birthday every year. Instead, she would invite him to spend a few hours at her house and she would treat him lovingly. Alone, just the two of them.

Faraz was so distracted that he didn't notice he had taken a route home along Firdausi avenue, passing the Joint Committee Interrogation Centre. It was dark, and the giant was asleep, lying like a colourless shadow. Whenever he'd passed it, accidentally, before, he'd remembered Forood, imagining him being tortured. Though twenty years had passed, it seemed to him that his cousin was still alive, waiting to be saved. But after his uncle's visit yesterday, somehow, he was sure that Forood was no longer there in anguish but in the mass grave of Khavaran.

Chapter Four

JOINT COMMITTEE INTERROGATION CENTRE, JUNE 2002

On Saturday, Faraz walked along the wide road, one side of which belonged to the interrogation centre. The wall was eight or nine metres tall, built of yellow and brownish bricks, now darkened to various shades of grey. He reached the green door of the interrogation centre and rang the bell. There were buildings on the other side of the road and a few cars parked here and there.

'Who is it?'

'Faraz. I'm here to see Rohulah.'

'Come in.'

The door started to open, but there was no one around. He had heard from ex-prisoners that they were invariably blindfolded before going through this door. He wondered how differently he would feel if he were a blindfolded prisoner. His heart started beating faster as he stepped over a barrier half a metre high in order to cross the threshold. Inside, there was a courtyard with an empty, round, blue pond in the middle and a three-storey building surrounding it. Each level seemed to be about three metres tall and the balconies were protected by grilles with long signs that read 'SS' welded onto them.

He waited near the pond, semi-hypnotised; the image of Forood standing there, blindfolded, flashed across his mind. He heard the sound of a door opening and looked up as an official came and asked him to enter and wait for his uncle. As he led Faraz along a dark corridor he said, 'Mind your head', a courtesy Faraz guessed was denied to prisoners. He was taken into a room and told to sit on a chair. He realised he had to step over a barrier to get through every door he passed. How would a prisoner wearing a blindfold get over these barriers without falling?

'Your uncle will be with you soon. He's busy with other people.'

The room was almost bare, except for a table, a few chairs, a cabinet and a picture of Khomeini on the wall, watching him. He remembered his father telling Forood, 'All pictures of the Shah and Farah were removed from every classroom in the school. Pictures of Khomeini replaced them.'

After a while, his uncle appeared. His clothes were grubby, which suggested he was busy working on something.

'Are you ready?' he asked.

'Yes.'

'Come with me.'

They walked upstairs and entered a room with several doors leading off it. His uncle led him through the only open door and into a long corridor with cells on each side of it. Faraz felt anxious.

'This wing needs to be painted. There are ten cells and two sets of bathrooms, which are at the end. Everything is to be renovated by removing the existing surface and applying a layer of plaster over all the graffiti. Do you think you can do it in three months? Or shall I bring in another person, so you can work together?'

'I can do it on my own. There isn't too much. I'll let you know if I run into any problem.'

'Fine. Let's see how the others are working, so you know what to do.'

Faraz found himself on another wing without going out through the door they came in. Men were hard at work there and greeted them as they entered. The radio blared out over the whole place. His uncle took him to one of the cells and said, 'You see, they haven't prepared it by removing the plaster altogether. They've just sandpapered off the graffiti. It's less messy and quicker. You've done plastering and painting before?'

'Yes. I painted our house last summer.'

'Good. Come with me and I'll show you where to find plaster, paint, brushes and other things you might need.'

As they walked back to the ground floor Rohulah said, 'This building is circular, with nothing around it and nothing inside it, in order to keep it cold in winter and warm in summer. The designers were German. Reza Shah ordered it in 1932 and it was ready in 1937. They designed it in such a way that no one could escape from it.'

Faraz knew that two people had escaped from it in the early years of the Islamic regime, when there had been a high number of arrests. Perhaps others had escaped, too, but he had not heard.

They reached the storeroom. 'See whatever else you need,' his uncle said. 'Make a list and give it to me by noon. You can start work now.'

Wiping the sweat from his forehead, Faraz asked, 'Is there a fan on the wing?'

'No. I'll make sure you have one tomorrow.'

'Thanks.'

'Shall I turn the loudspeaker on, so you can hear the radio?' Rohulah asked, starting to go.

'No, thank you. I don't like noise while I'm working.' With the radio on, how could he hear if anyone came on to the wing, Faraz thought.

Rohulah left him in the room. Faraz walked back to the wing and glanced inside each cell one after the other, as if looking for someone or something. The first thing he saw was that the cell floors were covered in worn-out carpet and he could see faded, dried blood on some of it. The cells were of three sizes: small, only two metres by one and a half; medium, two metres by three, and a few large cells that were three metres by five. There was no bedding, only a few blankets in the corner of each cell. There was no means of heating the cells, just one big stove in the corridor. He wondered if Forood had been kept in any of these.

He looked closely at the inscriptions and drawings on the walls which were to be scraped and painted over. There were dates of arrival and departure from as early as 1970, up until recently. As he looked closer, he saw half-faded markings and arrangements of lines. The first six of these lines were upright, the seventh ran diagonally across them, bottom to top, left to right. That must mean a week, and four of them meant a month. He could not understand some of the writing on the walls. He could see that there were poems or short phrases and some of the messages overlaid others.

The names were mostly female: Axtar, Banafshe, Nasrin, Shadi, Nahid, Shohreh, Bahar, Narges, Ziba, Simin, Noshin, Zohreh, Fariba, Zahra, Farideh, Shekofeh, Monireh, Masoumeh, Nazli, Farkhondeh, Hori, Xavar…

On one of the walls he read, 'They took Mahvash away three days ago. Today they gave us the newspaper, so we could read her name among the executed.'

The first day passed slowly. He walked from one cell to another, just looking. He did not know what he was searching for and he found nothing except the hard walls, which bore witness to the regime's use of the place. He decided to look for Forood's handwriting, but then, as if all the writing on the walls was laughing silently at him, he gave up. He realised that in cleaning the walls he was going to wash away memories of the last twenty years as well as years before that. For a moment he felt suffocated by the enormity of what he was about to do. He stood in one of the bathrooms, sluicing water over his face to feel better. Looking into the mirror in which thousands of prisoners had seen themselves reflected over the years, he couldn't make out his image clearly. It was as if the sum of prisoners' pain had worn down the mirror's ability to reflect what was in front of it. *So, this mirror has seen them all and is now watching me.*

He turned his back to the mirror, as if escaping it. What would his excuse be if people accused him of collaborating with the regime in an attempt to cover up evidence of torture? Leaning against the side of the sink, he looked at the toilet cubicles in front of him. He went inside one and tried to look at it with the eyes of a prisoner who had just taken off his blindfold to be able to use it. No matter how hard he tried, he could not see the place through a prisoner's eyes.

To reduce his anxiety, he read more of the handwriting on the walls. There was anti-regime graffiti on the bathroom doors. There were names on the walls with dates of prisoners' arrivals and departures. Some were partly faded and unreadable. There were poems by Bertolt Brecht on the walls and some poems by Iranian poets, too. There were messages to give hope and strength.

This, too, will pass... Torture is not painful, don't fear it... The pain of torture will not last more than a few days, while you'll remain the people's hero forever... It's four months now that I've been in this hole and I have not seen anyone except the jailers and interrogators... Don't sleep, don't think negative; walk... I'm not sure any more how long I've been here, and how much longer I'll be here. One morning after six months, I got tired of making a line on the wall to count the days. So now I'm lost in time. What does it matter how long I've been here? But it matters how much longer I will be here, though there's no way of knowing that. The only thing that matters is that you're waiting for me. You wonder how I would know that without any visits. I know it, my heart is telling me that you're counting the days of my absence and you're waiting for my kisses...

Walking from one cell to another, he heard men working on other wings, hammering or pulling at something. He heard the echo of tools falling on the floor, cutting across the sound of the radio. He thought, this place was used as a theatre of terror, torturing people to confess and to accept things or to collaborate. It was a small theatre set inside a larger one, where public torture or execution took place every day. Now they were transforming it from that theatre of terror into a theatre of warning, in order that people should see scenes of torture and learn that if they spoke out against those in power or tried to set up unions in their workplace, they, too, would end up somewhere like this. It was also a stage to show how some of those in power suffered on their way to power and were therefore entitled to get away with whatever they were doing now. Faraz thought about the extent to which politics is theatrical in Iran and wondered if it was the same in other countries. He realised that religion was no longer a means of keeping people quiet with the hope that, when they died, they would attain what had been stolen from them in life. He suddenly felt that all the walls were speaking to him, and they would be heard only if the doors were opened to the people who didn't know what had happened here. And now they were going to be silenced, as the people who leaned on them to write their names had been.

He sat down behind a desk in the small room that connected the wing to the rest of the building. He was contemplating what he was going to do, when a sudden image of all those prisoners who had entered this interrogation centre flashed into his mind. He held his head, as if to stop it from exploding, but then his eyes fell on the writing on the desk under his hands and a smile came to his lips. There were anti-regime graffiti on the desk. He imagined the prisoners were given pen and paper to confess to their activities against the regime, but they wrote on the desk instead of the paper. The scars on the walls were no more than a snapshot of what prisoners had felt or left there. How could he see beneath the surface and within those walls, which had a specific smell he had never encountered before?

He finished his first day without doing much work and returned home, haunted by the cells and the writing scrawled on their walls.

Chapter Five

OMID

A couple of days had passed since Faraz started work in the interrogation centre, and he felt uncomfortable at home. His parents looked stern whenever they were all together.

He heard his mother talking on the phone and at the end of the call she told his father that four of her paintings had sold. She sounded cheerful. Three months earlier, Faraz had gone with his mother to one of the underground exhibitions in north Tehran, where she had wanted to leave a few of her paintings for sale. Together, they had looked at the work of other artists, which was already on display for a public who would come and see it by invitation only. From the outside, the place looked like any ordinary house, but inside, all the walls were covered with beautiful and astonishing paintings. Ana didn't like selling her paintings but every year she had to sell a few, in order to manage the New Year and summer holidays. During the New Year holiday they usually had lots of guests and they needed extra money. They needed money for the summer, too, to go away somewhere together. Every summer they would go to a place they hadn't visited before.

Faraz opened his inbox and found an email from

his brother Omid, who was living in Germany. He was happy to see it. Usually his brother had some news for him when he wrote, otherwise they talked to each other on the phone. Was Omid sending him an interesting article, Faraz wondered? Then the words hit him between the eyes. As he read, anger rose inside him like a flame burning his chest painfully.

Faraz, I've called you several times in the last few days, but you were not in. I told Mother to ask you to phone me, and she said she'd told you, yet you haven't called. Now I understand why, because it's true, then, that you're collaborating with the regime. I wanted to hear it from you directly before judging you, but you didn't call. You don't even have the guts to talk about it. Don't tell me that the phone isn't safe! What risk is a phone to you any more? Now everything is safe for you, because you're on their side. You're washing the blood from their hands. Congratulations, man. Well done! How much are they giving you for re-writing their history?

I never thought what had happened between Father and Uncle Rohulah would ever happen between us. With Uncle's lust for power and money they drifted apart after 1979. But what is it that's aligning you with those murderers such as Rohulah? Money? Or perhaps it's not money, but fame? Are you going to stand for Tehran's next mayor? And after that, are you going to make yourself a candidate for the presidency? Why not? You might even be approved by the 'leader', having Uncle behind you. Yes, the ladder has been put there for you and you have a long life ahead of you to go up to the top. I hope somewhere on your journey to power, you come up against the image of Forood.

How would you wash the disgrace of your name from history? Would you pay someone else to do it for you, as you do it for them? I'm sorry for you.

To be frank, if I was one of our parents I would kick you out of my house. They're being too kind to you, as usual.

Faraz was transfixed. He could not believe Omid was treating him like this. He could see no point in writing back to his brother. Although he had not consigned him to quite the same fate as their uncle, Omid had clearly made up his mind about him. He remembered Omid saying, 'Since we didn't have freedom of expression during the Shah's time, we were after unlimited freedom in toppling the Shah, but what we got was unlimited despotism.' Faraz felt that despotism had rubbed off on Omid, too, otherwise why would he treat his brother like this, just for working on the conversion of the interrogation centre into a museum?

Chapter Six

A DOOR TO THE PAST

Faraz touched the scars on the prison walls, as if examining a wound on the face of someone he knew. Most of the writings were not done by pen or pencil, they were engraved. Drawings seemed to have been made by the actual body parts. A face looked distorted in the act of sticking to the wall. He felt the pencilled outline of an eye watching him. Someone seemed to have left her hand hung on the wall; a flower on the wall seemed dried up; a heart bleeding white, bearing an arrow that pointed to a love poem, prompted him to touch it to make sure it was not beating. He stopped in front of a mark which was neither painted nor engraved. It looked like a slap on the face of the world with a bleeding hand. He put his palm against the bloody hand mark. It didn't fit but disappeared under his hand for a moment, so it could not be the handprint of Forood.

Faraz was distressed. He was well aware that all these images ought to be preserved in a museum as a field for future research. His head ached for killing those prisoners a second time by silencing their last surviving words. It was his choice to take part in his uncle's attempt to convert the interrogation centre into a prison museum, but he found it painful. He had worked there now for a few days and every day his curiosity gave way to anxiety. When he agreed to take part in this project, he hadn't known what he was going to see, nor had he known what he was going to be required to delete from the face of history. He remembered his brother's email, mocking him for being a history teacher and agreeing to wash the regime's bloody hands. His whole family were against his helping to expunge the fact that the Islamic regime had also used this place as an interrogation centre. Even his girlfriend was quieter since he had been working there and seemed upset about it. He missed his class and his students. Some had parents who had been tortured here, and he wondered whether a few might end up in a place like this themselves in 10 or 20 years? Not only were there still many other prisons in existence, but new ones were being opened near factories, to house those workers who refused to accept the punishing life they were forced to lead.

It wasn't easy to wash away all this evidence, as some histories had been washed away. That's why his uncle had said that the walls should be scraped before applying a layer of plaster and then painted over. They didn't want to simply cover it up for now, afraid that one day people would remove the new skin to expose the true museum beneath the show museum.

Looking into each cell, he could almost see prisoners engraving their names with their fingernails, or the spoon they ate with. He wondered how prisoners could bear being in those small cells behind closed doors day after day, in heat that seemed unbearable to him. He imagined how it would be if all the prisoners who had passed through those cells during the last thirty years were there at the same time, and realised the wing could not contain them all at once. This interrogation centre was a transit facility, where prisoners were not kept long. Just long enough to force them to cough up their information - although most did not. It was a factory for extracting information from humans by pressing on their bodies, to stop their minds from functioning normally. But despite what the rulers used to say, Faraz knew that it wasn't a successful factory, because their subjects were too stubborn.

Who were these people who wrote the poems or short love stories they wanted to tell someone, but kept locked inside themselves? Who were the artists of this giant body whose guts seemed to have been made by its captives?

Indeed, the wing looked like a library and the walls were books, written by the hands of those people who had been locked away from society in order to eliminate their influence upon it. Many of the writings could be read only by touch, rather than by sight, as if, over time, they had become part of the building. Faraz had agreed to kill them by removing them, as if they too, like their creators, were made to aid the enemy. They had to be destroyed, as many of their creators had been, and were now in a grave, a place of memory for their families to visit. What would happen if the museum kept this wing and others intact as they were, and the door was left wide open to the public? How many visitors would come every day to see the pierced skin of this creature which was undergoing an operation to lose its identity? How would the families of those who were mostly dead, react? What would they do? How would they feel? They might prefer not to visit their loved-ones' graves any longer, but visit them here, where their names were written by their own hand, and the air they had inhaled still carried something of their essence. The carpets on which they had sat to eat, sleep and clean, still covered the cell floor, stained with their blood. Their relatives, who were familiar with their smell, their personality, would be able to find them on or within these walls even in their absence. What would their families' reaction be if they could see this place before its transformation? And what would Rohulah do to him, if Faraz did not carry out the essential part of the work he was paid to do?

He had to know when his uncle was in the interrogation centre. After all, besides transforming the prison into a museum, his uncle had five jobs and would have to attend to some of the others. Like so many in power, despite not studying at university, his uncle held a position in one. To have more jobs than they could even handle was to have more income, and it enabled them to run the country the way they wanted, while other people were searching for work and committing suicide when they couldn't find any.

Wearing a dust mask, Faraz began working on the first cell. He took a piece of sandpaper and started to rub at the wall. Then he went downstairs for the supplies he needed. In order to get out of the wing and downstairs, he deliberately didn't bring up everything at once.

He had done half of the first cell when he heard his uncle's voice, 'Are you okay?'

'Yes.' Faraz stopped working and watched Rohulah as he entered the cell and inspected the walls.

'Good. Let me know if you need anything.'

He realised not only did other men not check up on him but, as if he were an extension of his uncle, they even kept away from him.

A couple of days later, before noon, he was scraping the walls of the second cell, when he heard his uncle's voice again, 'Faraz come out. I want to take you to a good restaurant. I'm sorry you eat here, in all this dust, and not downstairs with the others.'

'I eat when I feel hungry, that's why I eat on my own.'

Faraz couldn't tell his uncle that none of the men who were working there looked like builders. From their demeanour he felt they could have been prison guards in the very same building that they were now being paid extra to reinvent. He even felt some of them had the look of Islamic Guards. It wasn't difficult for Faraz to tell what people's jobs might be when he passed them in the street. And here they all seemed to have put aside their guards' faces only for the duration of this job. He knew that to build a prison they used construction workers, but his uncle wouldn't bring in anyone who didn't know this place to see things that people shouldn't see. Once again, he asked himself why his uncle had chosen him to come and witness what had happened to Forood in here.

'Okay, now let's go out and eat.'

He didn't want to go anywhere with his uncle, but he didn't know how to refuse the offer. What if people or his family saw them together? He realised Rohulah's suit was clean and pointing at his own clothes, which were covered in dust, said, 'I feel embarrassed to go to a restaurant like this.'

'Fine. Another time,' Rohulah said, but he didn't leave. Faraz didn't know what to do. He was wondering if he could tell his uncle to piss off, when he heard him ask,

'How is your grandmother?' Rohulah was watching Faraz's face. 'You see her. Don't you? How is she? Is she in good health?'

For a few moments Faraz was lost for words. What could he tell his uncle? Could he say that in the twenty years since Rohulah had seen her she had become another person? Instead he pulled himself together and said, 'She's fine. She's doing well.'

'Good. Say hello to her next time you see her,' Rohulah said, and left.

'Sure,' Faraz heard himself say, and wondered if his uncle had heard him. Then and there, it occurred to him that the motive for Rohulah recruiting him must be an attempt to get closer to his family, especially his mother, whom they all knew would not live another twenty years. So, the torturer was missing his mum, he thought, and realised he didn't know much about this kind of creature.

***

By the time Faraz finished the second cell, he realised his uncle was not coming to check on him every day and was in the interrogation centre only in the mornings.

As the days passed, Faraz made sure he did the scraping, plastering or painting when his uncle was around, and in the afternoons searched the wing for hiding places. Faraz was working with great care not to miss anything, as if the walls were made of glass and might break under his hands.

He had seen men walking around – taking things they needed from the room that was allocated for tools – but he had not seen any women in this future museum. He wondered if it was made by men only. Was it run as a place of torture by men, too? He thought there must be something wrong with workplaces without women.

Looking at the walls closely, touching them to feel the uneven parts that might have been covering up a hiding place for a last letter, he thought of Forood. Did he write a letter before they killed him? Where would he hide it if he was on this wing? He wondered if a day would come that marked the last letter of the last letters, when capital punishment would stop and never take place again. While his hands prepared the walls for painting, his mind was somewhere else. He could not work out what was behind his anxiety. Was he worried he would not find anything of Forood? Could his cousin have even spent time in one of these cells? There were other wings and cells in this building and other men were erasing all trace of the prisoners who had been locked up in them. Who were these men, who were destroying a history that could not be retrieved? He felt that every scrape of every mark on the wall added to the pain that had been inside him ever since he had lost Forood.

***

One morning, Faraz was scraping a corner of the wall, when something shifted under his fingers. As he removed the loose pieces of plaster to repair the wall, he discovered a handmade cavity. As if a door to a new world was starting to open, he felt himself entering the real prison behind the facade. In the cavity he found a small package. Puzzled and excited, he took it out. The covering was nylon and fastened with a thread. Rushing to one of the toilet cubicles in the bathroom, he closed the door. He felt his heart swell up inside his chest and beat painfully, as if not having enough space. His hands were shaking, and he couldn't open the knotted thread around the small package. He went back to his tools to cut it. Suddenly he heard his uncle asking him if he was all right. For a moment, Faraz was speechless, composing himself. He said he was fine, wondering how he had not heard his uncle enter the wing, or his footsteps. Rohulah walked into the first two cells and glanced around, and said, 'Let me know if you need anything.' As soon as he had left, Faraz rushed back to the toilet.

There were three small pencil drawings. One showed a blindfolded mother with a baby in her arms, feeding at her breast. The baby's eyes seemed to be searching her mother's face. The second was a drawing of a number of women sitting in a small cell with bars in front of them. The third drawing was of a woman with her ear and her right hand pressed to the wall, and Faraz wondered what it meant.

Faraz couldn't pull himself together and go back to his work. He felt the drawings were shocking - more shocking than some of his mother's paintings.

Later that day, he handed the drawings to Nasim, and watched her while she looked at them one after the other, again and again. She was speechless for some time.

'What are you going to do with these?' she asked.

'I'll give them to Bahram.'

'Why?' she demanded.

Faraz looked at her in surprise. She had never responded to him like this before.

'Don't you think we should publish them on the internet? Don't you think everyone has to know about this evidence?'

Faraz caressed her and tried to calm her down, 'I'm sorry if you're angry with me, but you cannot put your life in danger. You know that they'll stone you to death if they arrest you. Don't you?'

'It's not only you who's in prison, working there. I'm in prison, too.'

'What do you mean?' Faraz gasped.

'Look at our relationship that once made us happy and kept me safe, too. Now it has become a prison, because we're not married and therefore I'm subject to torture and death if I get arrested. So, I have to watch myself all the time and not do things that might get me into trouble, or put you and your family in danger.'

'I'm sorry for what you feel about our relationship. But we love each other, and we can bear all these obstacles. Can't we?'

'How much longer do you think we can live outside the law?'

'As long as we need to, and we are strong enough not to let it get to us.'

Chapter Seven

THE PENDANT

Faraz realised that he never heard his uncle's footsteps coming on to the wing. Was Rohulah trying to catch him in an illicit act? Faraz laughed at his own imagination. Still, he had to do something to make sure he would hear the sound of the door whenever his uncle entered. He inspected the relevant doors and realised the door to the balcony was permanently locked. He shut the only other door each time he came back from the storeroom. Every afternoon, he placed some tools behind this door with a piece of wood on top of them, that would fall whenever someone opened the door. He thought this would make it safer for him during the afternoons, when he didn't expect his uncle and was looking for hidden things.

***

One day, Faraz was scraping walls when a small piece of plaster slipped to the floor to reveal another tiny handmade recess. He found a small package inside it, which turned out to be a pendant, a prison-made necklace. Upon examination he could see it was made of red stone carved into a heart shape and there was a drawing of three birds on one side, with a date on the other: 1.5.1982.

After work he went to the Art Café where his friend Bahram could usually be found at that time of day. The Art Café was on Revolution Road, near Tehran University. Faraz peered in, but the crowd and the smoke prevented him from seeing if Bahram was there. He opened the wooden door and heard the jingling sound of wind chimes and as he entered the smoke hit him. He looked over at one corner, towards the table beside the tank with its long bamboos and fish swimming in the water. Bahram liked one particular dark blue fish and used to sit next to the tank and say, 'This fish is very happy among these bamboos because, swimming around them, he feels he's living in a big pond, rather than this watery cell.'

Faraz went to the counter. He sat down and asked for some tea. Looking at the pictures and paintings on the walls, he realised they were new. The ones he had seen last week must have been sold. He looked at one of the pictures. It was a black and white tree in the middle of a vast green landscape. It spoke of loneliness. Watching the crowd, he saw Mr Farahi was at his usual table, the first on the right, with his papers in disorder. He must be working on his script. He was sitting alone now. Mr Farahi, a 45-year-old writer, was tall and well-built. He was balding and what hair he had was grey. His script had been rejected by the Ministry of Islamic Guidance, and so now he was trying to censor it himself in a way that they would approve. In front of him were wooden stairs that led up to the crowded first floor. Under the staircase he saw the same young woman he had seen last week. She had her jacket on and was getting ready to go. Before leaving, she came to the till. Faraz saw her offering money to the man at the till but he wouldn't take it and said, 'Yours is paid for.'

'Whenever I come here, you say the same thing. Who is paying for me?' the woman asked sharply.

'I'm sorry, I was told not to tell you,' said the waiter.

The woman said nothing and left.

'I wouldn't be disappointed if someone paid for me,' the waiter said to Faraz.

Faraz replied, 'Some people are living romantically.'

He opened the wooden menu and traced the engraved words 'Art Café'. The same technique had been used as for the pendant in his pocket. He looked at the white pages between the wooden covers, at the list of sandwiches, cakes, and hot and cold drinks. He heard his stomach rumbling from hunger, but he had no appetite. The music combined with the noise of the people - all of them talking - made him think of the silence of the cells where he had spent his day. His throat was burning from the smoke. He looked at the 'no smoking' sign on the wall, which was hardly visible. Faraz was thinking about going home when he heard Bahram's voice.

'You look like a prisoner already. What's up? Lost your appetite? I bet you can't sleep, either.'

'I'll be fine in a few days.'

'I hope so. What did you feel when you went into the place?'

'I was scared.'

'Were you scared of what you were going to see?'

'I don't know.'

Faraz took the pendant out of his pocket, 'Look at this.'

'Wow. Did you find it there?'

'Yes.'

'It's amazing. I wonder what happened to whoever made it. Who made this, and for whom?'

Bahram could not take his eyes off the stone and examined it in silence.

'Can I keep it for a few days?'

'Sure. Don't mention where it was found. Here are some sketches, too.'

Chapter Eight

XAVAR AND AZAD

One afternoon, when he was sure Rohulah was not at the site, Faraz was searching the wall of one of the toilet cubicles when his hand felt an uneven surface behind a waste pipe. Though his hands weren't large, it was difficult to reach behind the pipes. He took a tool and scraped at it. A hole appeared, which seemed to be a narrow opening into a handmade space behind the pipes. The entrance was not more than an inch wide, but the space was big and inside he could feel another package. He closed the door to make sure no one would come and find it and take it away from him. He tried to lift out the package, but he found it difficult; every time he grasped it, it slipped from his fingers back into the hole. He thought he heard footsteps and left the bathroom, surprised at not having heard the door opening and the sound of the wood falling on the floor. But no one was in the long corridor and he walked to the main door and realised it was shut and the piece of wood still in its place.

He picked out some other tools to help him get at the package. Once it was in his hands he looked at his watch. An hour had passed since he had started trying to remove it. Cleaning it, he undid the wrapping and realised it was a miniature handmade notebook, two inches by three, with pages covered in small handwriting. The depression that had been eating away at him over the past weeks lifted slightly. He couldn't wait to read it. That day seemed endless and he looked at his watch every few minutes to see whether it was six o'clock so that he could go home. At the same time, he was anxious as to how or where to read it. If he took it to his room Nasim would see it and demand to read it too, and he couldn't cope with her wanting to publish it on the internet.

***

As soon as Nasim was asleep, which he could tell from her breathing, Faraz got out of bed and went downstairs to the sitting room, where newspapers lay on the table and would make a useful cover for the notebook. His parents were asleep. He turned the side light on, so he could see. As he opened the little book with shaky hands, he saw at the top corner of the first page a number in brackets.

What does (4) mean? He asked himself, turning the notebook this way and that.

The pages seemed to have been torn from a larger exercise book, cut down to this size and stitched together. The paper was thin and of poor quality and the writing was in blue pen. On the last page it said: "My love, I looked through my notebook again and saw that – like the other notebooks I made for you - there were lots of interrupted lines, sentences and subjects. This is because I had to stop writing and hide it whenever I heard a noise. When I could write again I started to write about something else."

Faraz resolved immediately to look for those other notebooks.

JOINT COMMITTEE INTERROGATION CENTRE, 1984

Azad, my love. My neighbour left me more paper in the toilet cubicle, so again I'm writing to you. It's Friday, when not many guards are around, and we'll be warned when one of them comes on the wing by a prisoner in the first cell, who'll make a noise by dropping a plate on the floor. I'm glad, though, that you will never find this little notebook, because talking to you is only a pretence for me to write my life story, our love story. Darling, how is the weather in the outside world where you are? Summer must have started, because it's about three months since my arrest. Isn't it strange? I feel it's a long time ago that I was outside and in your arms. What would it be like to put my head on your shoulder again and listen to your soothing words, while you run your fingers through my hair?

I remember you used to say, I'm reading in your face that you want me to make love to you. Or you would say, I'm reading in your eyes that you're not happy. What would you read in my eyes, my face, and in every part of my still painful body if you could see me now? One thing I know, that you would read how much I miss you and how much I need you to take away my living nightmares with your kisses. And I would take away your pain of not being with me by returning your kisses.

Azizam, one thing that strikes me here day after day is how these men - and even the women guards - hate women. Looking at these female guards, I cannot see anything feminine in them. I feel they're ashamed of being women. It's not only in covering themselves up, but in the way they walk; they reduce themselves to tiny, insignificant creatures when they talk to male guards or the interrogators. And the men? The interrogators and guards show their contempt and disgust whenever they see us, and I wonder where this kind of mentality comes from. I've never seen such hatred towards women in my life, as I see here. They must have got it from their upbringing. Education - or lack of education - is part of it. And religion, of course, which was (and is now even more) interwoven with education. I wonder if all religions state that man gives birth to woman, as is said to be the case in Islam? Perhaps the reason that in Islam the first woman was supposed to have been created or born from the first man is the revenge of men for being born of women!

Eshg-e-man, I wish I had our photo album with me so that I could look at your photos and the places we went together. I wish I could see photos of our friends and family. I think about those photos in our album and I remember some of them more than others. One that I often think of is the picture of the young girl about ten or twelve in her wedding dress, beside a big man, in his wedding suit, who looked forty or fifty. She is putting the wedding ring on to his fat finger in the picture and looking at the camera at the same time. There is something in her eyes, as if they're screaming, fearfully though silently. Unspoken words are flowing out of her eyes. At the same time, it seems as if she's trying hard to conceal her fear behind an indifference to what she is being forced to go through. Looking into her eyes in the picture, I had the feeling that she was thinking about the nightmares she would have to live with every day and every night from then on; their wedding night, their honeymoon and every day until her death. Remember, love? You said it should come under the title 'portrait of a forced marriage', or 'photo of the violation of children's rights'. Every time I looked at it, I found it impossible to translate the feelings in her eyes into words. We found it in the room we rented, after we had our brand-new birth certificates with our marriage certificate. It was a one-bedroom flat, and when the owner took us there to look at it, I saw that picture lying in the rubbish. I asked the man if he knew whose picture it was, and he said, 'The last tenant left it and I don't know where they've gone, to forward it to them. You can throw it in the bin.'

***

Faraz stopped reading and said almost out loud, 'Brand new birth certificates? Marriage certificate?' Then he realised he should have thought of getting a new, forged birth certificate for Nasim, so they could marry. Their relationship could then be more relaxed, and they would enjoy more freedom in public with fake documentation than with nothing. Faraz had heard about agents who smuggled people out of the country. They must be able to forge a birth certificate, too. Why hadn't he thought of it before?

***

Remember, Azad jan, I kept that picture and put it in the last page of our album, so I could look at it when I was unhappy, to remind myself what real sadness might be. I used to look at it and cherish the girl in that picture, as if she was my little sister who I could not know and help. I wonder what's happened to the girl in the photo, and why they left it there when they moved away. Did she leave it behind, or did he leave it? And why?

The other picture in our album that I sometimes think about is the picture of us with my uncle Babak. We took that picture the first time you met him at our little party, in spring 1979. Remember, love, how passionately he defended Khomeini, and you told him to wait and see? He patted your back and said, 'Khomeini is a real anti-imperialist and a real revolutionary, otherwise people would not follow him.'

I remember you smiled at him and said, 'Don't let people fool you with their numbers and don't add to their numbers with your amnesia about history. And try to enjoy this wine you're drinking, because it will be banned soon.'

He laughed at your words and said something like, 'You are very pessimistic.'

Then you asked him what he thought an Islamic state would give him.

You two talked and joked with each other and laughed over your wine. Do you remember?

He was a member of the Tudeh party and pro-Russia and he spent three years in prison during the Shah's reign for that. He told me he was interrogated in this prison which is now known as Evin's wing 3000 and Towhid prison. He was released by the people's uprising in 1978, and he was very soon active again.

Then in 1982, when the regime asked members of the Tudeh party to inform on themselves, he went to one of the Islamic Guards' offices. I remember seeing him at my parents' house a few days before, and he said he wanted to go and inform on himself. I said to him, 'Don't do that, they might detain you because you were a prisoner during the Shah's time.'

He laughed and said, 'This Azad is affecting you with his pessimism, my darling. Don't worry at all, some of my friends have already informed on themselves and nothing bad has happened. Besides, my name has been mentioned by those who've already informed, and they'll come for me if I don't go.'

He had no fear, nothing to be afraid of. He had fought against the Shah's regime and he was one of those who looked forward to seeing Khomeini in power. He had defended the Islamic regime from the beginning. Like the regime, he had called the opposition groups traitors and Israelis or American spies for wanting freedom of expression or union. When the war broke out, he organised money, food and even youth to the front. He was proud of what he was doing, which was all helping the regime to build its foundations. So, he had nothing to hide.

Anyway, he went to the Islamic Guards' office and told them on reception that he was there because of the requirement to inform. He was asked to sit in the corner and he was interrogated the whole day. The interrogation didn't involve any violence, because he was happy to help and gave them all the information they needed. That same day he was transferred to Evin and he was executed a month later.

My love, I know I should think of happy

memories, but you can't choose what to think about. The mind has its own logic and makes its own choice. You know what? Though I have to be careful that the guards don't see me writing, I feel it gives me an important sense of freedom. No matter what I'm writing about, writing to you helps me escape from this place for a while. I'm aware that you already know some of the things I'm writing 'for you, but the pages, the pen and the cell which I'm in don't know. So, I like to write about things that I have feelings for and pretend you don't know or

***

Azadam, today I know that you're thinking about me. Not that you don't think about me on other days, but I feel sure that I'm in your mind right now. Because today is my birthday, I'm now 28 years old and it reminds me of my last birthday. Remember, we went north, to the Caspian Sea? You knew I loved to be there and asked me in advance to take a day off work, and you did the same. What would we do today if I was free? I want to

***

My love, today is Friday again and I like to imagine that one day you're going to read this letter and I want you to follow my story. I want to write about the first time we met, so bear with me and do what I ask. Yes, this is the story of us and how we fell in love at first sight, and how that love has warmed our hearts right until I ended up in here.

I wonder if my account of the memory is like yours. Here is mine, but before you read it, try to remember for yourself. No, write it down, and then read mine and see if our love stories and our initial feelings are similar, or whether I have fantasised it.

How long did it take you to write it down? Now that you've written your version, you can read mine. But let me write about our encounter as if it wasn't my life, to take us back to the people we were then. What would someone else see? Let me write the script of our first encounter and let me recall the first day as if I was watching a film about someone else.

One sunny Friday morning in autumn 1978, Xavar stopped at a bus stop on the outskirts of north Tehran, with a newspaper in her right hand and a pencil in her left. She was nervous, but it was early days in a time of transition and it was safe to do these odd things.

A man approached her with a smile and said, 'It's all too obvious that you're waiting for someone to give you the password in order to pick you up!' She laughed, although she didn't know if this handsome man was the guy she was waiting for.

'And what's the secret word?'

The man looked at his watch and said, 'You're five minutes early. So be the princess for now and I'll be the frog.'

Xavar could not help laughing.

You remember that, don't you? Have you noted it down?

Anyway, she tried to stop laughing and looked at him from head to toe for the second time and thought, *He is too handsome to be single*. She would kiss all the frogs in the world to turn one of them into a man like him. For the first time in her life in such a situation – on seeing a man for the first time – she had the desire to kiss him.

It seemed he was busy reading her mind. Quietly, looking into her eyes, he spoke the password and in a teasing voice continued, 'Every secret word like this is a key to enter someone's world, which is fascinating, and it's a privilege for me to know you. I really appreciate it.'

She didn't know what to say, and just looked at him.

'I think we should go to a coffee shop while we wait for the others. Agree?'

She nodded, and they walked away.

My love, now I want you to think about the differences between our two scripts, and what similar words we both used to describe that important day. Stop reading and think back to that day and our body language.

How long did it take you to write? I would like you to concentrate – now that you're aware of our different versions of that day – and read the rest of my letter with this in mind: do we agree on the moment of that first physical connection between us?

Before continuing with our encounter, I want to ask you if you knew my colleague - the one who gave me the message about our meeting. I don't think I told you, but about two weeks before we met, I found a leaflet in the changing room at the factory. It suggested that we should organise ourselves into something like a union, an independent organisation. I was holding it when I came out. I gave it to some other workers and told them where I had found it. I said, almost to myself, I wish I knew them. That day after work I was waiting for the bus, when one of the men came up to me. 'Are you serious about wanting to meet someone from this group?'

'What group?'

He laughed. 'You've forgotten already! You said you would like to meet one of the people who wrote that leaflet.'

'No, I haven't forgotten. Do you know them?'

'I know someone who knows them. Do you want me to send them a message and tell them that you'd like to see them?'

'Yes.'

A few days later, he came up to me and gave

me a small package. 'Here you are, they've sent you this.'

My love, I still remember the message, I opened it excitedly. It said: 'Next Friday, at 7 in the morning, come to Tajrish roundabout, stand at the Darakeh bus stop. Have a newspaper in your right hand and a pen in your left, so that I can recognise you. Then I'll approach you and ask, do you have my friend's pen? You should ask me, who is your friend? I have to tell you the name of the person who gave you this piece of paper.'

You know, Azad, before coming to our meeting I thought I would see an old, wise man, who had read a lot and would share his knowledge with me. I didn't expect to see a man as young as myself, who was a good listener and asked lots of questions.

Remember, in the coffee shop we talked for a while and planned how to distribute leaflets among the workers. Then two of your friends joined us and we went walking in the mountains, while talking and planning for the publication of our agenda. That day I didn't notice the mountains or care about the natural beauty around me. My mind was focused entirely on you and your words; the way you were laughing, concentrating, and I wanted to feel your eyes on me. In the evening when we got back to the bus stop and had to say goodbye, it seemed we had known each other all our lives. That was the first time I realised that I wanted to stay with you. It was only the fear of ruining our relationship that made me walk away.

Azizam Azad, if we were not so busy with everyday political work and had time to talk about everything, would we tell each other these things?

I couldn't believe my feelings. I had never before felt that I could go to the ends of the earth for a man. Oh no, it wasn't the first time I'd fallen in love; but this time it was different, very different. You know that I was seventeen when I fell in love with Morad and that we married when I finished high school. I started to work in the National Shoe Factory and he was already working in General Motors. But the Friday I met you, I didn't want to go back home to Morad. I felt my heart was with you. For more than a year I'd been living with him because he was my husband, not because I loved him. My love for him had gone out, like a candle, as if love has a set duration. You and I never talked about Morad. He was a good man, and we were good friends, but I wasn't in love with him any more. And for several months I had had such a strong desire to fall in love again that sometimes I was frightened, and worried that something might be wrong with me. I was thirsty for love and he could not give it to me. Like me, he was pro workers' rights, and in 1978 we exchanged any news that we heard about what was happening. The revolution changed us all.

Before going to my meeting with you I'd no idea I was about to fall in love, so I had told Morad about it. When I went home he asked me how it had gone, and I didn't know what to say. I couldn't tell him that I had fallen in love, but he sensed something new in me and wouldn't stop asking questions. 'How many people went into the mountains? Were there women as well as men? What did they look like?' and so on. Clearly, he wanted to know what was on my mind, but I didn't want to talk. To get rid of him, I had to lie and say I had a headache.

I remember feeling like this! I saw you two days later, and I counted every moment of those two days. One minute I was telling myself, *he has feelings for me*; the next I was telling myself, *no, he would prefer someone who is good at analysing and talking about politics*; then, *no, he wouldn't want someone just like him.* How could I be sure of that? Most people fall in love with someone like themselves, as if they fall in love with themselves again and again. Or their self-love doesn't allow them to recognise those who are different, who might make their lives more interesting. And finally, I was worrying that you might be married. I even thought you looked at my hands to see if I had a ring on or not. You don't know, but I had to sell my ring and Morad's ring too, when his mother fell ill and needed to stay in hospital. This happened about six months before we met, when I was not in love with him any more, and I suggested selling them, which he didn't want to do, but we had to!

My love, my mind is worrying over my relationship with Morad. At what moment did I lose my love for him? I can't remember how my feelings for him faded. I remember struggling with myself to love him and being successful for a while. Then came a time when I just couldn't any longer, and I felt a huge gap between my feelings for him then, compared to when we had first married. It was at that point I began wondering if I would fall in love again. Sometimes it seemed impossible.

My final argument with him was when I asked why he hadn't come to the divorce office as we had arranged. 'Who's this guy you're leaving me for?' he asked.

'Does it matter?'

'Well, I would like to know the man who is after my leftovers.'

I was furious. 'I never realised that you were so backward. I wouldn't have stayed this long, had I known that you see human beings as *leftovers*.'

Then I started packing, intending to leave him for good. While I was packing, he kept pleading, 'I'm sorry, I didn't mean it. I'll come and sign the divorce. Please don't leave like this.'

I refused to listen. He was still talking as I left with two small suitcases. An hour later I was in your house and I felt happy and free. Not only did your love make me happy, but freedom from him made me happy, too. I never told you what had happened with Morad because I didn't want you to know what kind of man I had been living with, or that I had decided to leave because of the way he talked. I always spoke of Morad as a good man, but someone I was not in love with any more. Perhaps he is a good man, after all, and that day he was so angry and bitter because he wasn't himself.

Do you remember those times as clearly as I do?

You asked if I had my divorce and I explained that Morad hadn't come to the office.

'It doesn't matter,' you told me. 'I'll make a divorce certificate and pronounce that you and Morad are no longer husband and wife.'

Now that you've read my version of how we met, what do you think? How similar or different are our versions? I want to read yours. No, I don't want to read it. I would like you to tell me or read it to me.

Looking back, my love, I feel that I didn't understand Morad and the sadness that the idea of separation caused him. Now it has hit me, the pain of separation, regardless of the reason for it - whether voluntary, like my separation from him, or forced on a couple, as it has been between the two of us. After all, he loved me, and it was natural to get upset and try to stop me leaving. Imagine how distraught I would be if that were to happen in our relationship; if one day you came and told me that you liked me, but you didn't love me any more and you wanted us to separate! Though I might not say anything to hurt you, I would be heartbroken. Perhaps it was the same for Morad, but I didn't understand it at the time. Though I feel I would prefer not to stay with you if you didn't love me the way I wanted you to, I would still be completely crushed. But Morad, like so many other people, preferred to stay with me, despite me not loving him. For my part, although I didn't love him any more, the reason I didn't leave him was because I couldn't afford to live alone. My salary wasn't enough to rent a place and manage my expenses. It was the same with so many women that I knew, and whom I questioned about why they were living even with husbands who were abusive.

Azadam, I wish I had access to music. I really miss the music of water, music of the sea and rivers, music that is different every time you hear it: the music of the rain.

***

Faraz was still reading when he heard his mother leave the bedroom and, on seeing him, come into the living room. He covered the notebook with a newspaper.

'Are you okay? Couldn't you sleep?' asked Ana, concerned.

'I'm fine, just reading the papers.'

His mother went to the bathroom and Faraz put the notebook in his pocket and held up the newspaper, before his father came out of the bedroom. It wasn't possible to continue reading now that his parents were up and about. He couldn't wait to get back to Xavar's notebook. Although he found the whole experience of working in the interrogation centre shocking, he felt he was getting involved in a part of history that not many people were aware of. He realised that what the regime was destroying was only the surface of a history that would live forever in Xavar's notebook and between the lines of other prison memoirs. They were going to strip off people's prison writings, but some of those people were alive and were already talking about it.

That morning, which was Friday and they were all at home, Faraz tried not to show the excitement he felt after reading the notebook. He thought of people like Xavar or Forood as non-violent revolutionaries who tried to educate themselves and others about the civil rights everyone should be entitled to and were imprisoned or killed as dangerous to society. They were dangerous indeed, but only to those in power.

Faraz's mind was still busy with Xavar's writings, when he heard his father ask him, 'Do you see your uncle there?'

'Yes. Sometimes he comes up to check on how I'm doing, or when I go downstairs to pick up tools I see him.'

'How does he treat you?' asked Nima.

'As usual, formal, though I can tell he wants to be kind to me,' Faraz answered, before realising he shouldn't have said that. He didn't mention that his uncle had asked him out to lunch.

On hearing his father say, 'I see,' Faraz, looked up from his plate and saw Nima nodding, as if to say yes. 'And what about you? How do you treat him?'

'Father, there is a grave between us, Forood's grave, which will divide us forever,' Faraz said, watching him steadily. He felt hurt that his father should have such a low opinion of him.

'You don't trust me, Father?'

'Son, I have seen things in my life that mean I cannot even trust myself any more.'

'I don't understand,' said Faraz.

'I've seen people who were once good, change because of money. Money is dirty, and I can see how it contaminates those who have it or try to get hold of it. So it's no good getting upset that I don't like you helping your uncle to cover up what happened in that evil building. For twenty years it was used to torture people, and you're removing the evidence with your own hands.'

Faraz turned pale. Staring at his father, who was now shaking with rage, he replied, 'I don't help my uncle.'

'Then what are you doing there, my son?'

Faraz didn't know what to say. Nasim, whose colour was also draining from her face, and who felt for Faraz, left the table. His mother, clearly distressed, looked at her husband and sprang to Faraz's defence. 'Don't you think you're being hard on him?' she challenged Nima angrily.

'He must have his reasons for working there. He said he wanted to find traces of Forood.'

Faraz's father stood up and left the room.

***

That Friday, they were invited to go and see one of Faraz's aunts in the afternoon and stay for dinner. He made an excuse and told them to go without him. First Nasim wanted to stay with him, but he asked her to go saying that he needed to be on his own. As soon as they had left, Faraz took out the notebook and sat behind his desk in his room and read.

***

I wonder which factory you're working in now and what name you put on your new birth certificate. What books are you reading and what do you write about?

My love, the last time I was taken for interrogation, I was asked about Saman and our two friends who were arrested and quickly executed in 1981 for possession of papers. I said I didn't know them. Now I remember how much we enjoyed that time when we rented a photography shop as a cover for printing pamphlets in 1980. How is

***

Sometimes now I think about all those forbidden publications that would mean death for us if we were arrested with them. All we were saying was that workers should have the right to organise themselves independently, which of course was counter to what the regime and mass media were saying. We believed that only by organising could workers defend their rights, such as the right to protest, publish, and to speak. These rights are fundamental in some parts of the world, and yet elsewhere, such as here, people die in the attempt to acquire them.

***

Faraz wanted to tell Xavar that things are no better for workers now; many are not paid for the work they've done and may get arrested when they ask for their wages, or fired and replaced with the unemployed. He also remembered his brother Omid's answer to his question about why the workers in democratic countries don't stand up for their rights, either. Omid had said that, if in countries like Iran people are silenced by the fear of arrest and execution, in the West the media dictates their opinions and what they ought to do. Faraz missed his brother and longed for the discussions they had had over the past couple of years.

***

Azadam, it's a week since I wrote these last few pages and hid the notebook somewhere safe. I took it out this morning, Friday, to continue writing, which makes me feel free and closer to you. You know, darling, in one of my interrogations they asked me if I knew Abtin and I said no. Since then, I have been thinking about Abtin. Let me first remind you how I was introduced to him. Remember? Once we were talking about the situation and I asked you, 'Have you read Abtin's latest article?' You looked into my eyes and asked, 'Do you know who he is?'

'No,' I said.

'It's rubbish,' you snapped.

I was puzzled and asked, '*What* is rubbish?'

'His article,' you said.

'Why do you say that?' I asked, worried. I had expected you to support the article.

'Why not?' you said, trying not to laugh.

It was only a few days into our friendship, which is why I didn't understand your attitude. I said, 'Well, he has provided a real foundation for his argument rather than using jargon to argue that we have to do this or do that. He doesn't have to use books to prove that the Islamic regime is backward or against women; he shows it simply in the regime's influence on everyday life. Why do you think his article is rubbish?'

'I didn't say I *think* it is rubbish; I said it *is* rubbish.'

'Yes, but why did you say that?' I asked, annoyed.

'Because I wanted to see how you'd react,' you replied, laughing.

'Well, now that you know what I think, I want you to tell me why you don't like it!'

'I like it,' you said, smiling broadly and pulling me towards you to kiss me. 'That's my article,' you said. 'My pen-name is Abtin.'

Eshg-e-man, even now I can feel the joy I felt the moment you said you were him.

As I sit here in solitary confinement, thinking about you and remembering people's reactions both to your writing and to you as a person, once they knew it was you who had changed their views, I have a different feeling about Abtin, the writer. Your fame went before you, and people's celebration of you made me feel privileged. A writer such as yourself is able to talk to people, to enter their lives, their minds, and change their attitudes towards things. You shape their opinions. You make friends of them – but sometimes enemies, too. I haven't forgotten that you had – and still have – enemies. You move on, you change through your writing, and each new relationship you make becomes a note in the music you hear in your head. Now I

***

Azadam, it seems they have taken – no, stolen – all our books, because the other day the interrogator asked me why we had so many English and Arabic books. Why did we have books in three languages? His question seemed irrelevant to me at first. But then I realised that they must hate books, because they're against thinking, talking and discussing, and books are nourishment for the mind. As they are against freedom of expression, they must also hate books because they lead people to think and question things, which is the greatest threat to their power. Questioning is not allowed; whatever the leader says is right and everyone must follow it without thinking for themselves. My love, I didn't tell them that we both loved languages and that you were fluent in English, French and Arabic. It would not be useful to tell them that we both liked to compare different translations of a text to help grasp the full meaning of the original, and how it can be translated. I didn't say that sometimes when you were studying different translations of a book, you would burst out laughing and look over at me and say,

***

My love, now it's raining. Not a shower, more like a drizzle. I can't hear it, but I can smell it. Though they have taken away the rain by locking me up and covering the window, they cannot lock out or take away the scent of the rain! As the scent of the rain envelops me, I hear you saying, 'Take a deep breath, darling, this is life, the earth's perfume.' You come into my cell with the smell of the rain, the cold, food, water, and as I feel them, I feel you deep inside. They try hard to empty my heart and my brain, but they won't succeed.

Once a week, I get the chance of a ten-minute shower, and as the water runs from my head to my toes, I imagine it's you. You become water. You are each drop of water that washes me and caresses me. Your hands, your fingers and your caresses were as soft and as soothing as water. And now that my skin is too dry and cries for a shower, the water soothes it as if it's your kisses.

When they bring food to the wing, before distributing it to the prisoners in their cells, the smell reaches me, and you come with it, saying, 'What would you like for dinner?' And I hear myself telling you, 'It's some time since you made Mirzagasemi. I miss that dish of aubergine that you make.' You answer, 'I'll buy aubergine and garlic tomorrow morning and make you Mirzagasemi.' I begin to imagine the smell of grilled aubergine mixed with the garlic and eggs and hear your voice, 'Come on, it's ready!' Oh darling, is it ready for me? Make it ready for me. I'll come and eat it. One night when everyone's asleep here, I'll come to you forever.

The night turns cold, and there you are

telling me to put on my jacket. Except that now I don't have a jacket with me and instead I draw the blanket over my shoulders. You touch my hands and say, 'It's cold, let me warm them.' And you clasp my hands and rub them until they're warm. You see, you're here even though they were not able to arrest you.

You know,

***

I feel I can see things now that happened years ago, but I didn't see them or understand them then. Isn't it strange that sometimes understanding comes to us a few years later? Does it mean that I'm changing? If we ever see each other again, perhaps we shall be two different people. How would we perceive each other's changes? Or perhaps something else is happening. That is, I'm thinking more in here than when I was free! Outside these walls I was busy working and spent my little spare time reading politics and I didn't have time to think. Perhaps not learning to think and not being used to thinking is another reason why so many people are frightened of solitary confinement. Apart from the fact that being alone doesn't have a good reputation in our

***

My love, a few days have passed since I wrote

to you and today is Friday again. Not only are Fridays safer to write to you, but since they were the only day we didn't work and could spend together, I can now see that Fridays are when I miss you most, and writing helps me to imagine us together. Now I would like to tell you something strange, which has been preoccupying me over the last few days. For some time, I'd been hearing sounds from the cell next to mine and I thought, there's more than one person in that cell. A few days ago, I could hear clearly that the prisoner in the cell next door was talking to someone and was saying, 'Now try to sleep and I'll take care of your hand. You'll be fine tomorrow.'

My love, I thought, poor girl, they must have damaged her hand under torture. Perhaps they whipped her hands and that's why the other prisoner is trying to help her. Then I heard her say, 'I'll fix it with a bit of sugar and water, don't worry. Sleep well.'

Darling, I could not understand what kind of injury it must have been that it needed to be fixed with sugar and water! I tried to listen more closely, but the voices weren't audible. Then in the early morning when I was sure that the guards weren't on the wing, I called out to her: 'What's your name?'

'My name is Behi.'

'When were you arrested?'

'Ten years ago.'

'What? But the prisons were emptied when the Shah's regime collapsed. And that's only a few years now.'

'Then I don't know how long I've been here. Perhaps it's less than that.'

'Are you alone, or with someone?'

She was silent for a while. Then she said, 'I'm not alone. I'm with a friend. What about you? Are you alone?'

'Yes, I'm alone. I wish I was with someone, too.'

'Don't worry. I'll make you a friend.'

'What? You'll make me a friend? I don't understand!'

'I'll send you one of my babies. But promise that you'll take care of her.'

'No, no. You can't give me your baby! What if she cries for you, or—'

She interrupted me, 'Don't worry, she doesn't cry. She is not that kind of baby, she is different. Give her a name and look after her as if she's your child. Will you promise?'

Darling, I was confused and didn't know what to say. I heard her calling, 'Are you there? Listen, tomorrow night when the guard takes you to the ladies' room, go to the right-hand bathroom and look behind the door of the first toilet. I'll leave a friend for you there. Don't forget to take her to your cell. And talk to her. Don't think she doesn't understand. She understands everything. Okay?'

'Yes, fine. Thank you.'

Darling, I couldn't wait for my turn to use the bathroom so that I could find out what she meant by leaving her baby for me.

Then last night I went to the designated bathroom and came back from the toilet with a model made of bread dough. It is small, about two inches long. My neighbour has left me this companion so that I am not alone. When I returned to the cell, I wondered if she had spent all this time talking to a little doll like this one. I had to ask her. As soon as I knocked on the wall, she asked, 'Did you find it?'

'Yes. Thank you.'

'You're welcome. Take care of it.' She sounded like an innocent child.

'Sure. But can I ask you something?'

'Yes. Go ahead.'

'Is it one of these you've been talking to over the last few days? Or is someone with you?'

'The older sister of the one I gave you is living with me. She looks like the one I made for you.'

'I see.'

'You have to hide her from the guards. Otherwise they'll take her away and make her a guard. You don't want to become a guard, do you? You prefer to be a prisoner than a guard, don't you?'

'Sure. Don't worry. I'll take care of it. Sweet dreams.'

'You too. Goodnight.'

'Goodnight, darling.'

My love, I feel miserable. How can they change a person so much that she speaks to a model made of bread dough? And yet she must be so kind to have offered to share one of her 'babies' with me. Don't worry, I'll be fine. No matter how long I have to be here, I'll come out of this place sane. I know what your answer will be, if

***

Eshg-e-man, what colour is the sky you can see? I miss seeing the sky, the sun, the moon and the world, but most of all I miss you. My feet are healing, except for one of the little toes which is still infected and is swollen and very painful. But other parts of my legs and feet are much better now.

Remember? It was early 1979 and a few days after the Islamists came to power when one day we walked past this interrogation centre in the middle of Tehran. As we passed its thick walls, you touched them and said, 'How many people are going to be tortured to death under the Islamic regime - in the name of god, this time?'

It was on that day that I learnt about the history of this place, not knowing that I would be in here myself in a few years' time. Then, when you saw my surprise, you asked me, 'Do you think it's the end of this Nazi-made building as an interrogation centre, or will it come back into use?' You went on, 'As you see, they're killing royalty very quickly now and the killing will not stop with them. They'll find others to kill. How can they secure their power without silencing people?' I didn't want

***

I've missed my work mates, those men and women who fought together for years to gain the rights we ought to have. What are they doing now? After toppling the Shah and while the regime was still in its early days, we talked about ways of helping women workers with children. They had to leave their children in the nursery in the morning and give them their milk in the afternoon. Those who were looking after the children were workers themselves and had no training in childcare. We demanded trained workers for the nursery and for children to be given some fruit during the day, as well as for their mothers to give them milk between mealtimes. It would only be temporary, but we could make things a bit better for them.

As you see, I've reached the last few pages of this small notebook. So now I'll hide it somewhere to save it. I'll carry on writing to you as soon as I can steal some more paper - next time I'm interrogated. Or my neighbour might be able to pass me some pages again. Do you know what? I have a good feeling when I write, as if I'm really talking to you. Sometimes I even look up to see what your reaction is, and I find myself surrounded by these walls, gazing back at me.

Now, thinking about the last five years of our struggle against the Islamic regime and the many people who lost their lives in this battle, I feel we had no choice other than to fight. Be your name. Xavar.

***

As soon as Faraz finished the notebook, he couldn't wait to give it to Bahram. Bahram was his oldest friend, the one person outside the family he could really trust. Bahram would know what to do with the notebook. He was involved in trying to build a teachers' union and always brought Faraz news that otherwise he wouldn't hear. Now Faraz needed his help – not only with Xavar's notebook, but with Nasim's predicament too. He was walking towards the Art Café, when he was transfixed by a small drama on the street and stood watching. A taxi stopped, a woman got out of it and as she slammed the door and the car started to move off, her scarf unwound from her head. Faraz saw that the end of her scarf had caught in the door. He started to run after the car, which was moving slowly because of the traffic, but the driver either seemed to be unaware of what was going on or didn't want to stop and have to deal with it. He accelerated away as the road was clear. Faraz stopped running and looked back. Now the woman seemed to be concerned about not having a veil, as she could get arrested. She seemed not to know what to do and hesitated at a corner of the pavement. Other people had seen her, and a woman offered to go and buy a scarf for her. Men started to stand in front of her, shielding her from the eyes of any passing moral police. The nearest shop selling scarves was fifteen minutes away. Faraz watched the men who had created a safe shield around her, saving her from arrest and a beating, or from paying a fine.

From outside the café, Faraz looked in. Bahram was sitting at a table on the left-hand side, near the till. Above his head, part of a tree trunk was fastened to the wall, holding four lit candles. The place was busy, as it usually was at this time of the day. Faraz sat down in front of Bahram, took out a box of cigarettes from his pocket and put it on the table. Bahram took it, opened its lid and smelt it.

'It doesn't smell very nice,' he said, putting the box in his pocket, 'I'll try them later. What is it this time?'

'A love story, the best I've ever read.'

Bahram laughed loudly, 'Did they get together at the end?'

'I don't know. I've only read the part that I found,' Faraz said despondently.

'Some young people blame our parents' generation for bringing this regime to power,' Bahram reflected. 'They don't realise that many people back then also struggled against the Islamists and were tortured or killed as a result.'

'How could they know? As ever, anyone who talks gets arrested, or butchered in their own homes. The regime is planting its own version of history into our heads,' Faraz said.

'We have to do something with these things you're finding in that place,' said Bahram thoughtfully.

'And end up in an interrogation centre?'

'Yes, like you're there now,' Bahram pointed out drily. 'One has to see it this way or that way. And I'm waiting to see it once you've turned it into a museum.'

'If I could get on to the other wings I might find traces of Forood. Otherwise they'll be covered up, if any of his writings are on the walls, or on a piece of paper hidden inside those walls,' said Faraz.

'But traces of him are inside you, man. The way you talk about Forood, it's as if he's still alive. And can't you go on to other wings?'

'No. Both times I tried, I ran up against the Islamic Guards. I said I was looking for my uncle, and they told me he wasn't there, and I should go to reception.'

'You look depressed.'

'I'm fine.' Faraz took a deep breath. 'I need to find someone who might be able to forge a birth certificate for Nasim and a marriage certificate for us.'

'Hmm, I'll think about it,' said Bahram, alarmed, 'Do you mean to say that the two of you are together without having any documentation?'

'Yes. How could we have documentation?' Faraz retorted.

'Don't you worry about what would happen to you both, especially to her, if they find you out?'

'How would they find out about our relationship?' asked Faraz defensively, well aware he had been too casual about this.

'Hey man, have you forgotten that we're living in a country where we need state permission to fuck? Don't you realise you could be arrested for any daft reason? I can't believe you, man. I thought you two were safe in your relationship.'

'Okay, please don't go on about it. Try to find someone who might be able to help,' pleaded Faraz.

'I'll do my best,' said Bahram, shaking his head disapprovingly.

'I'd better go. Please don't show the copies of that notebook to anyone you don't fully trust.'

'Don't worry. You look different, Faraz. You've lost weight. Are you okay?'

'I'm fine. Just lack of sleep.'

Faraz went home thinking about Xavar and her love for this man called Azad. Did Nasim love him in the same way that Xavar loved Azad? Did he treat Nasim as Azad treated Xavar? What kind of a man was Azad? How could he find his writing under the name Abtin, if he were alive and still writing under this name?

Chapter Nine

ARREST

The next morning, when Faraz went to the wing to continue his work, he started by searching for clues to Xavar. He found her name and the dates she had entered and exited cell number 3, which indicated that she was there in summer and autumn of 1984. Faraz couldn't understand this because as far as he had gathered from reading Xavar's notebook, she had been arrested in the spring of that year. Puzzled, he thought perhaps that if he found more of her writing, he would discover why the dates on the walls were not consistent with the dates in the notebook. But how could he find the rest of her letters, which would have had to remain hidden for decades? And as for Forood, he'd made no progress at all. It seemed to him that the male prisoners who spent time on that wing were prisoners from the Shah's era. The dates showed that prisoners here during the current regime were mostly women. How could he get to other wings to search for traces of his cousin?

Now he was no longer brooding about what his father or Omid thought of his work here, his head was full of Xavar and Azad. He remembered that his uncle had told him not to bother with the windows in the cells, all of which were covered with mesh. He went back to the first cell again and looked at the window. It was too high up and he couldn't reach it with his outstretched hand. He felt discouraged. Using a ladder, he climbed up to the mesh and tried to lift it off, but it was impossible to remove with his bare hands.

***

One early afternoon, when Faraz thought his uncle must have left the site, he went to the bathroom to look at the walls more closely. He examined the ventilation shaft, which was covered with mesh. He imagined being a prisoner trying to reach up to the mesh and he realised that by putting one foot in the basin he could get access to it. He brought in the ladder and, standing on it, tried to lever off the mesh, but again it was impossible. He would have to break it to remove it. He was perched on the ladder, absorbed in these thoughts when he heard his uncle's voice.

'Are you all right?' He was standing there, watching Faraz.

Coming down the ladder, Faraz wondered how long his uncle had been there. 'I'm fine, thinking about how to clean the ventilation cover before painting it.'

'Don't worry about it. These bathrooms won't be used in future. Just get rid of the writing on the walls.'

'Oh. All right, then,' said Faraz.

'Is everything else okay?'

'Yes, I think so,' said Faraz, trying to sound relaxed.

'Well, I'd better go then. Let me know if you need anything. By the way, you seem to have lost weight since you started working here.'

Trying to laugh, Faraz said, 'I guess I'm just not used to manual work, although I enjoy it.'

'Will of Allah. Bye for now.'

He accompanied his uncle to the entrance to check if the wood was on the floor, and it was. The tools were pushed away from the door. So his uncle had come through this door, but how come he hadn't heard the sound of the door opening and the wood being knocked on to the floor? He decided it must simply be because the bathroom was a long way from the entrance. And as usual his uncle had his creeping shoes on, so just as his prisoners couldn't hear him coming, Faraz wouldn't know when he was being checked up on, either. That day, he continued scraping the bathroom walls, which didn't have much writing on them. In the middle of the afternoon, on the excuse of going to the storeroom, he went downstairs to make sure his uncle had left. Then he came back to the bathroom again. He was determined to search the space behind that dusty mesh and see if there was anything there. He put his hand on top of the mesh and felt across it from one side to the other. When his hand touched the lower part of it, he felt something uneven. Using one of his tools, he tried to pull the string attached to the lower part of the mesh. It gave way easily, and he felt his heart jump out of his chest. He climbed down, walked out of the bathroom and looked out into the corridor to make sure no one was around. In his mind, he saw prisoners lying on blankets, blindfolded, with just enough space between them to prevent them talking to each other. It was the image that Bahram had painted in Faraz's mind of the early 1980s when the number of arrests was so high that even the corridor had been used to hold prisoners.

Faraz came back to the bathroom and loosened the mesh further. He pushed his hand inside the ventilation shaft with difficulty. It disappeared behind spiders' webs and he felt several things in there, took hold of them and carefully drew out a number of small packages covered in dust and dead flies. His heart was racing, his hands shaking, as he stuffed the packages into one of his pockets. He then rearranged the mesh back into position. Climbing down, he checked to make sure that nothing looked as if it had been tampered with. He went into one of the cubicles and closed the door in case someone came in. Then he examined the packages: the covering of one of them had been opened and damp had made the writing illegible. Here or there he could read a few words, but they didn't mean anything to him. He would have to wait till he got home before opening the others.

He wondered if any of them contained Xavar's letters. Before going home, he checked his appearance. His trousers near his pockets were dirty and dusty. He couldn't clean it off, so he spread the dust all over his clothes. Though he felt tired from the intense activity of the afternoon, he still couldn't wait to see what he had found.

As soon as he reached home, Faraz went to have a shower. He emptied his pocket and placed the packages on the bathroom shelf. Then he cleaned them up and made them ready for reading as soon as everyone else was asleep. But first he wanted to ascertain whether any of Xavar's letters were among them. Some of the packages he opened were the final letters of prisoners who were going to execution. These were letters written to lovers, children, partners, parents or friends.

But as he opened the wrapping of the biggest package he saw the mark (1) on a notebook, which was again circled. He knew it had to be Xavar's; it was the same size as her other notebook, roughly two inches by three, but this time written in black pen. The paper seemed to be of better quality and, once again, the pages were stitched together in the middle.

How many of these notebooks has she hidden? Faraz asked himself. *Where can I find the others she must have written?*

***

[illegible] These were letters written to X [illegible] personal correspondence.

[illegible] the very top of the biggest package [illegible] which was [illegible] the same [illegible]

[illegible]

[illegible]

JOINT COMMITTEE INTERROGATION CENTRE, SPRING 1984

Azad, my love. How are you, darling? You'll never guess which prison I'm in right now. I'm in Joint Committee, not far from where we once lived. Am I really writing to you? No. They'll never let me send my letters out. When I asked to call my parents to let them know that I've been arrested, Ghulam the interrogator said, 'Give us a person and we'll reward you with a phone call.'

Azizam, it seems the price of a phone call is very expensive here and you know I can't afford it. I wonder what the price of freedom would be? Not difficult to imagine. So, be patient.

Let me tell you about my first experience of entering this world – a place you can't possibly imagine. The car drove into the prison yard and they blindfolded me there, still sitting in the car. Though they had held my head down all the way, so I couldn't see anything except their legs, the blindfold was like closing the door on the world outside my body. By wearing the blindfold, my connection with the world was instantly cut off. I didn't

***

I wonder if it's because of his name that Ghulam constantly needs to demonstrate his power. He kept asking me where Farid is. When did you meet him for the first time? Did Farid fuck you as soon as you first met? It seems he doesn't know what your name is. He doesn't know your other names, either. I wish you would delete Farid from your list of names, because they know that you use it. So choose a new name to be called by. I like calling you Azad, because you told me about this name of yours when you said you loved me, so it's associated with the end of my anxiety as to whether you loved me or not.

My Azad, let me first tell you how I was arrested. Do you remember Shahla and Hamed, who were our neighbours in 1980? You must remember them, because one day when you came home, after throwing leaflets into the air at a demonstration at Tehran University, you told me, 'As I threw up the leaflets, I saw him watching me.' I still remember your worried expression, when you went on, 'I saw him too late, otherwise I would have moved to another spot, before doing it. I pretended not to see him, but I saw his hand grab one of those leaflets.'

We knew that they were with the Mujahidin and he was somewhere at the top of the organisation. We heard nothing more about them after we left that place. Anyway, the morning of the day I didn't return home, while I was at work, I heard the door open. I looked up and saw Hamed entering with two men whom I assumed were guards. He looked at each of the workers in turn, and the other two men watched him and us. I pretended not to know Hamed, but I was shocked and had a feeling I was going to be arrested. When they left, I thought they would come for me straight away. Then, as time passed, different thoughts were racing through my head. I was hoping he hadn't pointed me out, and in fact knew nothing about me, but what was he doing there except identifying anti-regime activists? I had to prepare myself for interrogation, but I couldn't think. I was worried and already missing you. By the afternoon, it became clear to me that they would arrest me at the door, when my shift was over. But I had no choice other than to leave by the main entrance. As you know, they guard this factory like a prison. Every time I went to the toilet, a member of the Islamic council followed me, to make sure I wasn't going to try to escape by climbing out of the window.

I finished my shift and went towards the door with everyone else, thinking they might not arrest me in front of the others. But before I could walk out of the main entrance, the security guard asked me to stop. He said some people were waiting to see me. My workmates, who I was walking with and talking to, to make sure I wasn't alone, stopped as well, waiting for me. The security guard told them to go on, so they said goodbye and left. I said, I'm in a rush, but he didn't let me leave. When all the workers had gone, the same two guards who were with Hamed, approached and told me to go with them. On the way, my mind was busy with Hamed. Was he going to every factory and university to identify people he knew were opposing the regime? When I got here, they asked for my address. I gave them the false address I had given to the factory, but they said they'd been there and wanted my true address. I couldn't reveal it and let them arrest you. I was silent. When they asked me if I knew Hamed, I said no.

'Hamed was your neighbour and knows that you are Farid's wife,' one of the interrogators said. 'You're trying to save him by wasting time. But we won't let you do that.'

Eshg-e-man, they started torturing me straight away and, though it's two weeks now, I still can't sit properly. Its spring outside, yet here I feel cold. No, actually I'm freezing. I want

***

When I talked to my neighbour who gave me this pen, I mentioned Hamed and she told me that he and some other Mujahidin had become trusties. She said they're showing their support for the regime by helping them with interrogations, and even executions and are calling this strategy tactical. I wish I could send this information out, so you could spread the word about him, to save others he knows. My neighbour promised she'd tell other prisoners and soon the word would get out about Hamed, because some of the others have visits and they can pass it on to their families. So, I hope I'm his last victim!

My love, let me write about the interrogator. I know I'm not writing about my arrest in a chronological order, but bear with me, because I can't think straight. Though his name is Ghulam, it is he who has all the power and he uses it as if to prove that he is no slave. I wonder how Ghulam feels about love. He is about thirty years old and wears a wedding ring. He even kicked me for not wearing one! I wonder if he fell in love with his wife. Do men like him fall in love? Or do their mothers buy them women to have sex with? The marriage mask fits him well. In his world, women are bought like pieces of furniture with sexual equipment. In society these men only touch a woman after a certain procedure called marriage, temporary or permanent. But here, behind these closed doors and barbed-wire walls, they touch whoever and whenever they want. And it was after he touched me that for the first time in my life I felt like committing a murder.

I wonder by what process a person becomes a torturer and loses the sense of empathy that makes us human beings. I don't believe they are born like this; it must be hammered into them in training, and a kind of brainwashing that makes them see people like me as the enemy who need be dealt with in a certain way. I don't know how one is transformed into the kind of animal he is now. But I feel that even if he was a good man before entering that room, the process of what has gone on between us has changed him. We are both transformed; he when he yells god's name with each lash of my body, and I, yelling to spit out the pain, humiliation and anger. I feel this place is a good example of how people change at the limits of their daily life or their work, torturing or being tortured. No, I don't believe he was born like this. No woman could grow such a monster in her womb. He must be schooled in it, little by little. Every time he tortures someone to extract their information, he moves a bit further away from the human being he was born to be. His superiors congratulate him for obtaining information, so he has to do everything in his power to prise out what he's after. No victor emerged from that room; he couldn't get what he wanted, and I am still overwhelmed with pain and the fear that I might lose the only living thing I have of you inside my body. But then I wonder if I am really pregnant, or whether it's a fantasy.

I told him that I'm pregnant, hoping the knowledge might make them easier on me. Ghulam said, 'Good, then I'm beating two people at once. Your baby is a criminal just like you.'

His helper said, 'Why should we care about your baby? If you truly cared for it, you would have told us your address when you first arrived here, and not made us force your mouth open. It's not too late, though. You don't want your child to be killed before it's born, do you?'

When I was full of pain and hate, pinned to the bed, I felt he was trying to make me like himself, a *ghulam* – a slave. And he was the king of the torture bed. Perhaps he is the king of the bed he shares with some other poor woman he has bought. A few times, he

***

I know we agreed to give out our address after a couple of hours if any of us got arrested, but when they took me to the torture chamber as soon as we arrived here, I lost all sense of time. When he was tired of beating me, and had given the whip to his helper, Ghulam squeezed my breast until it hurt. I was also worried that if I am pregnant, torture may hurt the baby. Remember, I told you on our last morning together that my period was a week overdue and how unusual that is? I planned to take a test the next day, but it isn't possible any more. All I can do now is wait and listen to my body and see if my periods start again, especially after this beating. Or see if my stomach swells.

After the beating, when I went to the bathroom, I thought I was having my period and I was very upset because I thought, I'm not pregnant. But then I realised that it wasn't my period. I was passing blood with my urine.

Sometimes, I could hear your voice saying, 'Don't resist for more than a couple of hours. If you get arrested, I'll run away. If I don't come back from a secret meeting, you have to leave the house before two hours is up and never return.' But each time I tried to tell them our address, I couldn't say the words because I pictured our friends who had the same arrangement, but when the interrogators went to their house, one of them was still there. She didn't have anywhere to go and stayed in the hope that her husband would not reveal their address.

I don't know how many hours I had been tied to the bed when I tried hard to turn my head and, from under the blindfold, I could see the window very far away, up in the ceiling. It was lit like dawn. All I could remember was that I was arrested in the evening and that it was dark. They were tired but continued beating me. Ghulam sat on my back and said, 'Shake your fingers if you want to talk.'

I shook my fingers and he told his helper to stop beating me. He pulled the blindfold up to my forehead. He was sitting in front of me, looking into my eyes. He was one of the guys who had come to the factory with Hamed. I felt as if I were seeing inside his head, and his eyes looked large, larger even than his brain. It seemed to me that his eyes were holding his brain in place and his brain not only looked like a dried walnut but seemed about the same size. He asked for our address, and I told him with a voice that came from the end of the world. I was still very scared that they would find you there. He ran out. His helper released my feet and my hands and took me to a cell and gave me some bread and cheese with a cup of tea. A woman guard was taking breakfast tea around to the prisoners in the cells. She stared me up and down and closed the door. I couldn't eat. I slept. I don't think I had slept more than a few minutes when the door opened. I looked up, and saw Ghulam coming for me. I sat and curled up, facing the wall to save our child. He hit my head on the wall and kicked me in the ribs, 'You bitch, you didn't give us the address before he had left the house.'

My body was in so much pain, yet I wasn't going to give him the pleasure of hearing me cry. I wanted to be seen to be strong, though inside I was petrified. When I was interrogated, I could hear the voices of other prisoners and realised that while some of us were trying to stay strong, others gave in. I heard someone crying and pleading not to be beaten again, and I guess that scenario is what the torturers are waiting for. Since then, I have felt as if there are thousands of hearts under my feet. With every step I take I'm causing them pain.

***

I guess, not making any noise made me popular among the prisoners, who heard Ghulam shouting, swearing at me and kicking me while he seemed to be out of breath. At noon when the wing was quiet, and the guards weren't around, I heard voices asking each other about me.

'Who was it who got beaten up?'

'She's a new one in the cell beside mine. She'd not given any information to Ghulam.'

'What's her name?' asked someone else.

'I don't know. She just came in this morning,' said my neighbour.

'Talk to her, before the trusties or guards come back,' another prisoner suggested.

'Okay, watch then,' my neighbour said.

'We're watching.'

I could hear whispers among the prisoners, but I was so overwhelmed with pain that I couldn't join in, until my neighbour knocked on my wall and, not getting any reaction from me, said, 'Are you okay? I heard Ghulam was really angry that you didn't talk. What's your name?'

'Xavar!' I said. They must have heard the pain in my voice.

'When did they arrest you?' she asked.

'Yesterday evening.'

'Why?'

'They're after my husband,' I said and, darling, my tears were streaming, as if they had been trapped. I couldn't say any more.

'Don't worry, they can't arrest him now he's escaped. Were you tortured right through the night?'

'Yes.'

'I'm sorry, you must be in terrible pain. I wish I was with you and could give you a bit of support,' she said.

'Hello, Xavar. We're sending our love,' called someone else. And I heard others saying the same.

'Do you need anything? I can leave it in the bathroom if you need anything,' My neighbour told me.

'I need a toothbrush, toothpaste, pen and paper,' I said and they all laughed. I asked, 'What's funny about that?'

'You said, they wanted your husband! What do you want the pen and paper for?' one of them said, still laughing.

'I'll leave them for you this evening on the

left-hand side of the bathroom. But you must be careful they don't see you writing,' my neighbour said.

I thanked her.

Then someone in a cell further away called, 'Don't you need money?'

'No, I had some money with me when they arrested me.'

'Where were you when they arrested you?' asked another woman.

'I was at work, at the National Shoe Factory, and yesterday morning someone called Hamed, who I know used to be a member of the Mujahidin, came to the factory and identified me.'

'Is he the same guy who identified Maryam in the street?' someone asked.

'He is,' another woman responded.

But then there was a noise, as if something hard had dropped on the floor, and the wing fell silent. I heard my neighbour say in a low voice, 'Xavar, don't talk now.'

***

Azadam, I'm writing these letters to myself in a way. It's like writing the screenplay of my life. And though my current life is a horror film, writing about our relationship reminds me of good days which I need to remember and hang on to. Two days after my arrest, when I was still in pain,

Ghulam interrogated me, this time differently. He gave me a bundle of paper and said, 'You had better write, if you don't want more of the same.'

As soon as I heard the door close, I pulled up the blindfold to see the room. No one else was there. I took a few sheets of paper and hid them in my underwear. I was worried he'd realise when he came back for them, but it was another guard who came and took the paper and guided me to my cell. He was warning me that Ghulam would call me again, because I hadn't written anything. So, I made this little notebook with those pieces of paper and I'm happy to fill them all. I still have some of the sheets my neighbour gave me, and I've hidden them in a safe place in the bathroom. My love, I like the idea of using these pages first, the ones they gave me in order to write a confession for them, but now I write only for you. Writing to you gives me the feeling I'm

***

Azadam, a few days have passed since I wrote the previous pages and now I've learnt when it's safest to write. Early morning is a good time to lie down in such a way that looks as if I'm asleep if the guard peers through the peephole, and I can write without making any movement. Fridays are also good days, when not many guards are around, and you know, when the guard comes to the wing to check on us, prisoners tell each other by making a loud noise. I find it heart-warming that even here people try to help each other.

Last night, I was fast asleep when I was jolted awake by the sound of the cell door opening. I woke up properly and looked at the guard. In a low voice she said, 'Come on. Interrogation.'

I stood up and groped for the blindfold and the chador that I had been given when I was brought to this prison on the first day of my arrest. She led me to the outside wing and there Ghulam was waiting for me. He took a corner of the chador and pulled me down the stairs, past the yard and the blue pond, and up another staircase. When we entered a room, he gave me some pieces of musical notation.

'Read them to me.'

'I can't. My husband played them.'

'Who were these for? How come you can't read them if you wrote them?'

'I didn't write them. My husband bought them.'

'From whom?'

'I don't know.'

'Don't lie. These are secret letters to the CIA or Mosad. You and your husband communicated with them in this coded language, so that nobody would understand. Tell me what the meaning of these symbols is, or I promise to God I'll beat you to death tonight.'

'These are just sheets of music! My husband used them to play the guitar.'

'We didn't see any guitar in your house.'

I was happy to hear you'd taken your guitar with you when you left our home forever.

'We'll find out when we torture you again.'

'Show it to some other people. Someone here must recognise music.'

'Shut up. Don't pretend to be clever, you whore.'

There was silence for a while, then he said, 'Write down how many men you've slept with and what you did.'

At first, I thought, I'm not hearing him correctly and so I asked, 'What?' He came close to me and shouted at me, 'You're not deaf, are you? Write about the men who fucked you and how they did it.'

I felt rage mounting inside me and a kind of desire to do him real harm. But I knew that he would retaliate, so I tried to stay calm. I only said, 'You can watch a video if you need to satisfy your desires. I don't have anything to tell you.'

He slapped me hard around the face and said, 'I can make you write.'

I said, 'You can't.'

From below the blindfold I saw he had withdrawn his fist, which had been near my burning cheek. He continued, 'I can if I want. But tell me why you're so shy about writing down what you did? Isn't it true that infidels sleep around and do not believe in marriage because they don't believe in God or in punishment? So, be brave and write about your filthy activities. You didn't write about your political activity, so you can at least write about this.'

My Azad, I don't know how long the silence lasted, perhaps about ten minutes, although he was playing with himself and making some noises now and then. Then he said, 'Okay, you can resist writing about your sins. But now you have to do some writing and I won't let you go back to your cell until you do. You said you don't know anything about your Farid's espionage activities. Fine, but you must know about your prophets, Marx and Lenin. Now write something about each of them.'

'What's the point? You can't arrest them,' I said.

'No, I can't. Although I would go to the end of the earth to kill them with my own hands if they were alive. Now don't waste my time. Write about each of them on separate pages,' he said.

He sat on a chair and I could only see his legs and feet, which had slippers on – the same kind of slippers I had been given to wear on the first day here, when they took away my shoes.

My love, I thought I'd better write about Marx and Lenin, which at least wouldn't harm anyone. I started to write and realised I don't know much about them. I couldn't even remember the dates of their births and deaths. I could only reveal that Marx wrote *Capital* and Lenin wrote *What Is To Be Done?* I couldn't even remember the other books of theirs that I've read. He left the room and came back after an hour. He looked at the pages and said, 'Is that all?'

'Yes. I don't know anything more than this,' I said.

'You liar. You have to write all you know,' he said and left the room again.

All I wanted was to go back to my cell and sleep. I tried the door, but it was locked. I hid some of the sheets of paper he had left for me inside my clothes and sat there waiting.

He came back in the morning and looked at the pages again and said, 'You haven't written anything.'

'That's all I know about them. I don't know the addresses of their graves,' I told him.

He said, 'I know what to do with you to open your mouth.' Then he led me back to the cell. Passing through the yard I could feel that the day had just begun, and imagined you kissing my lips to say good morning. I tipped my head back to see the sky from underneath the blindfold. He saw me doing this and pulled my chador hard, so that I stumbled. I was in the cell by the time the guard came around with breakfast tea.

You know Azadam, last night as Ghulam slapped my face, I saw his hand from beneath my blindfold, and I thought how is it that people come to use their hands for such different purposes? Some use their hands to crush, some to create. I recalled your hands playing the guitar. Sometimes I felt jealous of that guitar. Last night I was thinking about you playing your guitar and I remembered our neighbour. We were living in a flat in west Tehran and once when we went out of the door, our neighbour who was walking down the stairs, said to you, 'I enjoy hearing you play.'

***

Faraz stopped reading and thought of Ghulam, Xavar's interrogator. Who was he? What was he doing now? How did he feel about himself as an interrogator? Was he still in the same job? What about his uncle, did he too interrogate prisoners? Or did he just run the place and not deal with actual people?

***

Darling, I haven't been able to write to you for about two weeks, because of the pain and because the guard had to come and change the dressing on my infected feet. A few days ago I was taken for interrogation again. Since I'm thinking that we didn't know anything about this place and prisons in general, let me tell you what I heard from behind the door of one of the interrogation rooms, while waiting for my turn. I could hear noises from the room, but then I felt someone leave without closing the door. I could hear what was being said inside the room, where there was a person under torture. I could tell because he breathed with difficulty. Someone seemed to be boasting about his ability to break the prisoners under his hands.

'You better listen carefully. I used to be a welder. I used a torch to cut steel pipe. I used oxygen to weld metals. With you I'll just stop it reaching your body. You'll melt slowly in front of your own eyes. No, I won't let you melt. I want to make a welder out of you. We need you to weld the opposition to us, as I used filler for welding pipes and tubes. I'm going to make you into the filler and you'll fill the gap between us and your friends...'

Azadam, I couldn't believe what I was hearing, but then came footsteps and the door was closed again. Now I only heard noises but could not make out what they were saying. Time passed, and I was sitting there, thinking about the prisoner who was being tortured. Who was he? Had he just been arrested? Again, the door was opened and someone came running out. I heard the same voice.

'Where's the doctor? He's dying. Quick. Have we lost him?'

Azadam, my heart was racing for the poor

man under torture and I could hear running feet. Then after a few minutes, I heard a submissive voice.

'I'm sorry, I can't resuscitate him...'

I heard the welder shouting:

'You stupid... You came too late. Haven't you learned anything? How can you call yourself a doctor?'

My love, I was so distressed to think of the person who had died at their hands.

Then it was my turn to be interrogated and I was taken to a different room, some distance away from the room where the man was killed. Ghulam read a report, which was about a wall that the people in charge of one particular factory had built in the middle of the canteen to divide it in two, so that fewer workers could sit together and talk to each other about their problems while they ate. I remember that you were very angry and told me that if they succeeded in doing this, it would be difficult to gather the 2,000 workers together. But I learned that you were the person who told the angry workers that if they weren't happy with the wall, then they should smash it. Ghulam read from a report, 'Farid hadn't even finished speaking when the workers attacked the wall and destroyed it.'

When Ghulam had read the report to me, or part of it, he said, 'Farid is very dangerous,' and I believe him. That is why I love you so much.

Stay dangerous to their system and their orders. Do more of the same for both of us!

After he had read out the report, he was silent for a while and then asked me about it, and I said again that you hadn't told me anything about it.

You know, my love, that day when I came back from interrogation, my mind was on our activities and what I'd experienced during the revolution that I'd never experienced before. One image stood out. It was of the first time I saw a rain of literature in a meeting. I realised leaflets were coming down, dancing in the air, while my hands were among thousands of others reaching up to the sky to try and catch them. Those were the same hands that were fists against the Shah and that very shortly afterwards became fists once again, to condemn the oppression of the Islamic regime.

***

Faraz felt that the image of hands trying to catch leaflets was familiar. Where had he seen it? Then he remembered one of his mother's paintings, which was in their storeroom, though he had not looked at it for a few years. The painting was very similar to what Xavar had described: a scene of people with their hands up, trying to catch something, which at first glance looked like big flakes of snow, but then would appear to have been sheets of paper. His mother called that painting, 'The Rain of

Freedom'. Now he felt that since he had never seen that kind of rain, he'd never missed it. Until the internet was accessible to people, he didn't know the joy of freedom of information. It was only a year since the young had begun creating their own blogs and posting their spontaneous thoughts and articles or chatting with each other freely. Over the past year, hundreds of weblogs had sprung up, for teaching, political and cultural discussion, or for various magazines. He remembered the conversation he had had with Omid, who said, 'This is temporary; soon the Big Brothers will sell the technology to the regime to monitor and arrest those who use the internet, or blog to promote people's awareness of political events.' Faraz suddenly felt, once again, nostalgic for the conversations he had had with his brother and all that exchange of news.

He looked at his watch and realised his parents would wake up soon, so he decided to leave the rest of Xavar's notebook for the following night and get some sleep before going to work.

***

My love, I don't have newspapers, a radio, or a TV. All the news I hear comes from the interrogators, and they give me information that makes me anxious and tired. They try to make me believe the outside world is dead. Last time I was interrogated, one of them said, 'We have arrested everyone. All of your groups.' I wanted to ask: why then are you pestering me to give you information?

Azadam, remember to take care of your neck, which I know gives you pain. You shouldn't strain it too much when you read, then it will hurt less.

Now I'm certain I'm pregnant, because I have morning sickness. It's funny when I think our child must be as stubborn as you and me, because after all that torture she is still exactly where she should be.

Did I tell you that I asked for a bucket, so I can use it when I need to urinate? But the smell is unbearable! It's as if I'm living in a toilet, sleeping through its stench and eating beside it.

How does the skin of an orange smell, darling? I don't want to forget that scent. I only conjure up fruit in my mind; I haven't seen any since my arrest.

I can see the top of a tree from one of the bathrooms. The one which is on the right-hand side of the corridor. Even from behind the dirty window, it looks greenish at the top of the wall. When I go to this bathroom, I look at that tree as soon as I remove the blindfold. Otherwise the colour here is grey, and I never liked grey. I don't know why, perhaps because white and black are both lost in grey. I miss colour, especially the colour of your lips, which I used to kiss so often.

***

Faraz realised that he hadn't noticed that tree or had been indifferent to it. Once on the wing, his mind was focused only on those walls and he could not even look out of the windows to see if anything were visible. Though he always loved sitting or reading on the veranda at home, so that he could see flowers and trees whenever he looked up, he knew that he never saw them in the same way that Xavar gazed at the top of that tree.

He touched Xavar's notebook and looked forward eagerly to the rest of her writing, even before he had finished the one he had in his hands. She had written and hidden at least another two notebooks, numbers 2 and 3, which he had not yet found. Maybe more. He smiled at the idea that he was engaging in a kind of affair, reading a woman's letters while Nasim was asleep and, though they were not addressed to him, he read them as if they were written especially for him.

***

Azadam, I feel so alone in here. I asked my neighbour, Shirin, if she could teach me Morse code so we could communicate more easily, and she said, 'Don't worry, it's very simple. Just listen to what I tell you and then practise it with me on the wall tonight. Tomorrow night we will be able to chat properly.'

'Okay,' I said, and we practised for a while. Then suddenly we heard the warning signal, and the whispers and Morse tapping stopped immediately. Shirin said, 'We'll stop now.' A few minutes later the peephole cover was pushed aside, and a guard was watching me.

I wrote the letters in four rows on the wall and practised the Morse code with the fingers of one of my hands on the palm of the other, so as to be able to tap faster. At night, we talked again with broken Morse code, because I was very slow to understand and to tap correctly.

Azadam, I asked Shirin how was it she had pen and paper and knows Morse code, and she told me that she was arrested a few months ago and had been at Evin until now and had learnt it there. She told me that she had hidden needles, pen and paper in her belongings when she came from Evin. I was surprised, because I thought they were all recently arrested, like me. Shirin sent me one of her extra needles, which I used to stitch this little notebook with a bit of thread I took from my towel.

My love, I'm so glad that I now know how to talk to people here. The language of this world is Morse, and very different from the language outside. It's as if I've entered a different country, without knowing its language. It would be hard to survive if you didn't know how to communicate. The language here is not spoken, though it still has the quality of sound. It reminds me of a heartbeat, which is sometimes louder and faster, and it means that the guards are no longer managing to separate us. The first time

I heard Morse code, it reminded me of the day we were walking in the forest two years ago, when we both squeezed each other's hands at the same time to say listen, and we stood still. Then hearing the drumming of woodpeckers, we looked up at the tops of the tall trees. No matter how hard we looked, we couldn't see any woodpeckers, yet their tapping echoed around the wood. We asked each other how many there were but we couldn't tell. I wonder if the Morse code was learnt from woodpeckers.

Now that I've learnt Morse code, I can communicate with other prisoners at night. But what about during the day, when time feels endless and without any excitement? Now I understand why they use solitary confinement to break people. I feel as if in solitary confinement we meet ourselves, by being forced to think. On the outside, they have removed our capacity to think, by making us busy all the time with work or mindless entertainment on their television and then, in here, they leave us alone. And since we aren't used to living alone and thinking, we quickly get bored, and after that we become frightened.

***

My love, how are you? Don't ask me how I feel. It's a few days since I've written to you. I was taken for interrogation again this evening, and this time there was another so-called man acting as if he had some concerns about me.

He said, 'Is it true you're pregnant?'

'Yes,' I said.

'So why don't you do something to get yourself out of here? I know bringing your husband here is hard for you, but you should know that we won't harm him.'

I thought, *Sure you won't – just as you didn't harm me.*

He continued, 'Think about what kind of man your husband is, that he would let you stay here in place of him and his activities.'

Azadam, I had a desire to slap his face for not only insulting you but insulting me with words like this. Instead I said, 'I was told that there was evidence against me and that's the reason for my arrest. I wasn't told that I'm a hostage for my husband, which is what you are saying.'

'Well, it's not exactly that you're a hostage, but we'll let you go if he hands himself in. Your husband is thinking about his life rather than yours. If it's hard to tell us where he is, then you can help us in other ways and we can let you out very soon, even as soon as next week. What we want you to do is just go and live as before, continue with all your usual activities and go to all your meetings. All we'll do is watch from a distance. We might sometimes get in touch with you to ask you a few questions, that's all. But we won't let anyone know about it, you don't have to worry about that. I know how you would feel about being looked on as a spy. What we want from you is that you just act normally and take on whatever responsibilities they give you. Go and have your child and raise her yourself, rather than depriving your child of her mother.'

He paused for a moment and then said, 'I asked Ghulam to let me talk to you. Now go and think about my suggestions and I'll tell Ghulam not to disturb you for twenty-four hours. If you make up your mind to help us and want us to help you, let me know before this time tomorrow, otherwise Ghulam will summon you. And you know his method is different from mine.'

Azizam, I didn't say anything and wondered how much more they could beat me. I talked it over with my neighbour and she said, 'They won't beat you any more, because they've realised you're strong enough not to reveal any information.'

I asked her, 'So, what did the interrogator mean by saying Ghulam's method is different?'

'I'm sorry, but I think he was threatening you with rape,' she said. 'I'm telling you because you're a strong woman and I'm sure you'll bear it, and you wouldn't trade information for not being raped.'

I was so shocked, my hand dropped from the wall I was tapping, and I missed what she said after that. Then I heard her asking me if I was still there.

'Yes. I'm listening. But it's unbelievable,' I said.

'Xavar, nothing is unbelievable in here! People die here under torture, and they use any possible means at all to open our mouths and give them information. And by not telling them what we know, we make a statement to them and to ourselves that we have a different kind of power over them. So be brave. I know you're a brave woman.'

So, my love, I thought to finish this notebook today and hide it before tomorrow. I don't know what's going to happen and I hope my neighbour is wrong. I can't bear to think of any harm being done to our little child inside the frail cage of my body. Be with me tomorrow and I'll be with you. Be your name. Xavar.

***

His parents were still asleep when Faraz finished Xavar's notebook, but he sat there in their sitting room with the lamp on. He felt miserable and could do nothing to get away from the thought of what had happened in 1984 to this woman. He knew she was one of many. Now he could understand why his parents and Omid were so angry at the idea of his being identified with the regime. They had seen what had happened to people like Xavar; that's why they hated the Islamists and anyone who helped them. Even if that person was their brother, like Rohulah - or indeed, like himself. Faraz stared out into the room, sunk in thought, wishing there were some way he could exact revenge on Xavar's behalf. He had to go to work in a few hours and he hadn't slept. He was not sleepy, but he was tired. He felt very tired, as if a heavy load was weighing on his shoulders.

***

As soon as he reached the interrogation centre, Faraz wanted to search the ventilation shaft in the other bathroom, but he had to wait until the afternoon, to make sure his uncle was not around. On examining the ventilation grille, he realised there was nothing loose, and so he gave up. After a couple of hours, however, he thought to bring the ladder and climbed up to look at the ventilation area again. He felt the surface around it carefully. His eyes caught sight of a slightly discoloured patch on the wall a couple of inches away from the grille. He touched it to feel if there was anything unusual. It seemed normal, but the difference in colour puzzled him. He tried to pull the mesh off the edge of the ventilator nearest to the discoloured patch, but everything held firm. Disappointed, he came down the ladder and continued his work.

Then a thought flashed through his mind. He went back to the bathroom and again put the ladder up under the ventilation shaft and with one of his tools tried to peel off the discoloured part of the wall. As he was working away at the surface he heard a noise in the corridor. He tried to back down the ladder quickly, but it shifted and fell. Before crashing to the floor he jumped and hit the back of his left hand on the washbasin. His hand started to bleed but the pain wasn't too bad. He went into the corridor and walked to the entrance. No one was there, and the wood behind the door was in place.

After cleaning his hand and bandaging it, he went back to the bathroom. He began the process once again of removing the plaster from the wall. As he hacked off a small piece of it, he excitedly tried to force his uninjured hand into the ventilation shaft, but the area was too small. He could not give up now. He used some of his tools to make the small space wide enough for him to be able to reach inside.

Suddenly he heard another noise. He tried hard to hold on to the ladder and not to fall down this time. He listened again. Nothing. He was worried that his uncle or anyone else might come. He resumed his work, but again heard something. Coming down the ladder he went into the corridor to see that a sparrow had flown in and got trapped. Relieved that it was nothing else, he once again started work and this time found nothing. The space behind the mesh was empty, except for spiders' webs and dead flies. He took down the ladder and cleared up the messy floor. Looking at the hole, he was worried that his uncle would notice it if he came into this bathroom. What explanation could he give? He knew that he would be in grave danger if anyone noticed it, so he realised he would have to cover it up with plaster, which he swiftly did. The newness of it troubled him and so he brought in some paint and applied it all around the ventilation area.

He was soaked with sweat and his left hand was hurting. The sense of frustration he felt was so strong that his body couldn't cope with it. He ran his hand over his forehead and realised he could do no more work that day. He went down to reception.

As soon as he saw Faraz, the Islamic Guard who was in charge whenever his uncle was not around, asked, 'Have you injured your arm?'

'Yes. It's painful. Do you have a first aid kit?'

'You'd better go to hospital and make sure it's not serious. Inshalah it will be fine soon, but you must get it checked out,' said the man.

'Okay. I'd better go. It is quite painful,' said Faraz. He needed an excuse to get away from there. His head was screaming. He realised that since they knew he was Rohulah's nephew, they treated him as if he, too, had some authority, and stayed away from him.

Chapter Ten

ANOTHER PART OF TOWN

For the past few days, Faraz had not seen his mother when he came back from work. He went to her studio. Through the door, he could hear a loud passage from Beethoven's symphony No 9. He realised she was absorbed with her painting and didn't hear his knock. He felt Ana only wanted to hear that music and see nothing except the paint on her brush, stroking the canvas. He stood near the door, facing his mother's back. She was working just on one corner of the canvas, so he could see most of it. It showed women with their hands clenched over their heads, their mouths aggressively open, as if shouting with all their strength. The women's tongues in the front row were as red as the flags over their heads at the back, as if they were bleeding. Rain from grey clouds was washing their hair, sticking their clothes to their bodies, highlighting the curves of those at the front.

He felt the scene was familiar. He knew that his mother painted the images she had stored in her mind's eye, of the demonstrations which took place between 1978 and 1981. This one reminded him of one of her paintings of the women's demonstration a few days after Khomeini returned from exile and said that women should cover their hair. Faraz could not remember if it was his mother or Khomeini who said that the veil was the flag of political Islam, but he remembered Ana saying we could not get rid of a flag without getting rid of the politics behind it.

Faraz didn't disturb his mother by speaking or making a noise. He left her, wondering why she was painting this scene again. She had sold that painting to a friend of her friends. Why *was* she painting it again? She never painted the same scene twice. This one seemed different, though. Darker, with women's nakedness and rain. It seemed to him that she was making a point by doing it again, as if proclaiming that she was not like her son, a collaborator. Though Ana never said anything to hurt him, she wasn't talking to him as much as she had before he started working in the prison. Faraz knew that his mother escaped into her painting when she was troubled. Usually, she painted for four hours a day and the rest of her day was spent on housework, reading, or seeing family and friends. But now she was mostly in her studio, their spare room, which she had turned into a workshop.

He remembered that, ever since he was little, she had found consolation in painting when she was upset, and it helped her a great deal. She looked younger than most women of her age and was healthier. Looking back, he realised that Ana's painting had become political again. There had been a break of a few years when she painted other things. An example of that period hung in her bedroom: a painting of men and women in the sea. And there was a painting in their living room of a wooden basket full of books on a shore, with a few books lying here and there around it. Facing it was another painting of a suitcase floating in the sea. There were a few smaller paintings of hers in the corridor. One was a painting of an elegant neck wearing a necklace, and another of a pair of feet with a jewelled anklet. But for the past few years, after the assassinations of the opposition started, she had returned to her old political subjects. Recently, when news of assassinations dwindled, her work had changed again, this time back to nudes, which Faraz saw as an act of rebellion. But now she had re-started her political paintings, and they were becoming much bolder since he had begun his work at the interrogation centre.

Faraz thought they were all suffering and escaping into some kind of obsession. Some addictions, such as painting, didn't hurt the artist or anyone else, but other neuroses, such as obsessive cleanliness, might affect the person and the people around her. His grandmother was suffering from compulsive cleanliness, and it was killing her. Now he realised how much the social situation and the fact that one of her sons supported the regime had pushed her into this state. She cleaned her house every day and washed her hands so often that sometimes her fingers bled. Faraz believed his brother, Omid, was also suffering from obsessive compulsive disorder, though of a different kind. Omid was careful to stay clean politically. While Faraz was adventurous and liked to try new things, as long as they didn't hurt anyone, his brother wouldn't risk anything that might make people denounce him.

Faraz felt lonely; his family neither understood him, nor did they trust him any longer. He couldn't share with them the things he found in the interrogation centre because they were against his working there in the first place, regarding him as a rewriter of history, a censor of people's resistance. He couldn't ring his brother and talk to him, as he would have done until a few months ago. He couldn't reply to Omid's insulting emails. He felt Omid's poisonous tongue was turning his parents against him, yet he could do nothing about it. How fragile people's relationships were when it came to politics. His father's relationship with his uncle was never the same after Rohulah sided with the Islamists in 1979, and now Faraz was feeling a kind of rejection by his family as well. He could see all too easily how the atmosphere in their house had changed as soon as he started working at the prison.

***

Faraz began to read all the graffiti on cell walls that he had not yet examined. At last, in cell number 8, he saw Xavar's name and the dates she had entered in early spring 1984 and left in the summer. The writing was already fading.

After a few frustrating days in which he discovered no more of Xavar's letters, he went to the Art Café to see Bahram.

'You look awful,' said Bahram as soon as they had sat down.

'I can't find the rest of Xavar's letters. I don't know what to do any more, to work out where she hid them.'

'Perhaps you aren't looking closely enough.'

'I don't know. I'm tired.'

'Tell me, where did you find the notebook?'

'I found one behind the pipes and the second in the toilet ventilation.'

'What? You didn't tell me there's more than one.

You've found another?'

'I have, along with some letters from people who were going to be executed.'

'Have you brought them for me?' Bahram asked excitedly.

'Yes.'

'Good,' Bahram said with a sigh. 'You wouldn't keep anything back from me, would you now?'

'Don't worry, I'll let you know about everything, but you have to keep it all secret.'

'I know. But give them to me now, before you forget.'

Faraz took out a small box wrapped in beautiful paper and gave it to Bahram.

'It is a present indeed,' Bahram said, taking it from him and putting it in his pocket.

'Yes, and there's an extra present inside it. For your birthday. You'll like it.'

'There's another six months to my birthday.'

'Then it's your half-birthday.'

'Thanks. It seems this uncle of yours pays you well.'

'He does. Though only part of it is for my work. The rest is Forood's, Xavar's and other people's blood money.'

'You're right. Is it cash you're giving me?'

'It is.'

'Thanks, that's very good of you,' said Bahram. 'As a matter of fact, I'm really glad of it just now. One of my colleagues has been arrested. He's a young teacher with a wife and kid. So, there's no money coming into the family and we're supporting them.' He grinned. 'Bet your Uncle never reckoned on his dirty money being put to such good use, did he?'

Faraz smiled wanly. 'That reminds me,' he said. 'Today the receptionist told me that there's furniture stored there and asked me to look at it in case I wanted anything. He said they're going to get rid of it all. I didn't know what he meant exactly until I went with him to see it. He left me there and said I could help myself to whatever I liked. There was another man there trying to decide what to take. At first, I couldn't understand why all these sofas, shelves, books, computers and other things were just dumped there. Were their owners arrested, too? Then as I looked, I understood that these things had belonged to the prisoners. They had been stolen from their houses at the time of the raids and never returned.'

'Did you take anything?' Bahram asked, screwing up his face.

'Yes, I took a few things. I saw two pairs of glasses and took them. Here they are. Their owners must be long dead, presumably.' Faraz took them out of his pocket and handed them to Bahram, who examined them gingerly.

'And these two.' Faraz took out an English copy of a small-sized *Communist Manifesto* from his pocket and removed a pencil drawing of a mountain from between its pages.

Bahram took them and looked at them. His eyes filled with tears.

'I did think of those students of ours who are truly in need, but I couldn't take anything from there for them to use.'

They sat in silence for some time.

'The whole thing must be very depressing for you. I'm worried about you,' Bahram said.

'I'm okay. Don't worry.'

Bahram changed the subject. 'About the birth certificate you were after the other day…'

Faraz sat up with interest. 'What about it? Have you found someone who might be able to forge one?'

'Well, I think Nasim doesn't need a forged birth certificate. There are birth certificates around, which she can have and then make up her own story.'

Faraz frowned. 'I don't understand.'

'They're birth certificates of people who died in the Iran-Iraq war. She only needs to pretend that it's hers,' Bahram explained.

'But where can we find one?'

'I talked to some people and I was told there are two women's birth certificates, which I'll be sent in a couple of months, as they're not in Tehran right now. But there is one problem with them.'

'What's that?' asked Faraz.

'In both cases the owner is older than Nasim. If she is fine with that, then she can have one of them.'

'How old are the certificates?'

'Twenty-seven and twenty-nine.'

'I don't think she'll have any problem with that,' Faraz told him. 'Once we have it, we can register our marriage and stop worrying that we'll get caught and she'll be tortured or killed.'

'That's right,' said Bahram, smiling ruefully.

Faraz sat back listening to the classical music and looked at the long wall, which held a display containing newspapers from all around the world. He noticed a new one. It was a foreign newspaper with George W. Bush's picture on it, which was displayed upside down. It reminded him that, despite all the regime's cooperation with America in Afghanistan against the Taliban, Bush had now named Iran as part of an Axis of Evil.

'I'm invited to a party. Come with me,' Bahram suggested.

'No. I won't go without Nasim.'

'I didn't mean come without her. I'll be with my girlfriend, too.'

'No. I don't want any risk right now. It will be the end of her life if the guards raid it,' Faraz said.

'Don't worry. I wouldn't mention it if I wasn't sure that it's safe. It's one hundred percent safe. Come on, you need a break, man.'

'How do you know it's safe?' asked Faraz.

'They have parties all the time. It's nowhere near us, south Revolution or Freedom Road. It's in north Tehran, in one of those Hollywood-style mansions.'

Faraz blinked at him. 'How come you know people there?'

'I know someone there from university and I've been to one of their parties. It happens every Thursday and they dance, drink and smoke till morning. Sometimes they even sleep there, or should I say collapse there and go home on Friday.'

'What a life. No, thank you. I don't like going to that part of the world. I prefer to stick to parties on this side of the world, where our students live, and get arrested for trying to have some simple fun!'

'I want you to see it and have a bit of a good time too. I know it will make you angrier. I was furious when I first saw it but, man, we have to know about this. We need to see it. Otherwise, how can we explain where all the wealth that is produced in this country is going? We only see the poverty, unemployment and street children and try to save one in every hundred of them,' said Bahram bitterly.

After more persuasion, Faraz agreed to go. 'But are you sure Nasim would be safe?'

'Yes, very sure,' Bahram assured him. 'All these regulations and laws are only for the poor, not for the rich who are in power.'

***

Nasim decided to go as a boy so that, if anything happened, she could not be identified as Faraz's girlfriend. She felt she was safe as a boy.

As Faraz and Nasim drove into Tehran's northern suburbs, they felt as though they were entering a different country. There were no street children, no beggars, no one selling things to survive, hand to mouth. Instead, there were quiet streets with tall trees on both sides, screening from view the mansions set back from the road behind walls and gates.

At the party, they were greeted by Bahram, his girlfriend and his friend from university. Other guests, about sixty of them, all wore designer clothes and had arrived in BMWs. They seemed to have just come from London or Paris, though there were exclusive boutiques catering for them in Tehran. They were dancing to loud western pop music and drinking wine. Other alcoholic drinks were in evidence, too – not to mention the drugs. Bahram murmured to Faraz that people were smoking opium. Faraz noticed three very good-looking boys in bow ties making their way through the crowd, serving glasses of wine, gin, vodka and other drinks on a tray. They were helped by three young women whose job was to refill the plates of food on the table. He could see that they were paid to serve the party-goers and were not from the same class as the host. Some of the guests were already drunk, stoned or apparently hallucinating. Most of the girls were barely covered.

Faraz and Nasim listened and gazed around at the faces as Bahram whispered into their ears. They learned that these people were all the children of those in power or related to the country's ruling establishment, the millionaires. The fathers of some of them had become millionaires in just a few years as a result of having the right connections, gaining foreign trade licences to negotiate deals and set up joint ventures in oil or car manufacture. They had flourished during the last ten years of privatisation, when hundreds of businesses were sold off to those with links to the new elite.

Faraz knew his uncle Rohulah was one of those trusted people who had a hand in the 'Bonyads', which controlled the economy by confiscating companies from the Shah's regime. Like his uncle, these rich people had benefited from tax breaks and loans. Bahram was telling them who was the son of whom and married to the daughter of this or that minister or mullah. In a way they were all related, not only as part of the ruling class, but in terms of being family.

Watching the guests as they sampled different dishes, not because they were hungry but just out of curiosity, Faraz thought of his students who could not concentrate in class because they were hungry and malnourished. Half of the population was living below the poverty line and because of the country's economic problems the age of marriage had been raised. People could not afford to marry and lived instead with their parents or, like himself, had relationships outside the law. But many people were deprived of a natural relationship because they couldn't afford it.

While people of the opposite sex would be arrested if they were seen together in public places such as parks, here they were having all the fun without any of the risk. It seemed that some were living nearby, as they came without observing the dress code. However, if any guards dared to stop or arrest them they would pay the fine quickly and get away.

Bahram's friend asked Faraz and Nasim if they'd like to look around the house. In the kitchen Faraz realised all the knives were chained and movable only within one metre, so no one could take a knife out of the kitchen.

'How come all the boys and girls are so handsome? Where do you find them?' asked Nasim.

'You see that lady in the blue suit, the one who isn't drinking, just observing? She is the manager of a trusted company. She chooses the waiters and waitresses. They're all in high school or their first year of university and need the money. They're interviewed and then the successful ones get sent on a training course for a few days.'

Later, Faraz asked Bahram, 'Aren't they afraid that the waiters or waitresses might take a picture and publish it online?'

'Their bags and mobiles are taken off them before they're brought to wherever they're going to work for the evening,' Bahram explained.

Faraz thought that, like himself, half the population was under thirty and could barely remember the revolution, or life under the Shah. They'd grown up under oppressive laws and all aspects of their lives were scrutinised. He wondered if those young people whose parties were raided because they didn't have money to pay off the Islamic Guard in advance, knew about this life. What would they do if they learnt that freedom existed, but - like plentiful food - only for the rich?

Chapter Eleven

THE CASPIAN SEA

After a few days' intense searching for Xavar's letters, and not finding any more, Faraz woke up one morning in a sweat, gripped by fear and anxiety. He had been dreaming of being blindfolded and pushed around in the detention centre as a prisoner. Forood, his parents, Omid and Nasim had been arrested, too. At one point, Forood was laughing under torture and he looked as he had looked twenty years ago, without a trace of white hair or any sign of aging, as if time had stopped for him. While Omid, who was younger than Forood, had grey hair and was telling the interrogators that he had done those paintings. Yes, some of his mother's paintings had been confiscated, too, and they wanted to know who the artist was. The interrogators kicked the painting of a river of dancing people, as if kicking the people depicted there. The guards turned one of the paintings to face the wall, as if it would corrupt them all. It showed a woman whose head-to-toe black chador had dropped to her waist exposing half her naked body. In his dream, though he was there as a prisoner, Faraz's mind was busy looking for things in hidden places, such as behind cracks in the walls.

Though it was still early he couldn't sleep. He went downstairs and found his father reading a newspaper.

'Morning,' Faraz said, trying to hide his discomfort.

'Morning, Faraz. What is it this time? A political mission that you have to get yourself sacrificed for?'

'What are you talking about?' Faraz asked in surprise.

'Just look in the mirror and you'll understand what I'm talking about.'

Faraz regarded his father curiously. 'I don't get it,' he said.

'No. We don't have much to say to each other these days. You've lost weight and you look depressed. I bet you can't sleep, either. What's going on, my son?'

'Nothing important, I promise.'

'Tell me the unimportant things, then.' Nima was looking concerned. 'Ask for a month's leave and see if you feel better. Then go and finish the job. Don't you think you've already seen enough there? I don't understand why you're killing yourself over it.'

'I'm not killing myself. I've just lost my appetite, that's all. I'll be okay soon.'

'Please ask for some time off and stay at home. Or go somewhere with Nasim. Or we could all go somewhere together for a few days, if you wanted to,' suggested Nima.

Faraz was staring down at his hands. He looked up into his father's eyes. Nima's face was kind, very different from Rohulah's, which seemed twisted by so much hatred. How could two brothers be so different, as if they were born or raised in completely different worlds? 'I'll think about it,' Faraz promised.

'Your mother's worried about you. Every day she says there's food left over because you don't eat like you used to.'

'All right, I'll tell Uncle today that I want to take next week off. I'm sure there's enough time to finish the job,' Faraz said.

'When are they going to open their museum of deception for public propaganda?' asked his father grimly.

'In January.'

***

Faraz asked Rohulah for a week's leave, which his uncle agreed to, but before he was due to stop work he redoubled his efforts to find more of Xavar's letters. He looked everywhere, studying the walls carefully, but found nothing, except an elegant long string of prayer beads made from date stones. The search for Xavar's diary distracted him and he couldn't concentrate on what he was doing. While working and trying not to miss any potential hiding places, his mind was also dwelling on Xavar's interrogator, Ghulam. Since reading her letters, whenever he saw an Islamic Guard he wondered if it was Ghulam. He had heard from activists who had been arrested in recent years and spent time in prison that some of the interrogators had been around in the 1980s.

Faraz wondered what kind of a man Ghulam was and whether he was still an interrogator, torturing the next generation of activists. What would happen to his children? Come to that, what would happen to Rohulah's? His uncle had four children, two boys and two girls, who seemed to be out of Iran now for much of the year. Faraz was always hearing from his mother, who had talked to Rohulah's wife, that one or other of them had just come to

Iran for a month, or that she and Rohulah were going to this or that European city or were in America to see their children. In fact, he'd heard his parents talking about this just a few days ago.

'Your sister-in-law called and said Aida has come home for a short visit and they went to Mashhad,' Ana told Nima. 'Apparently Aida asked her to book the best hotel, which has a swimming pool, Jacuzzi, sauna, massage and so on. And they stayed there for ten days. She said Aida thought it was very cheap. She would have to pay fifty times as much for the same service in the UK. She was going on and on, and I had to tell a lie to get rid of her and say that I'd got someone about to arrive and would have to go.'

'Of course, luxury life is cheaper here than in Europe,' his father had said. 'But it's only for those in power, or who have dollars to spend.'

Faraz remembered reading an article about one of the governors of Evin Prison who was now living in a palace he had bought in Canada. Would Xavar's torturer, or his Uncle Rohulah, retire to Canada, he wondered? Faraz felt a bitterness he had never felt before. He didn't like it. This interrogation centre had changed him.

***

Ana proposed they all go to the North and suggested taking her mother with them, too.

'Wouldn't it be a problem for Faraz and me?' asked Nasim, concerned.

'Not in the least,' Ana assured her. 'We're going to my

friend's villa, which is in a closed resort called Sea Home, near Babul. Police don't go there. It has its own security guard, employed by the residents. There's nothing to worry about. I've been there a couple of times and you have to see it! Once we're there, you and Faraz are husband and wife and I'm sure you'll have a good time.'

Faraz didn't like the idea but had no reason not to go, and Nasim kept pressing him until he accepted. He had heard about Sea Home and other little towns which were enclosed and protected enclaves, but he had never seen any of them. These places had been built by contractors, who bought the land cheaply from the poor and developed it into a resort that only the rich could buy into or use. None of the rules regarding segregation in the sea, or swimming, or the hijab applied there, and no moral police patrolled the seashore.

When they arrived at the main gate, the security guard approached and asked who they were. Ana gave the name of her friend and the guard confirmed that she had telephoned. He opened the gate and let them in. They found themselves in a little community of twenty villas. Women in bikinis were swimming beside men in the sea.

'Has the regime collapsed?' gasped Nasim.

'No, darling. The regime is firmly in place, keeping the poor in order but not policing itself!' Ana replied, taking off her scarf and exposing her hair to the air.

'Well, I would believe it if you'd told me we'd come to a European seaside town,' said Faraz's grandmother. 'Not only because of the architecture, but because of the people. Some of them are naked!'

'But they're not naked, Mother, are they!' Ana said.

'When they stop women for having too short a scarf, or for their makeup, these women are surely naked by the standards of the moral police!' marvelled Nasim, gazing around.

They walked through the resort, passing a succession of villas. Some of them were mansions.

'How can your friend manage to keep such a place in this town?' asked Grandmother.

'Well, she bought this villa with her brothers and sisters. There are six of them and they bought it jointly, to come here together, or each with their own family. It's always occupied by the families of one or other of them. This was her turn to come, and she said we could use it instead. She could never have afforded to buy it on her own, nor could she pay the service charges, which include the security guard.'

'How are we going to repay her kindness? Shall we buy something from the town and leave it for her?' asked Nima.

'No need. I brought her a painting of mine, which she loved.'

As they unpacked, and his mother put the painting in a corner of the room, Faraz looked at it curiously. At first glance, it showed a sea in which different colours were dancing, but then one could see other things: scarves were diving into the water as if rivers of scarves were flowing into the sea.

'Mother, what does it mean?' asked Faraz, his eyes still on the painting.

'Well, imagine women are free to get rid of their compulsory veils and drop them,' Ana said. 'What would you see?'

They swam freely in the sea and Faraz's mood changed after a couple of days, as he raced Nasim in the water and she kissed him as they swam. They swam in the dark, when everyone was asleep and talked about the sea, which looked like a monster at night. She wanted them to make love in the water and they laughed at the idea of getting arrested for it.

They bought forbidden wine and drank it on the beach without worrying. Then they dressed conventionally and went to look at the other beaches, public ones, where people were trying to have fun. They watched men and women swimming separately. Moral police were patrolling the shores to make sure no one dreamed of violating the Islamic rules.

They came back, upset that other people couldn't enjoy the temporary freedom they had.

When they sat down together to eat, Faraz realised how much he had missed the relationship he had with his family – their talk about politics, social issues and the jokes they used to tell. He could feel that he was not his usual cheerful self, as if he had seen and read things that his brain just couldn't cope with. As his mother passed him the rice, followed by the aubergine dish, he tried to pay attention to what they were talking about.

'Mother went to the market with our neighbour and said they invited her to the restaurant that serves alcohol as well,' said Ana, passing the food to Nasim.

'Thank you, it's delicious,' said Nasim. 'Was she joking about the restaurant that serves alcohol?'

'No, darling. Last time I was here, my friend took me to two restaurants in Babul, where we had vodka with kebab. I asked her how they can get away with it. My friend said, the owners pay off the police and they're left alone. No raid, no fine!'

'If you told my family this, they would say it's a lie,' sighed Nasim.

'It's disgusting, but it seems no matter where one is living, if you're rich you can get what you want,' Faraz muttered angrily.

'Have some more fresh mint and parsley. They're from the garden,' Ana urged Nasim, as if trying to change the subject.

She spooned some yogurt seasoned with wild garlic on to her own plate and smiled. 'Your cousin, Leila, called this morning. She's staying nearby with her fiancé and asked if they could come and see us. I told her they can come tomorrow for dinner. Is that okay with everyone?'

'Sure,' Nasim replied, while Faraz and his father nodded their assent.

***

The next evening Faraz had just started to lay the table when Leila and Majid, her fiancé, arrived with a bottle of wine. She had a gown over her short outfit, which she took off as she removed the colourful scarf that had covered a small section of her hair. She was wearing heavy makeup and Majid's nose had a dressing on it. Noticing Faraz look at his nose, Majid grinned and pointing to Leila, said, 'She asked me to have a nose job.'

'Nowadays everyone's doing it,' Faraz responded, trying to be friendly.

While they sat and had a drink, he went to the dining room to finish laying the table. His mother and Leila walked into the kitchen. Ana said, 'The food is ready. I just need to make a salad.'

'Our wedding is next month. You'll get your invitation in a few days. I know it's only a year since my first marriage, and I remember you came to that, but you have to come again!'

Faraz heard Ana say, 'It's the first time I've met him. He seems nice. But are you sure he's good enough for you?'

'Of course, Auntie. You should see how much gold he's bought for me.'

'Poor man. You made him go under the knife!'

'Yes, but he said he'd do that if I made myself a virgin. And guess what? I did! And now I'm as brand new as a new born girl.' Faraz felt sick but kept listening. He heard his mother ask, 'Isn't it better to have it as a Venetian blind? So, you can leave it open when you want to, and close it the next time you need your virginity?'

'Oh Auntie, I never knew you were so clever!'

'Was his nose very large?' Ana asked.

'No, but he looks better now. You should see his surgeon. *He* had a nose the size of a water melon. I asked him why doesn't he fix his own nose? The surgeon said, "There's nothing wrong with it."'

Faraz had finished the table, but stayed in the room, staring out into the garden in order to hear what his cousin was saying. Now he joined Nasim, who was sitting in the late sunshine working on her computer.

'Sorry, I'm not helping with the food. I have to finish this design by next week.'

'Don't worry, there's nothing to do.'

Leila and Majid left soon after dinner and the family sat watching TV and chatting.

Ana said, 'Their wedding party is next month.'

'I don't think I'm in the mood to go to her wedding,' said Faraz's father.

'You didn't go to her wedding last year, either,' Ana teased him.

Since Nasim never went to big family gatherings, such as weddings, for fear of being recognised, Faraz said, 'I didn't know she was that stupid. I'm not going to leave Nasim alone at home and go to her wedding. If she calls again, tell her Faraz and Nasim are not in Tehran.'

'You can go if you like, I won't be bored at home,' Nasim assured him.

'No, I don't want to go. She got married last year to a man her own age and they separated two months later. It seems she has found another stupid man; otherwise how could he ask her to stitch herself up for him? How many times is she going to make herself a virgin and invite us to the re-opening ceremony?' asked Faraz, crudely.

'So, you heard us!' cried his mother.

'We shouldn't be surprised by such behaviour when mullahs are in charge of society, Faraz,' his father observed. 'What do you expect young men to see in women when the mullahs are telling them that you sleep with angels in heaven every night, and then in the morning the angels wake up virgins?'

***

As the days passed, Faraz felt the old relationship with his family coming back and he relaxed. He realised a silence had fallen over them since his work at the interrogation centre, which was at last starting to break. He began joining in their after-dinner discussions with his old enthusiasm.

'It's unbelievable, yet here's some good news,' Nima said one night, indicating the newspaper in his hand. 'It says here they took the girl to the gallows and got her ready to be hanged, then realised they didn't have the rope to do it!'

'What girl?' Faraz asked.

'Kobra Rahmanpour. She was arrested a couple of years ago for killing her mother-in-law and was sentenced to death.' Nima was reading from the report.

Ana had already seen it. 'The poor girl had only just turned 18 when she was married to this man who was 53, to help her family who were living in poverty,' she said. 'Two years later, she could no longer take the abuse of her husband's family and one day when her mother-in-law wouldn't stop pushing her around, she killed her.'

'They're saying she claimed her mother-in-law was threatening her with a knife and the girl snatched it from her,' Nima went on. 'Then she didn't know how, but she said her mother-in-law threw herself on to the knife repeatedly and died.'

'Young women commit suicide or are killed by the regime for murdering their attackers,' said Nasim. 'I hope her husband and his family let Kobra live and don't ask for revenge.'

'Interestingly, it's only her husband who is still refusing

to forgive her. Other members of the dead woman's family *have* forgiven her,' Ana said.

'If you have a law that asks the victim's family to decide on the fate of the killer,' Faraz pointed out, 'it turns ordinary people into murderers, doesn't it? Will the day ever come in this country when execution is banned, and they stop using it as a means of oppression?'

'Yes, it will come,' Nima predicted. 'But I don't see it any time soon. Not in my lifetime. I wish the abolition of the death penalty would happen overnight, but it won't. It needs an entire nation to oppose it, or even more than a nation. The whole world should rise up against this kind of barbarism.'

'But how could they have saved their Islamic regime without all those executions in the eighties?' Ana argued. 'It doesn't matter if the laws are Islamic or non-Islamic; they can be used to give to those at the top a licence to commit state crimes. Once they've helped themselves to other people's share, they have to kill in order to keep what they've stolen.'

'What has the death penalty got to do with it, though?' asked Nasim.

'Without execution and imprisonment, no one would work for nothing. No one would live as a slave. Imagine, right now, the regime announces that men and women have equal rights. From now on! What do you think would happen?' Ana asked her.

'A long queue would form outside the divorce offices,' Nasim replied, gloomily.

Faraz, looking at her, realised she was still suffering from the time she had spent with her abusive husband.

Otherwise, why should she relate only to the problem she had had when she had been stuck with him? It didn't seem to occur to her to mention any other injustice, such as the stoning of women for falling in love.

One evening when they were all talking over dinner, Faraz's grandmother spoke about her neighbours and how kind some of them were to her.

'The neighbours' son is not getting married,' Grandmother announced.

'Does it bother you, Granny?' Faraz asked, smiling.

'He is fifty years old. How much longer does he want to wait?'

'Granny, how about asking him to marry you? Then you won't be worried about him.'

'I have to think about it!' Grandmother said.

'Don't wait too long, Granny. He might marry soon.'

'Things are very different from our time. The other neighbour, who got divorced two years ago, still sees the woman. Can you believe it?'

'What do you mean by "seeing" her, Granny?'

'Well, I was in their house and the bell rang and there she was, and they sat there talking like old times. I asked his mother, why don't they live together if they get on so well?'

'Mother, they lived together for five years and both realised they couldn't stick it any more. What's wrong with being friends?' asked Ana.

'Well, the way they talked to each other was more loving than some couples. It's odd,' Grandmother said.

'Of course their relationship is odd. The norm is that

when you marry, you have to live together for the rest of your life. Even if you don't love each other, still you should stay together. Couples only separate when they hate each other, and one might kill the other. It seems odd to us these days that people can love each other without sexual desire because we can't imagine it any other way,' Nima said.

Faraz caught Nasim's glance at his grandmother, who seemed thoughtful, as if dreaming of having a similarly good relationship with her male neighbours.

'Before the Cultural Revolution, male and female teachers had good friendships with each other. We talked to each other about problems at home, or we talked about politics and everything,' Nima went on. 'Sexual attraction didn't come in to it.'

'Since the Cultural Revolution, and the moral police patrolling the streets to arrest men and women who are not related, they have also managed to change people's perceptions,' Ana reminded him. 'It's as if people have now built up moral barriers to fit the crude rule that the regime is imposing on them. If in those days we fought for equal rights between men and women, now, twenty years on, the law has enshrined the regressive culture that the regime was after, at least within some people's minds.'

'Law makes culture and culture makes law,' said Nima.

'I feel now that most men are running on lust, while women are running for their rights,' Ana concluded.

'I don't know what you're talking about,' complained Grandmother. 'What has my neighbour to do with the law? Oh, never mind.'

'Have some more rice, Mother,' Ana said.

They continued eating in silence for a while, until Grandmother said, 'Faraz, you mustn't treat me like your brother, Omid, if you ever leave the country!'

'I'm not going anywhere. But what do you mean? What has Omid done to you?' asked Faraz in surprise.

'Well, the other day I called him. And you know what? He talked to me in German. I asked him if he had already forgotten to speak Farsi, but he just put the phone down.'

'Mother, that was his answering machine. I told you before, that when he's not at home his machine asks you, in German, to leave a message,' Ana interrupted.

'Do you think I'm stupid? It was his voice, not a machine. Anyway, tell him I'm not going to learn German just to speak to him.'

'How is my sister? Did she have a good time in Malaysia?' Ana asked.

'Yes, she had a good time, but she was annoyed about the plane she travelled back on. She said there was a leak in the roof and water dripped on to her shoulder. She complained to the crew and one of them put some tissues in the hole and told her that they had had a lot of rain in Malaysia, and that's why the roof was leaking.'

They all laughed.

'Granny, you must be kidding,' Faraz said.

'I'm not, call her and ask her. She'll tell you the same thing.'

'Mother, why is there no picture of Sara's husband in all the photos my sister has brought back?' Ana enquired.

'How do I know? Ask her.'

'Well, I asked that when she got married, and Azar said she'd forgotten to bring a photo. And you were at

Sara's wedding in Malaysia with Azar and her family and you're not telling us why we haven't seen any pictures of this man.'

Everyone was looking at Grandmother and seemed interested to know.

'Well. They're separated,' she said.

'What? Why?' Ana was aghast.

'Well, you haven't heard it from me, but I heard Sara tell her mother that he married her because he liked Iranian food,' said Grandmother.

'Iranian food? Isn't he Iranian himself?' asked Nima.

'What can I say? Your sister told me not to tell anyone.'

'Why? What's wrong with being married to non-Iranians?' Ana demanded.

'She was worried the authorities would hear about it and wouldn't let Sara come to visit, or they might not let her go back if she did come.'

'What are you talking about? There are thousands of Iranians outside Iran who are living with non-Iranians,' Nima pointed out.

'Yes. But with all this *Down with America* business, they thought Sara might get into trouble if word reaches the authorities.'

'So he was American!' Ana exclaimed.

'Yes. He was. I think Sara fell in love with his eyes.'

'And he fell in love with Sara's cooking?' asked Nasim.

'No, he was already in love with Iranian cuisine when he met Sara and proposed to her,' said Grandmother thoughtfully.

'I'm glad Sara has separated from him. Polygamy

might be next on the menu if he's that kind of man,' said Faraz, and they all laughed.

'It's fine for you to laugh, but Sara has had a tough time the last six months. That's why her mother went there and stayed with her for a while,' said Grandmother.

'Of course she must have been in a difficult situation. Did Azar talk to him to try and find out the problem?'

'Yes. He told her that he married Sara because he had heard Iranian women are good cooks. Your sister asked him why he didn't go to an Iranian restaurant rather than marrying a good cook? He said, "Well, Iranian women are good looking, too,"' said Grandmother.

Silence fell again and Faraz thought to himself that every family has its lies. The day before his grandmother came to their house, his mother had asked him if he could please not talk about the interrogation centre, or that he was working there. Faraz said 'fine,' and understood that it was quite natural she didn't want her family to know he was helping the regime to wash people's blood from their hands. He felt that everyone - from those at the top to those at the bottom - is saying one thing and doing another.

'Has Hassan married, Mother?' Faraz heard Ana ask his Grandmother, and his attention returned to the room and to his family.

'No. He asked your sister to look for a nice girl for him.'

'You must be joking!' Ana retorted. 'After all these years over there, now he wants a virgin from here?'

'I don't know. Your sister told him that girls here are all stitched up. But he still prefers someone from Iran.'

'He has the same disease as the boys have here. Men here don't marry their girlfriends; they marry each other's girlfriends,' Faraz said.

***

One evening when it was wet and they had to stay in, Ana turned on the TV, saying, 'It must be our beloved mullah's question time now.'

The presenter asked the mullah, 'If in an earthquake a man falls from the fifth floor and lands on top of a woman who is sleeping on the ground floor and they engage in the act of copulation, are they *halal* to each other or is their act sinful in God's eyes?'

Faraz started to laugh out loud but stopped when his mother said, 'Hush, listen. It's important.'

'My answer is that they are not involved in a sinful act, because God brought them together through a destruction of his making,' the mullah declared.

'I wonder why god doesn't bring them together without destroying the building,' said Ana.

'They must be obsessed with sex. Otherwise why on earth are they thinking about sex when they're buried in the rubble of an earthquake?' Nima laughed.

The presenter continued, 'The next question is: what is the language of the world after life?'

The mullah coughed delicately and replied, 'The language that is spoken in heaven is Arabic. That means no matter what language we are speaking in this life, Farsi, English… if we go to heaven, we will all be able to speak Arabic. But those who end up in hell will speak the language they speak now, in this world. Except Arabic. I mean, the Arabic speakers of this world would not be able to speak Arabic in hell.'

As they all burst out laughing, Ana said, 'Quiet now. Let's hear how he answers.'

'This is our very own comedy! Woody Allen should come here to learn how to make people laugh!' Nima chuckled.

'It's not a comedy for some people. They might go and learn Arabic to make sure they're okay in the other world,' said Nasim.

They tried to listen again and there was a man on the phone asking, 'Do you agree with Sheikh Fazlolah Nori, who said girls' education leads them to prostitution?'

'Of course. Western societies have lost their morality because women have given priority to their education and jobs rather than to their families,' the mullah replied.

'According to the mullah, you now have to bring drinks for everyone, woman!' Nima instructed Ana. 'But I'll get them this time. Who wants wine?'

Grandmother said, 'Have you heard Hasani's recent sermons?'

'No, Mother, tell us. I adore his analysis,' said Ana.

'In last week's talk after the Friday prayer, he announced, "Women are born in three categories: those who don't observe their hijab are like buses, in that everyone can ride them. The second category belongs to those who are *bad hijab* and don't wear their scarf appropriately; they're like taxis, which means only a few can take them. And women in the third category are like donkeys, in that no more than one person can mount them - like my wife, who observes her hijab completely."'

At that, they all started recounting jokes they had heard. As usual, their favourite character was mullah Hasani, the Friday prayer imam at the mosque in the city of Uromia and the representative of the supreme leader in East Azerbaijan Province.

Grandmother said, 'Listen to what Hasani said two weeks ago: he said, "Those who say people in the West are more advanced than us, are stupid. We are in the year 1381, that is the fourteenth century, while the West is in the twentieth century. Were they more advanced than us when they were in the fourteenth century? Of course not. We will be more advanced than they are now, when we reach the twentieth!"'

They were all laughing when Nima cut in, 'Have you heard him on the name of Iran?'

'No. Tell us!' said Grandmother excitedly.

'He said we should no longer register Iran as a girl's name. When westerners swear at us, they say "screw Iran". Do you think it's okay to hear that?'

And so it went on, but Faraz's mind was elsewhere. He knew that mullah Hasani was someone like his uncle, except for the fact that Rohulah joined the Islamists after they took power. Hasani was with the Islamists before the people's uprising and could lead his followers wherever he wanted. He was always armed, and it was said that he shot at the nose of the Shah's statue in Uromia before the Islamists took power. Destroying the Shah's nose on a statue that was guarded, caused mayhem among the province's police and forced him to go underground, while the statue was removed under the pretence of being repaired. Hasani was also in charge of a massacre of villagers in Kurdistan in 1979, a few months after the Islamic regime took power; Gharna was the only village in which 68 people, mostly women and children, were killed. Like Rohulah, Hasani sacrificed his son, Rashid, who was an atheist, by taking part in his arrest in the early 1980s. Rashid was in Tehran. Hasani found out where he was living and called the Islamic guard in charge to ask him to send some gunmen to make an arrest. He told the guards to kill the prisoner if he tried to escape, otherwise to arrest him. Rashid was kept in Tehran for a few days before the Islamic guards sent him to Tabriz. Since Rashid had been active in Tabriz, he was tried and executed there. Hasani said he was not upset when he heard about Rashid's death, and that he had done his duty. Another of his sons was in prison for six years during the eighties for being an atheist and was killed in an accident, two years after his release. One of his daughters, Hamideh, committed suicide by setting herself alight. Hasani did not participate in her memorial, because he believed suicide was forbidden in Islam.

***

On the afternoon of their final day, when his parents were out sightseeing with his grandmother, Faraz sat on the beach with a book in his hand. He couldn't get past the first page. He couldn't concentrate. He watched Nasim who was in the water with some other young people, but his mind was on Xavar. Faraz looked around and saw a woman, about his mother's age, sitting nearby.

He found himself looking at her; it was difficult to take his eyes off her. Then he realised he had never seen a woman like her, or perhaps since women were always clothed according to the dress code, the limbs she was exposing would normally have been covered. She looked like a mobile bank or jewellery shop: several necklaces around her neck; her wrists, from hand to elbow, hung with numerous bracelets - all yellow. Perhaps they were gold and she wore them all the time to make sure no one would steal them; or perhaps she thought they looked beautiful together like that. What about their weight? How could her neck and arms bear to be weighed down like that? If they could talk, wouldn't these parts of her body complain of being abused, Faraz wondered. His thoughts returned to Xavar. What kind of clothes would she have worn? How beautiful was she? Would he find the rest of her letters? Was she alive? If she was, what was she doing now?

That night he stayed up late with Nasim, who was sad that the week had passed so quickly.

'If we were married, like other couples, we could walk on the beach or run in the forest, just the two of us. We wouldn't need to come here, we could go to the beaches where ordinary people try to have fun. I wish we could stay longer.'

'Are you behind with your work? I'm always seeing you working on your computer.'

'I can do my work here. It doesn't restrict me to a particular place. I sent off for a whole month's work with a single click. They liked what I did and said I'll get paid next week.'

Faraz had opened an account under his name for Nasim. She had the card and could use a cash point to keep control of her own money.

Chapter Twelve

LOST IN THE FOREST

A few days after returning from the Caspian Sea, Faraz woke early one morning and couldn't get back to sleep. His mind was fixated on Xavar's letters and he felt infuriated at not being able to find the rest of them. He got out of bed, leaving Nasim asleep, and went downstairs to the living room. He moved quietly as usual and sat on the sofa looking through the newspapers on the table. He realised his parents were talking in whispers, and because the city was still quiet, and their house quiet, he could hear his name. Although he couldn't hear every word they said, he was curious and listened.

'…I don't know why he doesn't quit the job.' It was his mother talking. 'I thought going to the north might make him reconsider, and he might not go back to it. He's depressed, and he's lost weight.'

There was silence before his father said, 'Remember, right from childhood, he was stubborn… always did things… didn't dare to do… but Faraz didn't care what other people said about him. I always feared he might lose his head over his stubbornness, but I never thought he might go against our wishes, our morals, our standards. Forood… What would he say to him, if he was alive?'

Now his mother was talking: 'I'm afraid he's suffering

but can't bring himself to quit the job for fear of showing that he made a mistake in the first place.'

'He thinks it was his own idea to work in that filthy place,' muttered his father. '...what if his uncle hadn't proposed it to him? ...wanted to make him like himself. They don't know each other... Rohulah would never offer such a job to Omid. Omid would kick him out of our house...'

Anger welled up inside Faraz and he went back to his room, lying down on the bed beside Nasim, wondering what she was dreaming of. Was she having a nightmare about being raped by her ex-husband, or was she dreaming about playing with her sister? He lay there fretting about his parents discussing him and comparing him with his brother. He thought, *if you think I'm the stubborn type, what do you know about Omid? Do you realise that he always needed an enemy in order to prove himself, so that if he couldn't find one, he created one? Now he's turned his own brother into a monster, so as to cast himself as the hero. Omid used to look for enemies and usually picked on the person who was the easiest to attack, knowing the weaknesses, strengths and all the other faults of the person closest to him.*

Though it was still early, he couldn't sleep and decided to go to the prison and start work. He could hear the rain pouring down outside, but he felt hot and needed to walk in it. He went out and was surprised to see that no one was around. As he walked, he saw a few people running down the street to get a bus or a taxi. The rain, streaming over his head, soaking his shirt and trickling down his spine, made him feel better. He passed a bus shelter, with people crammed under its roof in order not to get wet. He noticed their surprise at seeing him. He thought, *why do some people not like rain, when they wash themselves in water?* The rain took the heat out of his mind and body and the wetter he became, the calmer he felt. Drops of rain ran together with the sweat down his face and body and the chill of it changed his mood and cheered him up. By the time he reached the prison, he was not the miserable person who had set out from home.

***

That day, looking at the writing on the walls, Faraz thought about the prisoners who had passed through this place and stayed alive. Who were they? Were their minds and bodies also engraved with the physical and mental torture that they experienced here? How did this prison affect them? Are the effects of the place as visible upon them as their presence is visible in here? How are they coping with the memories and consequences of their time here? Just as some of the hieroglyphics on the walls needed deciphering, he wondered if the scars on their bodies also needed to be interpreted with an expert eye he didn't possess. He felt every wall to make sure it was not concealing a letter from Xavar, but it seemed to him that he was not going to find anything. He realised he was looking at the walls differently; he could see invisible signs now. As his mind was constantly focused on the question of where prisoners would hide their final letters, he found himself searching certain places thoroughly. In the afternoon, he went to the bathroom, looked around and checked each cubicle with his hands. He didn't notice anything unusual about the walls as he touched them. Exasperated, he sat on the floor and checked the area below the sink, and again there was nothing odd. He lay down to examine the space under the sink once more in case he might see something. He thought it must be safer for prisoners to make a hole here than in the bare walls. He used one of his tools to scrape the surface under the sink until he dislodged some pieces of plaster. Though nothing was visible, as if willing it to lead him to a secret prisoners' cache, he removed more plaster. As it fell away, his hands felt an unevenness in the cement between two of the bricks and he wished he had brought his torch. He was still removing cement from this dark space between the bricks when a small package dropped to the floor. He felt his heart drop with it and a pleasant anxiety flooded through him. He went to one of the cubicles and closed the door. He had to know if this was one of Xavar's notebooks. He thought he heard footsteps in the corridor and stood there listening, then flushed the cistern in pretence of using the toilet. He cleaned the surface of the package, tore the thread around it and opened the outer wrapping. His eyes caught sight of the number (2) on the notebook. Delighted, he put it in his pocket and came out to find that there was no one on the wing.

***

JOINT COMMITTEE INTERROGATION CENTRE, 1984

Darling Azad, the torture that I warned you about has passed and is now thankfully behind us!

Ghulam raped me, and to feel less pain and humiliation, I tried to not concentrate on his act and what was happening to my body. I imagined being with you. He raped me, but I didn't feel much - or I can say I didn't feel what they wanted me to feel, because I was thinking of you. I used you as a shield to save my soul. So, here I am in my cell, in pain, but not battered or humiliated.

I feel pain all over my body, but mostly I'm worried about our baby. Did she see or feel his rape, his invasion? Will she know what they did to me or to her? Will she remember this when she is born? I'm sure one day she will understand that it was for a better future for her that you and I fought, and the result of it was my being trapped by men who think they can act like gods.

I wished they had not fastened my hands and legs, so I could have kicked Ghulam and clawed his face and taken his eyes out of their sockets. To make it easy for him, they tied me to the bed before leaving me there for him. So there was no fight. He raped me the same as he does his wife, I suppose, except that her hands and feet are not fastened. I wonder if she knows that rape is part of her husband's job description.

Since that day I have been thinking about this insane world, the world of these creatures who enjoy crushing humanity by means of torture. The cry of people from pain, the grinding of teeth and the sound of a limb breaking as they strike it, must surely give them pleasure, as music gives us. Sometimes they add in another sound when they use a cable to thrash the prisoners. All this against a background dirge of religious wailing like the Azan, Allah o Akbar, the call to prayer, or someone reading from the Koran, or mournful songs by Ahangaran, singing for solders fighting on the front line between Iran and Iraq. I wish he himself would go to war and get martyred, so he doesn't record any more dreary songs to torment us! Even when I'm not under interrogation and I'm here in this cell and hear his voice on the loudspeaker, I feel torture, psychological torture. His voice has a quality of mourning about it and because of that it is torturous. When I hear his voice, I feel the ceremonial aspect of torture and think that pain is progress, and then I long for the final phase of it, which is silence.

I have heard that during the Holocaust when prisoners were taken to the gas chambers, the guards sometimes played music by Wagner.

I wonder how those who survived the camps reacted to Wagner afterwards, if they suddenly heard it on the radio or at a gathering. How would it feel to be reminded of their fellow prisoners who were put to death to that music? When I was free, I didn't enjoy hearing the Azan or Ahangaran's chanting, but now it isn't a matter of enjoying it or not. Now I cannot listen to these things indifferently. Now, for me, the sound of prayer is associated with torture and rape and conjures up scenes that I want to eradicate from my mind. I wonder how our child will react to these sounds in the future. Will they have a negative association for her as well? After all, her ears will surely remember it at some level. Do you agree? You know, love, I never knew how vulnerable we are in terms of sound. I can close my eyes and not see, but I can't completely close my ears and not hear.

***

Faraz put down the notebook and thought about Xavar. He knew that at that moment, in the middle of the night while he was reading those lines, other prisoners, the generation of Xavar and Azad's children, were being shut up in cells and raped for the way they thought, and that he and others were carrying on with their lives as if nothing was happening.

***

You know, having a lover or children means nothing here. As days pass, the space between my life with you and my life in here gets wider and wider. I wonder for how much longer I can cling to the memory of the life I had with you. It's as if we were standing in front of each other murmuring love songs, when suddenly the earth shook under our feet and a crack appeared between us. The crack is widening every minute, hour, day and I'm watching it with horror as it takes you further and further away from me. In the wide shot of this scene, our images get smaller and smaller, and now I struggle to keep you in my mind as I last saw you.

***

A few days have passed since that animal invaded my body. I don't want to think about the rape, but sometimes my mind can't avoid it. And I think about this animal called Ghulam, who uses parts of his body as weapons against his enemies. He uses his hands and legs to beat us and uses his penis to rape us. I wonder whether the next time he has intercourse outside the prison, he will be able to control himself and not treat his partner roughly. How does his sexual part know when to act as a knife and when as a means of pleasure? What about his hands? How does he touch his wife or his children with his hands? Do his hands caress them or beat them? Do his hands remember how to behave when they handle either enemies or his family? If he doesn't beat or rape someone for a while, won't these parts of his body miss doing it? What would he then do to satisfy them? Would he rape his wife or another prisoner and beat his children? After all, such acts must release some chemical substance in him and provoke certain feelings, and surely after a while his body must crave it.

Things like this were unknown to us, or at least we never thought to discuss them. While these creatures were living in our neighbourhood and perhaps even greeted us in the street, we never knew what they were up to.

***

My love, I'm worried about losing the precious part of you that's inside me. I'm afraid this will be my only chance to have a child with you, and I don't want to waste it. My feet are burning with painful blisters. They have created a hell inside me by not giving me medication. It must be part of the torture. Or is it torture beyond torture? Although they're not doing anything to me now, the pain and burning prevents me from sleeping, so the torture continues. You know there is a border between the two states of sleep and wakefulness. For the last few days and nights, every time I lose wakefulness, before I quite fall asleep, I can see a vast valley below my feet. Then I'm pushed out into it and I can see poppies everywhere, red and orange poppies, before I hit the earth. I struggle to grab hold of something so as not to fall into the valley, all the time thinking about the beauty of the orange poppies. I wake up with feelings of horror and amazement, thinking I've never seen such beautiful orange poppies in my life, and not wanting to die. Do I have this nightmare because I fear being executed? I know that poppies are symbols of being martyred, but I don't want to be martyred and there's no reason for this fear. My case is not so serious that they'll kill me, although they have killed many of our friends who were arrested for nothing more than carrying a single opposition newspaper. However, they don't even know about my political activities yet, and have only arrested me in order to get to you. I'm just a hostage. Would they kill their hostages? I don't know what will happen. I only know that I've never felt as miserable as I do now. I have you, though only in my mind. You are here, with me in this solitary confinement, and inside me as a foetus that is growing, I think.

Here in the loneliness of this place it is so silent when the guards are around, I yearn for the sound of a cuckoo or a cricket. I'm afraid I might be going crazy. Ghulam comes into my mind, as if he represents the whole regime, and

I can see his utter disgust towards women or womanhood. Especially towards those of us who have dared to fight for our rights, when we ought to be staying at home to cook and bear children.

My love, these people who threw acid into women's faces to force them to accept the compulsory hijab, now use rape as torture to make us talk! I know what you would say if you were here, that it's exactly what you would expect of them.

***

Faraz reflected on how the Islamic regime's anti-women laws had given men a licence to treat women as subhuman. Rape didn't just happen in prison; men were legally entitled to rape their wives. He thought of Nasim, who was frequently woken by the nightmares in which she relived her former life. He also thought of the newspaper articles about boys throwing acid into the faces of girls who refused to marry them. Where had they learnt this practice, if not from their rulers?

***

Azadam, I wish I knew how you felt and what you're doing. What did you do, where did you go that night I didn't come home after being arrested? How did you feel, during those two hours of waiting and when you realised I must have been picked up? If only you could visit me so that we could know these things about each other. Where are you right now? Don't make any mistakes so that you, too, end up here, in this hell. My love, my body, which was the vessel of joy and satisfaction, is used here as a means of pain and humiliation. And so, I begin to feel as if I no longer cherish but *fear* my body that's become an instrument of pain, and I want to get away from it. Sometimes I feel that each of us was a solo musical instrument, but together we played beautiful, harmonious music. And I long for that music again.

I'm thinking that by arresting me they're trying to transform me, which I will fight against. By manipulating both my body and my mind, they're trying to alter me as a human being, so I see the world through their eyes. Every time I come back from interrogation, I try and work out what they're getting at when they ask particular questions. Prison is a slow ongoing torture designed to convert us - but we resist. By questioning us, they try to disorient us, so that we come to see them as our only means of survival and thus hang on to them. This is not conversion yet, but it's the route to it. To rebuild us in their image, to drain out our humanity, they have to push us down this route. That is, first to abandon our own beliefs and grow dependent on our captors. They won't stop there and leave us with the potential to join the revolution again when the regime is on its knees. No, they continue their torture, and we continue our resistance.

My love, they can't force me to like them, which would be to become a primitive creature. But now I wonder, when I come out of this mad hell one day, will I be able to rely on my body again as a means of joy and satisfaction? Or whenever I try to find joy, will this same body of mine remind me of its betrayal, of the deep sadness it brought me as a result of the pain it went through? It wasn't only with rape that they used my body to inflict pain on my soul. When they beat me, or deprived me of sleep, they also abused my body.

But they cannot empty my mind of love and refill it with hate. They think with torture they'll be able to soften me, so I'll become like dough in their hands. They want to work on that dough to shape it in their image, to imitate their words or follow their instructions like a robot. I will not let them.

Don't do anything rash, my love, so that you get arrested.

***

My dearest, it's a week that I haven't written, but I talk to you in my mind and try to picture you answering me. Though it must be warm outside, I feel cold at night, and I don't have any warm clothes.

Although by concentrating on your face I was able to pretend that they weren't raping me, when I'm least expecting it, the flashback I experience is different. It's of me being raped by Ghulam. As it starts, a cold sweat covers my body. Today when the guard opened the door, and perhaps because it wasn't the usual time for washing or getting food, I felt she must be taking me for interrogation and suddenly I pictured Ghulam on top of me. I could only see myself, with my hands and feet bound and not being able to move. Isn't it strange? Because when he began to rape me, from start to finish in order to blot out what he was doing, I closed my eyes so that I couldn't see him from under the blindfold. At the same time, I was thinking only of you, but apparently my brain still processed what was happening to my body. It seems I couldn't deceive my mind; I couldn't avoid recording what was happening. The brain takes a picture and revisits it at any time, and the worst thing is that it can repeat the same picture thousands of times, which might drive one mad because it's as if it's happening again and again.

I don't understand myself, my brain and my body right now, and I'm worried about our little child who is imprisoned inside me. Perhaps time will help me feel at home in my body again.

My love, I still feel over-sensitive. It must be due to the torture and my pregnancy. I guess so. I tell myself that one day I'll be free, and we'll see each other, though the thought of it makes me anxious as well as joyful! I feel I'm not the same person who said goodbye one morning and told you to be home at eight o'clock. Perhaps you've changed, too. My arrest must have hit you hard, especially knowing I might be pregnant. Did I see two stars in your eyes, when I told you that I had missed my period? You kissed me and said, 'Let's take a test. I can't wait to hear the result.' Then before I went out, you asked if I could do the test that day, and I said, 'No. I'll do it tomorrow.' I didn't have time to ask if this made you happy, especially as you were always so careful. But you were very happy that accidentally we were going to have a baby. I read it in your eyes.

I was telling you about changes I feel in myself, and that you might have changed also with me gone. You would have had to move from our home, as well as finding a new job, in case they made me talk. Perhaps you're anxious you might lose me forever under torture, and lose our only baby, too. These worries must have changed you somehow. But what if our changes are in different directions? I have seen things in here that I should not have seen. How can I wipe them from my memory if I ever get away from this dreadful place? We'll both be different people when we meet again. Perhaps even now we're different from the way we were when we fell in love. I'm not a broken musical instrument. No, I'm not broken. But what if I'm unable to respond to your caresses any more, as I used to? 'So?' I can hear you saying, 'Wait until the time comes. Together, we'll rebuild our relationship!' And you're right.

You know how I feel? I imagine how I'll look in ten years' time if they keep me here, and it reminds me of that little plant we had - the one we forgot to remove from the hot, sunny windowsill when summer came. One day when you were watering it, you called me over to have a look. Its colour had changed from green to pale yellow, the leaves were dead. I said, 'It's dead. But it died beautifully.' You took it from the window and left it somewhere in the shade and said, 'It's not dead yet.' And then after a few days small green shoots appeared, and in a while little green stems came out from the middle and around the yellow stems, and it looked beautiful as well as unique. Yes, I will be green and yellow like that plant of ours if one day I get out of this place. What happened to our plants? Who's taking care of them? I wish I had that yellow and green one with me here so that I could look at it every day in my solitude.

You know I've lost weight; the skirt that I was arrested in doesn't fit me any more. This is despite me eating everything that I'm given, so that our child is fed.

Have I told you that during my last

interrogation Ghulam asked me how many months pregnant I am? He used the word 'bastard' for our unborn child and he thought I would be upset by his use of such words. He doesn't know that bastard babies are fruits of love in my dictionary. We're all fruits of love, and his kind are the consequence of rape. Don't you think so, love?

I close my eyes and imagine sitting beside you on Darabad Mountain and listening to the sound of a waterfall. Do you remember? We walked through the yellow leaves and sometimes when we saw piles of them you would jump right into them and bet which of us could make a louder crunching sound. Which was louder - mine or yours? I can almost hear it in my imagination! But I can't smell their scent, that wet, yellow-green odour. When our child is born, and I send her to you, will you take her to such places? Will you ask her to walk through yellow leaves and listen to their beautiful perfumed music, as she touches them? How would that feel? I mean, walking over those golden leaves and making that sound with her?

I wish I had music here. You might laugh at me, but I think that to be deprived of music is akin to torture. Don't you think so? I think it's because you listen to it every day and therefore it's part of your life, and when they take it away from you, you feel deprived of some form of sustenance. I long for Vivaldi's Four Seasons,

Beethoven, and for all the music in the world! I close my eyes and try to hear music in my mind and imagine myself in your arms.

Sometimes I feel that these dirty white walls are coming towards me. They're trying to get me, to suffocate me. I open my arms wide and push them to stop them closing in and then I feel safe. Perhaps the reason for these strange feelings is that I haven't been out of this cell, except to use the toilet and to be taken to interrogation. I try to walk, but the cell is too small, and I reach the wall as soon as I begin, and then I have to turn after a few paces, which makes me feel dizzy. I try to do some exercise, but it's not enough. I need to walk, to stroll along the pavements and look at people. I need to talk to people, even if just to ask the time. But here, all I see is the women who are my guards, swathed in chadors, and I feel sick seeing them. I talk to my neighbour, who's given me this pen, but seeing someone is different from communicating in Morse. I need to see fresh faces, innocent faces. I want to see the faces of people who wouldn't harm anyone, even if their lives depended on it. I wish I had books. Isn't each book like a human being? If I had the opportunity to read, I wouldn't feel so lonely here. You know I enjoy reading, because it's as if the writer is talking to me.

***

Faraz stopped reading. He was thinking that the regime must put prisoners in solitary confinement in order to induce this very feeling, and to break them. Human beings are social creatures, whose need to be with others is rooted deep in their history. He wanted to tell Xavar that in a small way he felt he shared her experience; that he, too, felt like a stranger within his own family, since working at the interrogation centre had introduced him to the pleasure of knowing her.

***

Azadam, how are you? How am I? Well, I'm pregnant, I feel sick and I long for food, sweets, fruit. But most of all I long for you. I feel hungry all the time and, believe it or not, if they let me out of the cell, even blindfolded, I could find the kitchen. The smell would take me straight there.

Today is Friday and I feel better. Perhaps it's because Friday is the one day there are not many guards around and I've never had an interrogation on a Friday. So, today I'd like to imagine that we're having a conversation, though silently and in pages.

What name would you like to give our child? Once, I remember we were at the house of some friends and they had a silly fight over the name of their child, which was due quite soon. They simply couldn't agree on the baby's name and we couldn't stop laughing at the way they argued. Eventually they appealed to us to solve their problem. You suggested we could put all the names they'd each chosen into a hat and we could draw one out, and that would be the name.

I said, 'But isn't it fairer if one of you chooses the first name and the other the surname for her?'

The father raised his eyebrows and said, 'That's not in question. Her surname will be my surname.'

'Why is that?' I asked.

'It's always like that. Have you ever heard of a mother's surname on the birth certificate?'

'Then automatically, your wife has the right to choose her first name. That would make it fair if she's to take your surname,' I said.

Remember, love? You kissed me and said, 'It's the best possible solution. I go with Xavar's suggestion.'

Our friend was angry, but couldn't help laughing when his wife said, 'You're right. If his surname is her surname, then I choose her first name, or vice versa.'

So, now I'm thinking about the name we should give our child. Have you thought about it? How could you, when you don't even know if I'm pregnant or not? I'm not sure what surname you use now but, whatever it is, she should take it. People like us who have to live with different names and surnames and carry different birth certificates at different times, can't afford to care too much about their children's names.

***

Azadam, in the early hours of last night I woke up from a horrible, frightening nightmare. It was about the night they raped me, but the nightmare was more frightening than the real event. You wonder why? Because in the nightmare you weren't there to help me and I was by myself. When I woke up I wished I could have had a long shower to get rid of their smell and their marks on my body, as if they had really touched me. I don't know, perhaps due to lack of food and exercise I've become psychologically, as well as physically, weak. I tell myself it will pass, no situation is forever; no matter what the end will be, it *will* end.

You know, love, before coming to this cell and watching the days pass, I was never aware of the mind's capacity to cope with hardship. If I'd thought at all about being in solitary confinement when I was free, perhaps I'd have imagined I wouldn't survive it more than a few days. But now I'm here, I see how the mind can travel elsewhere and free itself from the place where the body is trapped. Yet I wonder for how long the mind can survive like this, and is everyone's mind equally able to do it?

Azizam, I dream of waking up one morning

with the warmth of the sun on my face, and see the light coming through the window. Not this covered window, a different window.

***

Though Faraz found it hard not to finish the notebook, it was getting light and he thought he ought to go to bed before his parents woke up, and save the rest of her letter for the following night. As he lay down beside Nasim, she turned to him and, with her eyes closed, said, 'Kiss me.' Faraz, stroking Nasim's forehead with his rough fingers, kissed her.

'You have to start massaging your hands with olive oil,' she said, her eyes still closed.

'Of course, my love.'

'You're changing, becoming harder outside, tender inside. Now sleep. You have to go to work soon,' she said, and soon her breathing told him that she was asleep herself.

***

You know, love, today I remembered that time when we were with our friends, Mina and Dara. We came to know them through our political activities and one day the four of us decided to go camping in the mountains. When we arrived, after setting up our tent and having something to eat, I suggested a little walk. You were tired because of driving and Dara said he'd stay with you. So Mina and I set off towards the forest and we were so busy talking about the political situation, we forgot the time and which way we'd come. We were still talking when I said, 'It's time to go back. It's getting dark.'

'Yes,' she agreed. 'Though it can't be dark this early. Still, you know how it gets darker earlier in the woods.'

Then we looked around, wondering which direction it was. Which way did we have to go to get back to our tent? We were panicking but tried not to show it. We decided to walk towards some light, as if the sky in that direction still had a little light in it. As we walked on, getting increasingly lost, the darkness spread through the forest. By now we were both tired and couldn't hide our anxiety. It was three hours since we'd left you and Dara for a half-hour walk.

'They'll be worried, and they can't get help. There's no help around,' said Mina.

'If only we had water with us,' I said.

'What can we do if we don't find the way?' she asked.

'We will find it eventually, I'm sure we will,' I told her, but I wasn't sure at all. I only said it because I so badly wanted it to happen.

We set off in a different direction and kept walking. We'd been gone nearly four hours when we heard you and Dara calling our names. We called back and finally found each other. You and I clung together in relief. Then I heard Dara shouting. I looked round and saw Mina was watching us, ignoring this onslaught.

'How could you do that? You mindless...' Dara was raging.

I went to Dara and tried to tell him how sorry I was and that we didn't mean to get lost in the forest, and we were scared, too. But he was angry and wouldn't stop putting her down. Mina walked away and said, 'Don't worry Xavar. Let him bark. He's finding an excuse to pour out his bile.'

I was shocked to hear that, and yet Dara didn't care what she had said and launched into a whole litany of other similar occasions when she'd made him anxious. I went to Mina and hugged her, and she cried silently in my arms. I could hear you two talking but couldn't catch what was said, only your whispers mixed with the sound of crickets.

You know Azad, that night I fell in love with you all over again, not once, but twice. The first time, when we found each other, and you hugged me and kissed me and said, 'I thought I'd lost you forever,' and the second when I saw Dara's attitude to Mina and heard what they said about each other. That made me fall in love with you again, as I realised not only how different you are, but how good you are.

Was it that they didn't love each other? Was it Dara's selfishness? Why at that moment of joy at finding each other, after the intense fear that we were lost, was he not only unhappy, but he treated her like that?

What happened to them? Are they around? Or, as with so many others who joined the revolution and left it again like a tide going in and out, have they given up struggling for their rights? I wonder if Mina stayed with him, and why? Why would one person stay with another in a relationship like that?

***

My love, I'm glad my memories are so colourful. Perhaps no matter where we're living, we have two worlds: one external world and the other inside our head. My mind is a refuge, as well as a guide. There's a connection between the inner world and the outer, and I find peace in thinking about you and our time together. They can't stop me from thinking about you and they can't wipe my memory. They say that they're trying to re-educate me! And I try to imagine things that are very wrong in their eyes and find that I'm proud to own up to these supposed misdemeanours. In here I can see that bad is good and good is bad. Their good is a submissive woman who doesn't struggle for her rights, which seems very bad to me. My character, which seemed good to you and to many other people, is very bad to them. Well, it's good to be bad – and I prefer it!

One way of getting free of this place is by

imagining our life together: the three of us. I imagine buying clothes for our baby, getting ready for her birth. I imagine playing with her when she's one year old, then two, three, four, five, six and seven. I imagine going to the cinema or to a museum with her and I imagine giving her a pencil to draw with and teaching her to write her own name. I picture her as a teenager and when she first falls in love. Then I imagine my struggle to let her go for the second time. The first time would be her birth and the second would be when she leaves us to start a new life with someone else. What a wonderful life we would have if we could only spend it together and experience all these different stages.

Would we adore her? Or would we take her for granted? What am I talking about? I'm clearly living in a fantasy and can't accept that I'll have to abandon her against my will. Our child will be deprived of her mother for many years by this regime, by Khomeini as the supreme leader, Rafsanjani the president and Mousavi the prime minister. Yes, to maintain their deception of the people, they have to imprison anyone who is critical of what they stand for.

I was telling you about my two worlds. My external world is one of extremists, harsh words, violence and the hateful gaze of the guards. Darling, sometimes I think of these half-wit creatures called interrogators or guards and wonder what kind of families they were born into.

My love, though I distract myself with thoughts of you, I still can't wish away the thick walls around me. The faint sound of the Morse code, the gaze of the guard through the peephole and the muffled footsteps of the guards in the corridor, trying to catch the prisoner tapping the Morse, bring me back into this world. When I hear the clink of a cell door and the whisper of the guard telling a prisoner to prepare for interrogation, the hair at the back of my neck stands on end.

Do you want to know what prison smells like? It's not the smell of torture; it's different from that. These two smells are quite distinct, even though one arises within the other. I mean that you can smell torture in prison, but prison also has its own smell. Have you ever thought that torture has a smell? I never knew that, but it has. The smell is so distinctive that I can't compare it with anything else. It's not even the mixture of sweat, pain, blood, burning skin or... The smell of torture is different from all these. One would only ever find it in prison and I have no name for it. Perhaps its very vocabulary has died under torture. I see things here that are not explicable within the concepts or the language we develop outside prison. Imagine the smell of beaten flesh, which like burnt flesh is unique. I think I must stop writing about this.

***

This morning I woke up to the sound of cell doors that seemed far away, almost from another world. I lay there waiting for my turn, and when the door opened I held out my cup so that the guard – a woman, someone's daughter, mother or wife – could pour tea into it. I wonder if these women, who are guards, fall in love. Do they, my love? Or do we need to possess a special quality in order to fall in love? Or perhaps everyone can fall in love, but their kind of love must be different from our kind of love. Isn't it so, my Azad?

The rain is lashing against the window and I crave to be out in it. I feel thirsty for this rain that beats against my cell with its noise and its darkness. I wonder where you are right now. Are you watching it from behind a window, or are you walking through it? How I wish I could open the door or fly through the window and stand under this rain shower and watch the water run down my body and through my fingers. My love, while my nostrils are full of the smell of rain, my skin cries out for it and my lips long to taste it.

Darling, it's late and, as you see, I've reached the last page of my notebook. So, I have to prepare it for hiding. And you know what? Now I have a stronger feeling about writing than when I started. I feel it connects me to the future. Perhaps one day, when the people stand up against this regime, you and I will come here, and I'll retrieve these notebooks from their hiding places. Would I be able to let you read them? I don't know! Nevertheless, I feel that by writing these words, I am with you. I hope to see you in my dreams, but only at a time that means I'll remember it in the morning. You know that time between sleep and wakefulness, the place where you can still remember dreaming? Visit me then. That's where I'll be waiting for you, and it will fill my day. Be your name. Xavar.

Chapter Thirteen

SOCIAL MEDIA

The next time Faraz met Bahram, his friend made an intriguing suggestion. 'I have an idea,' he said. 'Do you mind if I upload Xavar's letters, and the images, so that everyone can read them?'

Faraz felt a dawning excitement. 'But won't that be dangerous for you?' he asked.

'No,' Bahram assured him. 'I don't use my real name on the internet and I always wipe my computer afterwards.'

Faraz was smiling broadly. 'Then do it! I think that would be really interesting. Do you need help with typing them?'

'No. I've already typed up everything you gave me. They'll be on the net with a single click. My only concern is that after a while the regime will read them, too.'

'Good, they might learn something!'

'Yes… But then they'll search for the source and they might trace it back to you,' Bahram warned. 'We don't want to put your life in danger, do we?'

I don't see any reason why the regime would know that it was *me* who found her letters at the interrogation centre,' said Faraz.

'What if they find out?'

'How would they? They might think that someone had

smuggled her letters out of prison and is now publishing them. There must be similar material on the internet,' Faraz reasoned.

'Yes, there are memoirs of those who spent time in prison during the eighties,' said Bahram. 'But they're written and uploaded by writers who are safely out of the country.'

'I see. But, all the same, I think we should do it and make them accessible to everyone,' said Faraz. He thought for a moment. Then he asked, 'Have you got the birth certificate yet?'

'No, but hopefully I'll have it soon.'

***

Faraz opened his email after a few weeks and read his brother's letters.

I no longer remember how many emails I've sent you, yet I haven't received a single reply. So, I assume this means you want nothing more to do with me – not even to acknowledge that you used to have a brother called Omid who was your friend! I wonder if you still write articles under different names against various violations of human rights in Iran. No, you won't be bothering with that any more. If you write at all, you could now write about how to delete a history of torture from a place like the one where you're doing just that, and the reasons for deleting it.

I wonder if you're still dreaming about our cousin, Forood. Are you? You used to say that sometimes you dreamed he would come to our house and tell us, 'You see?

I'm alive, I'm okay.' Remember, these are your words, Faraz, not mine! How can you do this to him, to us? I can't get out of my head the idea of what you're doing in that fucking prison. Are you really aware of what you're up to? Don't you realise it's collaboration with the regime to conceal the amount of torture they were involved in? Can't you get it into your head? Darling brother, this is for the future: they are deleting, or sanitising, their bloody history and you're their cleaner.

Congratulations on your new job and your new conscience, or perhaps it's not new, and it's only now that I can see it. I can't understand how you could have agreed to wipe out all trace of Forood and his friends, and their last remaining messages, from the walls of that prison. Don't give me that crap about their getting rid of it anyway. Yes, if you hadn't said you'd do it, they would have put someone else on it instead. The point is why you? Why did you go along with it? I'm ashamed of having a brother like you.

Every time Faraz read his brother's letters, they added to his pain and depression. He couldn't write back in the same vein, yet nor could he afford to lose his relationship with his only brother. Omid was also his only safe contact. Over the last few years he had published Faraz's articles under a fictitious name on websites, and in magazines. Omid sent him any book or political literature he asked for, so he could not afford to lose him. Above all, despite Omid's poisonous tongue, Faraz still loved him. At the same time, however, he felt Omid was full of anger and hatred and Faraz couldn't bring himself to step inside that world to argue on those terms. He believed that, because of the frustration people felt at not being able to change their situation, they built up a kind of bile that poured out at the slightest opportunity, even in communications between friends.

He decided that, as ever, Omid was judging him without knowing or hearing his side of story.

Chapter Fourteen

MAKING FRIENDS

Faraz was waiting for the right time to check the space under the sink in the other bathroom. Although he suspected Xavar might not have used that room to hide her letters, as she had used only one of the ventilation ducts, he felt it was worth checking. He had searched through the entire wing but could find nothing, yet he was sure that letters and small handicrafts must still be hidden there. He just didn't have the eyes to see them and felt everyone to be suffering from different degrees of blindness. He even carried his torch to work and shone it into cracks in the walls, as if it could somehow help him see things that were really only discernible by intuition.

One afternoon when he was sure his uncle was not in the building, he lay on the floor in the second bathroom with his torch in his hand. He hacked off the plaster from the entire space under the sink. The only advantage of that space was that there was no hurry to cover it up, because it wasn't visible. Having a torch made things easier and once the plaster was removed, he could see that the bricks were in place and there were no spaces around them. Disappointed, he cleaned up the mess on the floor and left the gash in the wall for the time being. He continued his work, but his mind was engrossed in trying to figure out what other hiding places Xavar and her fellow prisoners might use. After a couple of hours, he left off painting the wall in one of the cells and went back to the space under the sink to take a second look with his torch. There was nothing there. With one of his tools he tapped on each of the bricks in turn and when one of them shook slightly, his whole body jumped, and the torch fell from his left hand and broke. The wall went dark again, but he was not upset because now he was sure there was something behind the loose brick. Though unable to see, his sense of relief drove him on and he tried to dislodge the brick by making space around it. It took him an hour, and every now and then he had to go into the corridor to make sure no one was coming. Exhausted from the intensity of it and from his uncomfortable position lying on the floor, he at last removed the brick to find a package behind it. He didn't need to unwrap it to know it was Xavar's, and this one was the biggest he had found. Though covered head to toe in sweat and dust, he was overjoyed and felt like dancing, as if now Xavar was his lover and her letters were for him. He realised he did love her; with a different love than for Nasim, but nonetheless he loved Xavar a great deal.

Early next morning, when he looked at the notebook properly, he realised there was a number (6) on it.

***

JOINT COMMITTEE INTERROGATION CENTRE, 1984

Azad, my love, how are you? I have great news! From my solitary cell, I've been transferred to a larger one and I have cellmates. The good thing is that I can walk here without feeling dizzy or crashing into the wall after three steps! They allow us no bedding and at nights we must still sleep on the floor, as I did in the previous cell. Nor are there tables in our cells to eat at; for breakfast, lunch and dinner we spread out a cloth on the floor.

I've been here four days now and I've had no time to write to you, because I've been talking to my cellmates, learning why they're here and telling them why and how I was arrested. At night, prisoners are in communication with neighbouring cells using Morse code. Sometimes I feel the sounds are coming from another world, such as the men's wing below my cell. In here, I can see that two worlds run parallel to each other, or one inside the other. The regime is neither aware of them, nor can they eliminate them. I mean the world of Morse code, which allows us to communicate and keep our souls alive and keep part of us free. Here, writing to you is easier and I just stop when I hear the noise that warns us that the guards are on the wing.

Azad jan, yesterday after shower the guard took us to a kind of yard, which was exactly like one of these cells without the ceiling. We actually saw the sun peering over the walls! I stood in the sun and, for about half an hour before the guard came to take us back to our cell, I so enjoyed soaking it up for the first time in about five months. Its rays were not strong, yet it had a bit of warmth and its yellowness was beautiful. Its movement on the walls made me move with it. I had the feeling of being hugged by sunshine and I imagined it was you and your warm hands were touching my starved body. I wished I could have stayed there among the clothes lines for hours and hours and seen the sunset and then the stars.

There are three children in this cell. There's Ziba, who is three years old, and a boy, Nader, of eleven months. Their mother's name is Azar and she's twenty-five. Then there's Mitra, who is thirteen. One of the oldest prisoners, Nahid, is in prison with some of her children, and she's Mitra's grandmother. Let me write to you about Nahid. In prison she has developed severe headaches and sometimes the pain is excruciating. I asked her why she sometimes looks so desolate. I told her that I know being in prison is painful, but she should take it easy and try not to let her grief get on top of her. She thought for a while and then said, 'You're right, but I'm not sad that I'm here. Actually, it's a privilege to be among so many good people like you and Mahvash, although I wish Mitra wasn't here.'

She pointed to her and said, 'Her mother is in another cell and they won't let them see each other. But even that isn't the main reason I'm sad. The worst thing is that one of my children isn't on our side. She's on their side.'

My love, initially I thought her daughter must have been broken by torture, and I told Nahid to give her time. Then she explained to me that her daughter is a trusty and was in the torture chamber when Nahid was being beaten. She even asked her questions and told the interrogators that her mother was lying. I found it very difficult to believe that someone would hurt their own mother, especially in this way. Nahid's feet are still swollen from when she was tortured several days ago. She was originally arrested for putting up a few activists in her home and is now accused of being a spy. Her interrogator keeps asking her for the names and addresses of the people she helped, and every time she gives him false names and tells him that she never knew where they lived. Everyone lies like this in here and the interrogators can't really tell when we're telling the truth and when we're not.

One of my cellmates, who is my mother's

age and reminds me of her, is Mahvash and I'm very happy to have her for company. She looks after me and won't let me wash my clothes and warns me not to wear myself out. Let me tell you about her. She has a kind face with happy wrinkles – she doesn't have wrinkles between her eyebrows, which means that she never frowns. Her hair is mostly white from the roots down to her ears, and then brown from her ears down to her shoulders. It shows she used to dye her hair before she was arrested. I like her silver-coloured hair, which gives her a motherly look, and I asked her why she doesn't cut it to get rid of the brown. She smiled at me and said that the brown reminds her of the outside world, the life that she used to have and doesn't want to forget.

Another friend I have found here is Pari. She's thirty and was arrested because her brother and sister were active members of an opposition group and escaped arrest by going into hiding. Pari was living in France and was arrested at the airport when she came to visit her family. She speaks French and English fluently and I asked her to say something in French to Mahvash and me. I love the sound of it. You know, Azadam, she sang a love song for us and though I did not understand it, I felt its emotion and it really moved me.

I asked Pari whether people in France and other Western countries support our struggle against the Islamic regime. Pari said nothing for a moment and then, 'Do you really want to know?'

I was surprised by her question and said, 'Yes, of course. Why not?'

'Because it's very depressing to know that people are alone here. No one supports their struggle for secularism, gender equality or basic rights. Everyone sides with those who have power. You might not believe me, but as far as I can make out, the intellectuals, leftists and activists support the regime. They praise Khomeini for condemning Western governments.'

I said to her, 'We noticed this tendency here, among some groups. They couldn't see the danger of the Islamists taking power. They were pro-Russia, or disciples of Mao. But I hadn't realised that so-called "progressives" in the West also support the regime or believe in its slogans.'

'I don't know what you mean by "progressive",' she said, 'because progressive to one person might mean backward to another. But when I was in France, I didn't meet anyone who spoke against Khomeini and his regime.'

'Are they also pro-Russia?'

'Most of them aren't. They don't see Russia as a socialist country, but they support any anti-imperialist movement. And Khomeini took power on the slogan "Down with imperialism".'

I was really upset by this and asked, 'What would they say about all the executions since the Islamic regime came to power? I remember a recent photo of a line of young men in Kurdistan who were in the process of being executed after the regime took over, and it won an international prize and was published in hundreds of newspapers. How can people ignore or deny an image like that?'

Pari thought about this. 'Well,' she replied, 'they see this reality from behind a thick screen of ideology and they certainly don't see events in the same way as we do, who live through them.'

I said, 'They live in countries which have freedom of expression, and yet they support the execution of people who are merely fighting for the rights that they themselves already have.'

My love, Pari is a thoughtful person. I don't know what her sentence can be, or how long they will keep her here, as – like me – she's only a hostage. They don't have any evidence against her.

I told my cellmates how happy I was to be there with them and to be able to talk to them, and one of them said, 'It's temporary. Mahi will come back soon.'

'Who's Mahi?'

'A trusty, who's been with us for a month now and was just taken for "walkabout" a week ago. We'll have to live like zombies again once she comes back. No talking, no Morse code. Nothing, except wishing her dead.'

I should explain that *walkabout* means surveillance duties outside the prison. They showed me her belongings in the corner. I got very upset, because I had just found these women after so many months in solitary. I won't be able to write when she comes back, so I hope it isn't soon.

Eshg-e-man, this is the room I live in now. What's your room like? What do you do when you're not at work? How is life in the outside world? Now I'd better go to bed and imagine you in your new life, which is a blank page to me - and I can write it however I want to!

***

Looking at all these women who are denied food and comfort, I feel that they have not only imprisoned us, but stifled our desires. And what are we without those? We have to ignore our wants, the need for food and the need for pleasure. Azizam, I desire your hands, your touch, to forget where I am, and what I see.

Send me flowers, love, large red and yellow roses. Put one branch of jasmine around the reds, in a way that looks as if the little white jasmine flowers are kissing the red petals. You know the address, but I'll write it again, just in case: Xavar, Room 3, wing 3, Joint Committee

Interrogation Centre, Firdausi Avenue, Tehran. I know they won't give me the flowers, but I want to know that you sent them.

This evening, Azar, the mother of two of the children, was called for interrogation. She came back about four hours later but looked a century older. She sat in the cell, staring at the void. I asked other prisoners what had happened to her. They didn't know and said we'd better wait until she talks. I couldn't wait and went to her and asked if she was all right or if she wanted to eat her dinner that we had kept for her. She looked at me and then at my stomach and smiled, which wasn't like a normal smile. Then she told me that she had just had a ten-minute visit with her husband before they took him away to be executed.

When she told me, I automatically imagined you and me in that position. For a few moments I stared at her as if I didn't understand what she was talking about. Then I hugged her and we cried in each other's arms. Afterwards, she let me go and just sat on her own, perhaps needing to be alone with her thoughts of him during that hour of his departure. It was a moment, a precious moment for her to think about him and to know that he was thinking of her. Occasionally, I looked over at her and sometimes I saw again that smile on her face that wasn't really a smile. As I've told you before, my love, I sometimes feel I don't have the appropriate vocabulary to describe what I'm living through in this place. There should be a word for the expression I saw on that woman's face. And some other expressions that I see in here can't be described in the words we use outside. Perhaps the reason is that the world here is so different from the outside world, where words originate.

Azadam, I felt my heart burn when she told me about her ordeal, and the actual heat is suffocating me, too.

***

Faraz stopped reading. He needed to get the image out of his mind before he could continue. Then he thought about Xavar not finding an appropriate vocabulary to describe what she was seeing. Of course, the language of trauma was different and not everyone could read and write it. That must be the reason why people suffering from depression were not understood before they committed suicide. Their families, or those who were seeing them in their social lives, couldn't read their distressed faces or their faraway eyes, or comprehend their panic whenever they felt an intrusion into their world. He knew people who barely spoke and retreated into themselves for as long as they needed to grieve, while others needed to weep and let out their feelings in response to their traumatic experiences. What would he do if one of his family members were to be executed by the state, rather than dying naturally?

***

My love, I have not written to you in more than a week. Why? You can't imagine how difficult the last few days have been for me. Last Saturday I was talking to Mahvash and Pari about the time of the revolution, when we heard the warning signal that the guards were on their way. We continued talking, but the person who was communicating in Morse code, stopped tapping on the wall. The door opened and Mahro came into our cell and everyone fell silent. I realised the woman other prisoners called Mahi, was in fact our Mahro, my cousin. Ever since my arrest, I have been expecting to run into her at some point.

At the first family party we went to together, Mahro looked so pretty and all the young men were after her. Wasn't it about five years ago? She would have been 13 then and just loved wearing a short skirt and showing off her long legs. She was arrested with her brother last year and one day a friend called to let me know that my aunt, Mahro's mother, had had a heart attack and was in hospital. I went to the hospital and discovered she had died. The shock of it seemed almost to have killed my uncle Abbas. He didn't speak and didn't seem to be able to hear what anyone said. It seemed he only saw me when I actually hugged him, for then he looked at me and said, 'They killed him. They killed my boy.' I said that Mahro and Zagros are fine. Don't worry. He looked into my eyes and said, 'No, they've killed Zagros. They've given me his clothes and his grave number. That's why your aunt had a heart attack.' It was then that I understood what had happened and couldn't hold back my tears.

You know last Saturday when Mahro came into the room? At first, I thought I was mistaken and that she was someone else. She walked in as if she saw nobody in this crowded room. She didn't look around, she didn't say hello to anyone. Nor did the prisoners greet her. The minute she came in, I was struck by something about her that prevented me from rushing up to her as I used to when we were both free. There was something missing from her manner or from her look, something different from the Mahro we used to know. Before I could gather my thoughts and approach her, she put her black chador in the corner beside her things and went to the washroom. The guard hadn't closed the door when Mahro came in. In those few minutes that she went to the toilet, my cellmates scooped up anything that would be considered illegal. The chess board, which was made of paper and bread dough, was hidden away, as were all the pens and paper we use for writing or playing games together, or with the children. One of the prisoners told me, 'She is Mahi.' I wondered why they called her 'fish', and asked if she had told them that her name was Mahi. They said, 'Yes. And she is certainly fishy.'

She came back and spread her prayer mat in the corner of the room, put on a white chador, and started to pray. I watched her facing towards Mecca with her hands in front of her face, whispering. Then her hands dropped beside her body as she muttered something to her god. She then knelt to put her forehead on the *mohr*. This was so strange. You must remember that she never used to pray.

The prayers that should have taken less than ten minutes went on for two hours, as if she wanted to demonstrate how holy she was. Then she opened the Koran and took up her beads. She read the Koran, passing the beads between her fingers as if frantic to secure a place in heaven. I wondered if she was reading the *sura* that tells women to be obedient to their husbands. She didn't seem aware of me watching her.

I asked one of the other prisoners where Mahro might have been since I'd arrived in this room, and she whispered in my ear, 'Most of the time, especially at weekends, she's not on the wing.'

'Where does she go? Is she going home?'

'I don't know. There are rumours that these kinds of prisoners stay with their interrogators over the weekend, or even sometimes during the week.'

'What do they do?' I asked in horror.

'Well, as you can imagine, there's usually

sex involved – consensual or not. But I've also heard that they help their interrogators with arrests and other things. Even assisting with executions.'

My love, you can imagine how shocked and upset I was to hear all this, but I had to talk to her and find out what she had to say. I waited, but Mahro went on reading the Koran, as if this was the only thing she had to do in here. I went over and greeted her. She was clearly furious and looked up in contempt at being disturbed. When she saw me and realised who it was, she turned pale. She was speechless for a few seconds, as if she had been electrified. Then she dropped her eyes, which I think were full of hate, so that I couldn't see what she was thinking. She spotted my stomach and pulled herself together enough to return my greeting. With her eyes still on my tummy she asked when I had been arrested.

'Six months ago. I thought you'd have heard about my arrest and would expect to see me here.'

'Where were you up to now?' she asked.

'I was in one of the small cells in the little corridor.'

'Has Azad been arrested as well?'

'No, he hasn't.'

She was silent. Looking at her mat I said, 'You never used to pray. Is it the result of being in prison?'

She blushed and after a pause replied, 'I was too young and there were not enough good people around to show me the right way.'

'What about your parents? Were they bad, too? Is that why everyone loved them? You were in prison and couldn't see how distraught people were when they heard about your brother Zagros being executed. But they talked about him as a fighter, a hero. Your mother had a heart attack when they told her the news. By killing him, the authorities caused her death as well. You do realise that, don't you?'

She was silent for a few moments, then said, 'Baba came to see me, and he was carrying a carrier bag full of Zagros's clothes. I had never seen him in such a state. His trousers were wet and when I asked him why, he told me that he had wet himself when he'd been given the bag. They told him the name of the cemetery where he could find my brother's grave. He had come to see if I was really alive, or if they had killed me as well. He made me feel that I had lost my Baba as well as my brother. And then, later, I heard my mother had died. So, you see? I don't have a family now.'

For a few minutes her face lost that hateful expression and I sensed she was close to tears. I was struck by what she had said about my uncle: 'He had come to see if I was really alive, or if they had killed me as well.' And, my love,

I wanted to tell her that they *had* killed her. Not her body, but her spirit. Instead I pulled myself together and tried to reason with her.

'Don't you think you're making a mistake?'

There was a long silence before she answered in a shaky voice, 'It seems that what you used to say about religion being a personal matter and that you're only against the union of religion with politics was just empty talk. Otherwise you wouldn't question why I pray. In here, I've learnt that most of the things I was told before were just slogans and it makes me feel sick. I thank God for opening my eyes.'

'I'm sorry you feel sick, no matter what the reason. But to turn to god in prison isn't a private matter; it's a political one,' I told her. 'You wouldn't become religious if you weren't in prison and under pressure or being bombarded by religious propaganda. Besides that, the people who lock you up first convert you and then make you collaborate with them.'

She didn't speak for some time and then she said, 'That's a lie. I only pray to God.'

'Where have you been, then, for the last few days?' I challenged her. 'Will they let me out the same way they allow you? Is it true that the interrogators ask prisoners like you to attend the executions and fire the last bullet into the prisoners' heads?'

My questions made her turn pale, and her

lips trembled before her face took on a stony expression with a hint of violence.

'I've never witnessed any execution. And does it matter who fires the last bullet? Some prisoners do it just to prove their honesty or to earn the trust of their interrogators. They might act differently if they were free. But I don't think it proves anything. The prisoner in the execution line will die anyway. Far better she dies sooner rather than later. I really don't understand what all the fuss is about.'

My love, she was silent for a few moments and I didn't know what to say to her. She seemed a completely different person from the one I used to know.

Then she sighed and said, 'I've never harmed anyone. In solitary confinement God helped me to review my life. It was like I was watching a film, and I realised I had been wrong many times over. I saw how misguided I had been to pose as a fighter. I realised the reason for all that showing off. When I got here, I saw myself for who I really was.'

I told her, 'You're wrong, you only saw part of yourself: the part that they wanted to show you. It would be impossible to recognise yourself or anyone else fully in such an extreme situation as solitary confinement. Listen, you're too young for all this. Just eighteen. You have a long life ahead of you. Don't ruin it. Try to serve your sentence here like other prisoners, so that when you get out you won't feel ashamed.'

'I haven't done anything wrong. But those who told you about me behind my back have also turned my Baba against me.'

I didn't know what she meant. She continued, 'Baba won't visit me. Last time he came - it was eight months ago - he said that his heart was broken. When I asked why, he said that some families had asked him to tell me to leave their daughters alone and not to disturb them or beat them. Have you seen me beating anyone, Xavar? Why did they lie to my father?'

She was in tears and I didn't know what to say. After a pause I told her, 'I don't know their reasons for telling him that, but you can't judge everyone by a single lie, and you shouldn't debase yourself by helping the guards, just to get revenge.'

She stared into my eyes and said, 'I don't help the guards.'

I couldn't bear to remain in doubt any longer and asked, 'Did they question you about me? Have you told them anything about us?'

'They didn't ask me about you. Perhaps they don't know that we're family. But if my interrogator did ask, I would tell him that I don't want anything bad to happen to you. You were always good to me.'

Darling, I was shocked by what she said. 'What do you mean by telling your interrogator that you don't want anything bad to happen to me? Do you think they would listen to your opinion about who to harm, or not?'

'It depends. They're not all the same. My interrogator would listen to me.'

'Why? Why should he listen to you?'

All she would say was that he would listen to her.

My love, I didn't know how to respond. She didn't seem to understand me any more. Or perhaps her ears are too full of her interrogator's words for her to hear anyone else clearly. However, now that I know she hasn't told them anything about me, I feel better – for the moment. I'm glad they don't know I'm related to her. If they had known, surely they'd have asked her about me, you and our activities, or the people we were in touch with that she might know. What nags at me now, though, is the question of whether I can trust her. She knows you by the name they're not aware of. She knows we were both activists. She could do us both enormous damage and all I can do is hope that she won't.

Nothing of love or beauty is left in Mahro. Her eyes are full of hate, aimed at other prisoners who are fighters such as she used to be. I feel her hatred for the fighters is partly the hatred she has for her new identity. The strange thing is that she was so beautiful but now she doesn't look pretty at all. She has the same small nose and mouth, the same large eyes that seem to have a teardrop locked inside them, and yet hate has changed her expression. I feel she hates us because she was not brave enough to remain a fighter. Seeing us day and night is like seeing herself before she was broken. As if we are holding a mirror up to her past, the past that she couldn't hold on to and therefore doesn't love any more; the past to which she can't return. Even now, she knows she's become another person on the opposite side to us. She is with the enemy now – at least in the eyes of the prisoners.

Thinking about my encounter with her, I realise that we did not hug or kiss. Whenever we saw each other before, she used to run towards me and we would have a big hug and laugh. But here, neither of us had the same feelings that we used to, and we didn't react to each other with the love we used to share.

Azadam, while watching her pray I was thinking of my uncle Abbas, and I realised he lied to us. Remember? It was two weeks before my arrest that we saw him, and we asked him, 'How is our pretty cousin doing?' As usual he said, 'Mahro is fine. As much of a fighter as ever.' But sitting there at that moment, watching her, I could see nothing of this. This creature who finds refuge only by kneeling to god retains neither the fighting spirit nor the beauty of that innocent young girl. And my uncle? I feel when his wife died after losing their son, part of him died, too. And that deadness has soured all his remaining relationships. He will never be the same again.

My dearest Azad, during the last few days, Mahro has left the room early in the morning when the other prisoners are still asleep and returned late in the evening and gone straight to bed. She has rarely eaten with us and I haven't been able to bring myself to talk to her again. I wouldn't have known what to say to her, and she hasn't looked at me or at the other prisoners. It's obvious that she's been playing a role, intent on showing everyone that she was deliberately ignoring them. I could see that she wore a mask to hide her pain, by which I mean the pain of not being able to stay true to what she used to believe in and was proud of. She must also feel wretched that her father, her only surviving relative, no longer visits her. I feel in future, whenever she looks back, there will be a turning point, the moment she became a collaborator. Even if she doesn't continue to collaborate with the regime, after her release it will stay with her for the rest of her life. In a way, she'll be released from prison, but she'll never find freedom from what she's done in captivity. I asked other women if she was the same before she saw me, and they said she was, that she treated them as if they were untouchable because they didn't pray.

Anyway, Mahro left this morning and a few hours later the guard collected all her belongings. So, I won't see her any more. Perhaps this is for the best, because seeing her with her head on the *mohr* gives me a horrible feeling. You know, I realised she called the guard 'sister' and I asked my roommates about it, and they said that prisoners call the guards 'sister' or 'brother' if they're broken or a trusty or pretending to be penitent. But we, the ones who do not agree to collaborate, or don't pretend to be collaborating, always call them guards.

When Mahro was with us, we could no longer talk about politics and just sat and stared at the walls or read the rubbish books the regime allows us to read, such as Makhmalbaf's, or the Koran. Sometimes, when she was praying we sat in a way that she could not see us, and we talked to each other in Morse code, without making any noise. Two days after Mahro reappeared, Mahvash had some news about her husband. She got it illicitly in the bathroom, read it there and destroyed the note. She told us that since her husband had not collaborated, he had been transferred for imminent execution. Mahvash was very upset and we couldn't talk to her or support her. The prisoners believed that Mahro was there to report back to their interrogators on whatever they said, and their respective psychological strength or weakness. If Mahvash's interrogator discovered she knew about her husband's ordeal, they would interrogate her about it, and she'd be forced to reveal how she had found out. We used our hands as if patting our laps to say things to each other, which sometimes made some of us laugh involuntarily. And Mahro looked at us with contempt when her praying was over. Perhaps she thought we were laughing at her. She could not see that her situation wasn't funny at all, it was a tragedy - and I even pitied her for what she had become.

***

Faraz sat there thinking about Xavar and what all those women and men went through once they had been freed. He remembered a man who had spent two years in prison and told him that some of the trusties were released and some were executed. What had happened to Mahro? Was she alive? What was she doing and how did she feel now about her time in prison? People like Mahro, who became trusties in prison, might never have collaborated had they not been arrested. While those like his uncle, who had helped establish this regime or collaborated with it from the beginning, were now stepping out of the picture without having to face the humiliation suffered by those ex-prisoners who had started to collaborate under pressure.

***

My love, the little boy in our room, Nader, is very sick and his mother asked the guards to let her send him home. They said they'd ask the prison governor and get back to her. After a couple of hours, they said that the governor would let him go only if in return she gave him her sister's address. Nader's mother told them that she doesn't know where her sister lives now, and I believe her. Her sister wouldn't stay at an address that the regime might get hold of. Yet whether she knew it or not, I'm sure she would never have given it to them – not even to save her beloved child. He's in pain and didn't sleep last night or the night before that. He coughs all the time and breathes with difficulty. He has none of his usual energy.

***

Faraz was deeply focused on Xavar's notebook and didn't hear his mother coming out of her bedroom. He jumped at her voice. 'Are you okay? Can't you sleep?' Ana asked.

'I'm fine. I just came down to read the newspapers,' he said, and covered the notebook with the nearest paper before his mother reached him. He felt her looking at him with an expression he hadn't seen before.

'You'll let me know if you need anything, or there's anything that bothers you. Won't you?' asked Ana kindly.

'Sure. Don't worry,' he told her.

***

Oh, my darling, I'm happy, very happy. As you will know, I had my first visit yesterday from my parents and my grandmother and it was marvellous. My parents said that you send me your love. They gave me the scarf you sent, and I'm wearing it now. I love it, not only because it's beautiful and bright red, which is a contrast with the greyness of my prison cell, or that it's made of silk and its softness contrasts with this rough place, but because it is from you. I touch it as if I'm touching you, and I hold it in my hands and close my eyes and put it across my face as if it is *you* touching me! My mother said that you told them to tell me you wished you could send me things I like, such as perfume, chocolates, flowers and champagne. Oh I wish I had all these things here; they would cheer me up and make me happy. Though without you, my happiness wouldn't last.

Darling, now that I've had my first visit, they might not take me for interrogation any more and harm my child. I hope so. This visit really lifted me, and I feel I'm entering a different phase of my imprisonment. Mother asked me to loosen my chador and let her see my belly, then she said she thinks it's a girl and I told her I feel the same.

A female guard was standing next to my parents to make sure there'd be no secret communications, so my parents referred to you as my grandpa and told me that you were very worried about me.

Azad jan, if they were not after you, you

could come and see me, too. Wouldn't that be wonderful? I want to show you my bump now that my pregnancy is obvious. I wish you could put your hands on my stomach and feel it. I'm sure you wish you could put your ear to it and listen to our child's heartbeat and talk to her. Sometimes I imagine our reunion in one year, two, or three, or perhaps even longer. Do you have these daydreams as well?

I was so happy to see my grandmother. She belongs to the generation of women who were the first to fight for equal rights with men. Although I know you love her and you used to say that you enjoy talking to her, I realise now that you don't know much about her. My grandmother's mother was one of the freedom fighters during the Constitutional Revolution, that led to the establishment of parliament, and she was always under pressure from the mullahs. My grandmother followed *her* mother's ideas and adopted her behaviour, which was to act as though being free was her birthright and no one could take it away from her. At one time, two decades after the Constitutional Revolution, my grandmother had to leave town to save her own life. The fundamentalists wanted to kill her. They believed she was turning their wives and daughters to prostitution. They burnt down her house, but thankfully she had already left with her family a couple of hours earlier. The plan to set it on fire reached her from one of the men who attended the fundamentalists' meetings in order to keep tabs on them. He asked his wife to go and tell my grandmother about what they'd decided to do, and that they planned it for the following morning after prayer. My mother was very young at the time and doesn't remember living in Mashhad and fleeing in the middle of the night.

Do you know what my grandmother said to me today? She said that I am her. By arresting me, they have taken revenge on my parents and my grandparents. She spoke about how she is no longer young and so isn't worth arresting. She told me not to worry and that the family will take me back. I was so glad to see her, for she told me a lot about her life and her fight for freedom. I remember once she told me

***

Xavar's interrupted sentence brought Forood to Faraz's mind and he wondered if he, too, had visits. Did anyone go to see him? His father didn't want to see him, but what about his mother and his siblings? He realised that, despite thinking about Forood frequently, he still couldn't get beyond the superficial fact of his arrest or trying to imagine the life he had led between those now-familiar walls. He was grateful to Forood, because the search for him had led to the discovery of Xavar's notebooks.

***

Eshg-e-man, I'm happy because we heard today via the Morse code that someone has been released and it's cheered us up a lot. Her release means that some of us will get out one day, so we won't all end up dead! You know what I think, love? There are hundreds of thousands of us prisoners, and the regime can't kill us all. Perhaps they will kill thousands of us, but still many will return to the real world. I wonder what prisoners take with them when they leave. What does the regime want them to take? Submission? Desire for revenge? Fear? Hate? Frustration? Anger? Hopelessness? Depression? I'm sure you would add a great deal to this list. We witness the cruelty with which we're treated, and it makes me wonder who will repeat this cruelty, and in what form? After all, cruelty is contagious in many ways and might manifest itself long after one's exposed to it. I wonder if we can go through this process and not need to perpetuate similar cruelties of our own in later life.

Is it possible to heal the scars by being kind to others? We don't learn that here, of course! No, I'm wrong: some of us are very kind to each other. For example, Mahvash's relationship with me is all about kindness, isn't it?

Sometimes when I look at all these women, I see new things in them. Before my arrest I felt fear and recognised it in other people; but the fear I experience here and see in these women is different. In the outside world I saw fear, such as the fear of losing one's job, or of losing loved ones through separation or illness. But in here the fear is constant: fear of our loved ones being arrested, fear of being interrogated again, fear of losing friends because of execution or transfer, fear of our own execution.

Azadam, I imagine the moon is liquid sunstone and I wish I had wings and could fly away to it before coming home to you. I would peck at the moon with my beak and make a hole in it so that its yellowish quality would spill over, and I would bring you a drop of it as a gift, to hang in our room and watch it day and night.

Today, I was talking to Mahvash when thirteen-year-old Mitra, who has already been in prison for a year, came and asked if she could sit with us. We welcomed her gladly and I tried to make her laugh because she gave us such a bleak smile. Mahvash drew an interesting parallel, which I felt Mitra appreciated as it seemed to set her thinking. Mahvash said that the three of us have something in common: we are each in a unique situation of hormonal changes in our bodies that make our environment even more difficult to cope with. She told us about the hot flushes she has because of her impending menopause and said that sometimes she bleeds for weeks and develops a headache that lasts for several days. I had noticed that she was not sleeping well at night. Then Mahvash talked about the hormonal changes that occur during pregnancy and the different effects of these changes. I described the physical and emotional impact of carrying our child. After that, she asked Mitra if she wanted to tell us about how she's becoming a woman and the hormonal changes this brings, and Mitra did. I was so moved by her admission that sometimes she cries in silence; other times she pours cold water all over her hot face and head to wash away the maddening feelings that she can't contain. Sometimes she needs to cry or scream.

The other day Mitra had made a mouse out of a washing sponge and was playing with it with Nader and Ziba, until one of the guards opened the door on hearing the children laughing and confiscated it. I could tell that Mitra was very angry but didn't look at the guard. She just stared at the ground to hide the hatred that was streaming out of her. Mitra reminds me of those fish, born in the sea but captured and left in a tank, that hit the wall or the glass every time they try to swim as far as they used to. Mitra's situation is like theirs and I'm worried that every time she hits the glass, something inside her breaks. She misses her mother a great deal and longs to be with her.

In the mornings, when the door is open for the washroom, the children wake up with everyone else, but they don't open their eyes. I look at Nader, who is now better despite having no medication, and he clings to his mother with closed eyes, as if he's sick of his environment and doesn't want to see it any more. He cries if his mother tries to move away.

Today when the guard opened the door, everyone looked up to see who was going to be taken for interrogation. The children watched as well, fearful the guard might call on Azar, their mother. Ziba, who was sitting beside Mitra listening to a story, ran to her mother as soon as she heard the guard tell her it was her turn. As Azar was getting ready, putting on the chador and the blindfold, Ziba clung to her, deathly pale, and Nahid told her, 'You'd better stay here until your mummy comes back. She won't be long.' But Ziba resisted, shaking her head nervously and holding on tightly to her mother's chador. Azar herself was so preoccupied that she said nothing to her daughter about whether to stay or go, and it was Mitra who observed, with an insight no child her age ought to have, 'It's better she goes with her. They won't beat her so severely in front of her little girl.' Ziba's jaw was trembling as she accompanied her mother out of the room. They came back a few hours later. Azar had been beaten and Ziba was very agitated. Her mother lay down and Ziba sat beside her and caressed her with her little hands.

Nahid made a doll out of unwanted clothes and gave it to Ziba, who took it and hid it behind her, but didn't know what to do with it, so unfamiliar is she with toys.

When a prisoner comes into the room with dressings on her feet and can only walk with help from other prisoners, Ziba stands still to watch what's going on. She stands by the wall, pressing hard against it with her back. That wall would carry the imprint of her if it were made of softer material. She talks to her mother and asks why the prisoner has poorly feet.

And our baby? She has started kicking. I don't know if she's hungry or if she is telling me she feels trapped. Perhaps she just wants to hear your voice

***

Faraz thought of those children who were in prison with Xavar. What are they doing now, he wondered? How do they look back on those days, weeks, months or years they spent in prison? What about Xavar's baby? He could see that those of his students who were born during the Iran-Iraq war were severely affected because their mothers had suffered so much stress during pregnancy. What were the effects of Xavar's situation on her baby, who was experiencing it directly as she developed inside her?

***

I'm hungry. Everyone's hungry. We're all waiting for our dinner, which for reasons unknown is delayed tonight. Some prisoners are trying to eat a bit of dry bread that we always keep aside for times like this. You know, azizam, I miss the smell of bread. Bread here doesn't smell the same.

Two prisoners have been transferred to our cell. They're called Goli and Behi, and they believe they won't be staying with us too long. They say their interrogation has finished and they've been told they're about to be executed. They were both in solitary confinement downstairs, where most of the cells are occupied by men. They're happy to be together before having to face their ordeal. I can't believe how relaxed they are.

Azadam, let me tell you how Goli and Behi were arrested and interrogated. Goli said, 'They came for us when we had a meeting at my house. They must have watched and followed one of us. They interrogated the whole group in the same house. They wanted to find out where my husband and Behi's husband were. We said we didn't know. Of course, our husbands had escaped and by then we knew that they'd reached the guerrillas in Kurdistan. Anyway, each of us was interrogated separately in the bedroom, and we heard the beating while we sat silently, looking at each other with the two armed guards watching us. Bahman's left hand was broken when he came back from his interrogation.'

Goli was too upset to continue, so Behi

said, 'I don't know what they did to Shabnam, because we didn't hear the sound of beating, but heard her shouting and screaming. The guards in the room didn't let us talk or help each other after the torture. So, we could only watch her when she came into the room and leaned against the wall, keeping her eyes closed. After two days they took us to the sea, the Caspian Sea, and to the same shore where we used to swim. They kept Goli and me in the car and told us to watch. They said they needed us to catch our husbands. I don't know how people heard about it, but a crowd came running to the scene. There were so many guards with Kalashnikovs, pushing people back when they came close. Then, in front of some people who were trying to get to us and save us, they took Maryam, Shabnam, Bahman, Reza, and Saied out of the car and told them to swim. They didn't move, they held each other's hands. They were not frightened, or perhaps I was so frightened that I couldn't see it in their faces.'

Behi broke down at that point and Goli took up the story again: 'Saied had a smile on his lips. Bahman shouted, "Long live freedom," and they all took up the cry, which was when the guards shot them - before they'd finished. Their words, "Long live—" were in the air when I saw their bodies fall on the sand, and seconds later a wave washed them away.'

Azadam, they were both silent for some time

and I was wondering about their friends on the shore. Were they still alive and aware of the water?

After a while, Behi said, 'When the bullets hit them, and they fell, I screamed. Goli hugged me and we sobbed in each other's arms. The guard in charge pointed to our friends' bodies and shouted to the crowd, "Families of these anti-revolutionaries can come and take their children's bodies when they've paid for the bullets. However, they cannot be buried in the cemetery because they are infidels."'

My love, Goli said, 'I imagine our village has a new cemetery now and perhaps, in future, everyone else would prefer to be buried there.'

Behi said, 'I'm so glad that our husbands are with the Peshmerga. Now they're safe.'

***

Azizam, this afternoon Goli and Behi were taken from our cell and after that Mahvash was very thoughtful. Before I could say anything, she whispered, 'Did you see the faces of those two girls when they were taken to be executed? They didn't show much emotion, did they, when they were kissing us and walking towards the door? Is this the art of dying? Did we know how to live, that now know how to die?'

Azadam, Mahvash was talking about Goli

and Behi, but I looked at her slender pale face and said

***

My love, they gave us a newspaper today and it really cheered me up. It's more than seven months since I came in here now, and in all that time I hadn't seen a single newspaper. However, I was surprised that my cellmates were not happy about it until I was told that they had given us today's paper in order to let us see Goli and Behi's names on the list of those who had been killed. Yes, darling, they have executed those two beautiful young girls. My eyes are

***

They've taken Pari away. She was a good, wise friend who was easy to talk to. Mahvash and I are both very sad to lose her. Yet they haven't given us the newspaper since they took her. I wonder why not? Perhaps there's a chance they haven't executed *her*, at least.

***

I haven't been writing to you for the last few days. Today I spent several hours in a state of anxiety, because they called Mahvash for interrogation and, as she was going, and she saw how the colour had drained from my face, she said, 'Don't worry, they're not going to execute me right now.' Then she smiled and kissed me and said, 'I'm staying alive until your child comes into this world, then I'll give her my place. They're going to have to wait for her to arrive before they can take me away. I want to see her before leaving for good.'

She didn't wait to hear my objection, but just left. I sat waiting for her to return, worrying the whole time that she wouldn't come back. Although they hadn't removed her belongings, which they always do when someone is taken to be executed, I was still anxious. They could have put her in solitary confinement and I would have lost her.

While I was sitting near the door, Ziba was perched beside it as well, waiting for her mother to come back. Usually she goes with Azar to interrogation, but today the guards wouldn't allow it, and this probably meant Azar was going to be tortured.

I continued to keep an eye on Ziba, who was crouching by the door as if willing it to open. After an hour she'd grown drowsy, and I didn't know if she was just short of sleep or whether the tension of the situation was making her sleepy. I asked if she wanted to lie down in my lap, but she shook her head solemnly.

After three hours, Azar returned and Ziba

was whispering to her, demanding to see her feet. Her mother uncovered her feet and Ziba insisted she take her socks off, so that she could make sure her Mum really hadn't been tortured. Azar removed her socks and tried to smile, but I could see that she was making an effort to hide her pain and I wondered which part of her body they had beaten. Ziba clasped her mother's hand and asked what they had done to her. 'Nothing, they just asked me some questions,' Azar replied. Ziba went to hug her. But as soon as her hands touched her mother's back, I saw a stab of sharp pain cross Azar's face. She then asked Ziba to sit and hug her because she was tired. Later on, when

***

Azizam, I try to imagine what you had for lunch, and what you're going to have for dinner. We had abgoosht for lunch but there was no meat in it. Perhaps they made it with the fat because it was merely a yellowish water with a few peas and a small piece of potato for each person. For dinner we had eggs, and some prisoners left me their share. However, their bodies need food as much as I do and so I begged them to eat it themselves, but they didn't listen.

***

Faraz thought about this kind of love, in which people share what they have with those who need it. It's a love that debunks the individualism constantly promoted by those in power via the media. They have to suppress this communal love, which might make people stand up for each other's rights and put an end to the injustice in this world.

***

My love, I can hear the sound of shooting in my head. Don't ask me who they're shooting at. They're shooting straight at my heart. Tears are blinding me.

Azadam, tears are blinding me, I can't see the page well enough to write.

Eshg-e-man, they killed Mahvash. Again, tears are preventing me from seeing the page.

My dearest, they have executed Mahvash, my friend, no, my *mother* here in prison. She was more than a mother or a dear friend to me. When the guards called her, she was paler than usual. As if they knew she would not come back again, everyone stood up to kiss her. No one talks at these times, they only exchange kisses and watch as the prisoner is taken away for good. Then everyone continues whatever they were doing before, as if nothing out of the ordinary has happened and we have not just lost a friend to execution.

I hugged her, lost for words. I tried so hard not to cry but I couldn't hold back my tears and so it was she who tried to give me hope before leaving forever. She told me to think of you and our child and to stay cheerful. She kissed me and wished that I would 'stay alive' as she went. 'Stay alive' are the last words uttered by those who go to be executed to us who are still living. They are the same words, spoken in different accents and with varying degrees of fear, hesitation, anxiety, confusion, or even happiness that I have heard so many times here. I didn't want to let her go and held on to her hands tightly. She kissed me once more and said she had to leave, pointing to the guards waiting for her, and told me to be brave and let her go and not to make them angry so that I would end up in solitary confinement again. I whispered, 'You said you'd stay with me until my baby's born.' She smiled and said, 'I'm going to give her my place in this world. Look at it that way. Try to be happy.' She kissed me for the last time and I finally let go of her hands. But I could no longer hold myself together as I knew now that I would never see her again. I sobbed out loud. Then I had to stop crying, for the sake of the children here more than for the adults, although my heart was weeping inside.

My love, they killed her three days ago and yesterday they gave us the newspaper with her name in it. Darling, as I write these words tears are streaming down my face and I cannot keep them in. I even still hear the shots aimed at her heart, as if they are still killing her again and again. I don't know if it is to do with our unborn child, or the fact that I've lost a most valuable friend here that I needed so badly, but I feel desolate. I wish I could fly away and be by your side. I need you so much right now.

The children are asking for Mahvash and wanting to know where she's gone.

My love, did you see her name, in the way that we used to check the newspapers to see the names of those who had been executed? I hope her family can stand this terrible ordeal.

***

Faraz felt suffocated. It was the same feeling that had taken over his body when they killed Forood. Forood was his first loss, and the pain remained inside him and reawakened now and then. How did Forood spend the time in prison before his execution? How did he feel or think? Who did he talk to before facing the firing squad?

He couldn't read any more. He needed to get away from his feelings. Wishing to grab a couple of hours' sleep before going to work, he went to bed and found Nasim awake.

'Can't you sleep?' she asked.

'No. What about you?' Faraz enquired, trying not to show his distress.

She blurted out, 'I'm pregnant!'

Faraz stared at her as if he couldn't register what she was telling him. After all that care they had taken, it had happened. He hugged her, lost for words.

'What are we to do?' she asked, trying to peer into his face, which was buried in her chest.

After a few moments he looked up at her and said, 'We should celebrate our first baby!'

With tears in her eyes, she cried, 'You seem to have forgotten that we're not married. They'll kill us both after the birth. What will happen to our child?'

Faraz stroked her hair. 'For some time now, I've been looking for a birth certificate for you, so we can marry and live like other couples. I'll get one soon. Don't worry. Try to enjoy our pregnancy.'

Nasim smiled, repeating his words, 'our' pregnancy, rather than 'your' pregnancy and gazing at him in surprise.

'But supposing you do get a birth certificate and we marry, they'll realise our baby is due before we've been married for nine months,' she reminded him, still shocked.

'We'll work that out. Don't worry. You know in this country you can do anything if you have money. I'm sure we can find a register office that'll agree to put last year's date on our marriage certificate and our birth certificates. How about that? And my parents will help us if the bribe is large.' Faraz smiled at what he had said. He felt he was no longer the same person.

'You've changed,' Nasim told him. 'Or perhaps I still don't know you. I thought you'd be very upset.'

'Life's too short and we have to enjoy it. Why should we be upset for having a child when we're not married? It's no one's business how we decide to live and organise our relationship and our life. So, if they don't recognise our basic rights, we have no choice other than to get around these laws with bribery, or however we can.'

'You're right, but I'm still worried.'

'How long have you known?'

'I did a test a few days ago. I didn't know how to tell you, because you seemed depressed.'

Faraz caressed her. 'I'm sorry. You should have told me. Now try not to worry about it. Have you talked to my mother?'

'No. She sensed I was anxious and asked me if everything was okay and I said yes. I didn't want to talk to her before talking to you. I was trying to work out how to end the pregnancy. I thought you'd agree to get rid of it, because of our situation,' Nasim said, still shaky.

'No way should we get rid of it! Why would we throw away our child? What did she do, to be treated like that?'

Nasim was still looking at him in disbelief, when he said to her, 'We have to think of a name.'

***

I had another visit. Darling, it must be due to the sudden loss of Mahvash that I feel so emotional. My last month of pregnancy is adding to it. Every time the child inside me moves, I think of you. Since my parents' visit, my mind has wandered more to the world outside and to you. My parents said you send your love and that you're fine. I'm glad to know that you are, although I'm not sure what 'fine' means any more. Perhaps our vocabulary and the meaning of words has changed. If we see each other again, we may have to consult a new dictionary to understand the words we use!

Once the phone was disconnected, meaning that our visit was over, my mother gestured to me to open my chador, so she could see my pregnant belly – maybe they've already told you this. I did so, and she kissed me through the glass in front of her. I tried to put my lips exactly opposite her lips on the glass, knowing that we looked slightly ridiculous! I watched them force themselves to walk away from the visiting booth and I wished that the glass was not between us so that I could touch them and kiss them goodbye. I longed for their hugs and their company but, for all our sakes, I tried hard to conceal my need to see them.

I'm wearing one of Mahvash's scarves as I write to you. It's one that I once told her I admired for its beautiful pale orange colour, which reminds me of the autumn sun. Two days before they took her away, she gave it to one of the prisoners and asked her to give it to me when she was gone. I think she must've known how soon she would be executed but she couldn't talk to me about it. When we lose friends like this, I realise that we are not simply waiting for our own deaths.

Azadam, I wonder what you're doing at this moment. Are you asleep, or trying to sleep? Do you have difficulty sleeping since my arrest, or do you sleep like a child, as you always used to? I hope your sleep has not been affected and that you get a good night's rest. I can't sleep that well because of my pregnancy, the lack of space, air, and food, as well as the lack of you and the lack of freedom that is essential to our wellbeing.

***

As if Xavar had been addressing Faraz, he wanted to tell her that he had slept very badly since starting to read her letters. He was constantly preoccupied with finding the rest of them in the limited time still left to him, as well as with dwelling on their contents.

***

Azizam, I wonder if life goes on outside as before. Do people still dine in restaurants? Is red still the colour of freedom fighters? Do people still go to mountains on Fridays? Are *love* and *freedom* still forbidden words?

Sometimes I think of all the changes I've been through during the various stages of my life and I can see that I was a different person before 1978. The people's uprising against the Shah changed me and changed us all. That year we all grew up so fast. For a couple of years, I was two different people, grappling with competing ideas and tendencies. Then I became one person again - but a different one! I can see that you, too, have changed. When I was arrested, we were not the same people who had started living together in 1978. Up until then, I'd been more interested in dancing, singing and just having a good time. Like most other young people, I wasn't really interested in politics or the issue of censorship, though as a worker I was unhappy with the conditions. Getting involved with workers' rights, in a way, educated me. By 1980, I could no longer accept certain things, such as seeing homeless people or knowing that freedom of expression was under threat. It was getting more difficult to close our eyes to the injustices that the new regime seemed to be forcing on us: children being beaten by their parents, or the inequality between men and women.

***

My love, I haven't been able to write to you for the last few days. Up to now, I always believed that one day I might be released, because they don't have any evidence against me. A few days ago, I had a court hearing which has changed all that. The judge first asked me to remove the blindfold so that he could see me. He was a mullah.

'You haven't given us any information.'

'I don't have any.'

'You expect us to believe that you don't know any spies? Do you think we're stupid? We know that all your friends are infidels like yourself, but we can't arrest them without information from you, and you choose to collaborate with them rather than with us, who represent the will of God. You will pay the price for your satanic behaviour.'

A few minutes passed while he read my file.

'What kind of husband do you have, who won't even hand himself over to let you go free? Isn't it interesting that he is sacrificing you to stay alive? Where is your husband? Why won't you reveal his whereabouts? Is he worth dying for? Would he withhold information about you if he was in your position? I'm sure he would give us your address as soon as we requested it.'

Azadam, I couldn't tell him that I have principles and wouldn't sacrifice even my enemy, because he just wouldn't understand. They're too selfish to realise that there are people who would live in poverty rather than harm anyone, while he himself is living comfortably off the money he's being paid to sentence people to death.

He looked through the file in front of him once more and added, 'You'll be stoned to death for adultery.'

I was stunned. 'I've never committed adultery.'

'You're lying again. And besides that, you fought against the government and the will of God.'

'How?'

'By not giving us your husband's address and his place of work, you fought against our holy government.'

My first shocked impulse was to tell him to go to hell, but I took a deep breath and said, 'I was married. I don't understand what you mean by adultery.'

'Your file says that the certificate is fake.'

A ludicrous image came into my head of a file *speaking*. I said, 'It's not true, there must be a mistake.'

'Enough of your lies. You'll be beaten for those before you die. You were married to Morad and left him for this spy called Farid,' decreed the mullah, glancing up to see how I was taking it.

My love, I didn't know what to say. Who had told them about us? Was it Mahro? No, surely, she could have given them that information before I was even arrested. Yet how else would they have found out about Morad? My mind was in a jumble when I heard him speak again.

'However, it's not too late if you want to repent. Confess all your sins and tell us where your friends are living, and we may be able to ask God for His forgiveness. Otherwise, you'll be stoned to death, which is what your interrogators recommend. Now is your chance to change their minds.'

'I didn't know that you stoned political prisoners to death.'

'We don't; you aren't a political prisoner. We don't have any political prisoners. You're a whore and your cellmates are spies. Incidentally, by stoning you to death we will absolve you of your sins. Otherwise, we must answer to God why we granted you an easy death in front of the firing squad, sending you to Him still filthy.'

He looked at the guard and motioned him to take me away.

I was left speechless by his reasoning and pictured him throwing the first stone at my head. My love, what is the origin of this evil? Why do they enjoy inflicting pain and find pleasure in it?

The mullah wants to wash away my sins, but these so-called sins have made me who I am and are part of my identity as a woman who wants the same rights that civilised people enjoy throughout this world. As he was talking, I felt that he had come from another planet, or that I had been dragged back into the past. I sensed a great chasm between us; our perspectives on things could not be more different.

As you see, my love, I have no choice; they might kill me and there is nothing that I can do to stop them. I say only that they *might*, because other prisoners have told me one cannot be sure if and when it will happen. Any decision that the court makes must be sent to Khomeini's office for approval. So now I must wait and see what he decrees: whether I'm to die or not and, if so, whether by firing squad, hanging or stoning.

Eshg-e-man, before this court hearing I didn't think of my own death, not truly believing it possible, but now it's constantly in my thoughts, as if I'm waiting for them to take me away to be killed at any minute. Thank goodness I'm pregnant, as they'll at least have to wait until she's born, although I've also heard that they do kill pregnant women. Perhaps, in my case, I'm too close to giving birth for them to execute me. So, in a way, it's not just me giving life to our child; she's keeping *me* alive, too. I'm not sure, but I think she's due in a couple of weeks now. I wish I could postpone it for as long as possible. Her birth will signal the end of my life.

I wonder what my daughter will think of me. Will she blame me for not being there as she grows up, or will she blame only the regime for taking me away from her? I hope she understands that I needed to be with her as much as she needed me.

I'm tired, love, very tired; tired of everything, and now wish for an easy death. I need you so much right now to remind me of what happiness is. Azadam, I've forgotten the meaning of it.

Azizam, how would we feel if we were suddenly face to face? I would want to tell you how lost I have felt since losing you. Sometimes

I can't remember the outline of your face, the very face I kissed and touched every day. Not being able to picture your face frightens me. I try and recall the way you looked in that childhood photo and then try to imagine you last year, two years ago, or when we first met. But I can't get past the image of you as a child. It seems that by locking me up, they've not only taken you away from me, but they've also erased the treasured images I had of you.

I'm not fully aware of how my days pass here; what I do or think. I feel that our lives have been frozen. My life stopped the day they arrested me and held me captive. Now I live in an endless nightmare that never stops, except for the times that I'm still able to dream about you, even though my memories of you are fading. If they kill me, you'll have to fight for the two of us in future. You will, won't you? I need to know that our struggles won't stop with my death. I feel as if my body has become a fist and I have a desire to hit the dome of the world.

I wonder if stoning is done by men, like other methods of execution: shooting or hanging. It seems these are men's jobs and I wonder how they can do them. Why didn't their mothers teach them to act like human beings with true morals? Aren't we, as women, the first teachers? How then do they grow up to be so violent?

Until a few months ago, time in prison passed slowly. Some days it even felt as if time had stopped. But now I don't want the time to pass. I can live with this uncertainty now, or perhaps I should say I prefer it to dying. I feel that the day when they come to take me to my death isn't far off, because I'm due to give birth soon. I wish I could keep her inside my body forever. I want to be with her and if it's not possible to be with her as two separate bodies, then let her stay inside me! If only time would stand still, and we could live together always. I know that she wants to come out, and I'm not blaming her, but is she ready for her birth and the death it will bring me?

You know, Azadam, at least I'm happy that they will let her live and won't kill her with me. Some other women haven't been as lucky; they were stoned to death with their babies alive inside them. I don't know how long their babies would have survived after their mothers were killed. Perhaps the mothers were buried with their babies still living. So, like me, our child is lucky. Perhaps I should look at it differently. When our child is free from the confines of my body, I, too, will be free from prison because death will put an end to my captivity. She'll begin her life on earth, and I'll feed the soil so that more poppies can grow. I wonder if the places where stoning to death takes place are full of poppies like the sites of battles. It's said that poppies grow in great numbers on battlefields, where the soil has been nourished with blood.

My darling, shall we call our daughter Baran? I wish her to grow up to feel loved and I hope she learns to love me when she is told about me and my death. You should tell her that she was made of love, and this is why I was stoned to death as soon as she was born.

My love, I'd better hide this notebook before I'm due to give birth to our child. Now again, I think increasingly about freedom and its value. During all these months in prison I've worn my right to freedom like a badge of honour. This is the freedom I was born with. It's the freedom that connected me to you and made me flee a plainer, unthinking life. The prison authorities have tried to skin me of my freedom. They've used physical and psychological torture to make me relinquish it, but they can't take it away from me and so they'll have to kill me for it. They'll kill me because I'm evidence that they have failed. They know by killing me they hurt you and my family deeply, so it's a revenge on all of you, too. Stay Azad. Xavar.

***

Faraz finished Xavar's notebook but sat there in an agony of not knowing what had happened to her, hoping against hope that the sentence had not been carried out, and more determined than ever to find the rest of her letters. He was glad that today was a national holiday on account of someone dying fourteen hundred years ago.

As he lay beside her, he realised Nasim was awake. She kissed him. Faraz returned her kisses and, cuddling her, tried to sleep.

'Make love to me,' she whispered.

He knew he could not. His mind was overflowing with Xavar and her baby. He didn't know what to say to Nasim.

She looked at him, her eyes full of sadness. 'Are you in love with someone else?'

'I'm only in love with you. Now let me sleep,' he said, still holding her.

'Don't you think I know that you're sleeping only a couple of hours every night before you go downstairs? What is it, then, that you can't sleep, and you can't make love to me, if it's not love for another woman?'

He silenced her with a kiss and tried to sleep in her arms, but she freed herself and sat up in bed, gazing at him. Watching her, he couldn't remember the last time he had examined her face as closely as this.

'You look upset,' he told her.

'So, you realise. At last!'

He looked at her in surprise this time. 'I'm sorry if I didn't realise it before. But what's wrong?'

'I'm angry with myself for listening to you. I should have got rid of my baby. What can I do now? It's too late for a termination and look at our relationship!'

'How can you say such a thing about our baby? And what's wrong with our relationship?'

'You don't love me any more,' Nasim said, with a catch in her throat.

'What are you talking about? Of course I love you!' Faraz held her, both of them in tears now. They lay like this in each other's arms for some time and Faraz felt better for having wept.

'I'm sorry if I've done something wrong that's upset you,' he said, caressing her head.

'We barely see each other. When was the last time we made love? I want to know if you still love me. I don't want to stay with you if you're not in love with me any more.'

'Please, don't say such things. I really love you and I'm sorry if I haven't been treating you well these last few months.'

'What's the problem then, that you don't seem to see me any more? You're somewhere else when you're with me. I feel your body beside me, but your mind is with another woman.'

Faraz couldn't help smiling at this. Yes, the last few weeks he had been immersed in thoughts of Xavar. He didn't know what to say. He didn't want to lose Nasim. He was looking at her hands as they lay in his, not realising she was waiting for his response.

'I have to know, Faraz!' She pulled her hands away and cupped his face. Looking into his eyes, she said, 'What's going on?'

'I don't know. I feel depressed. That's why I don't make love to you.'

'Is it your work in the interrogation centre that makes you depressed?'

'I guess so.'

'Leave it then! You don't have to see it through.'

'I can't. I need to finish what I'm doing.'

'Why?' Nasim demanded.

Faraz was silent again.

'What is it about this work that's so important to you, that you don't care about losing your relationship with your brother? You know what your parents feel about it and I'm not exactly proud of what you're doing there, either. Yet you're choosing this job over *us*. It seems your commitment to your uncle means more than anything else to you. I'm sorry, I don't think I can bear to stay with you any longer. You ignore me. It's as if I don't exist. So, I'd better go away and leave you in peace.'

'You're wrong. My uncle is nothing to me. I don't even like him, I never did,' Faraz protested angrily.

'Why don't you quit the wretched job, then?' Nasim was shouting now.

They heard Ana out in the corridor. 'Are you two all right?' she called.

Faraz stood up, opened the door and apologised to his mother, who was hovering a couple of metres away.

'Come and have breakfast downstairs,' said Ana.

Faraz took Nasim's hand and led her out of the room. They ate their breakfast, but Faraz sipped his tea slowly and didn't join in the conversation.

***

That evening, when Nasim had been unusually silent, Faraz took her hands in his, and said, 'Please bear with me a little longer. I accept I haven't been a good partner to you since I've been working at the interrogation centre, but I need some more time. I can't walk out of the job right now.'

'You don't need to quit the job. I'll quit our relationship. I can't bear it any more,' Nasim said, without looking at him.

And at last Faraz realised he could no longer keep silent. No matter how powerful the need for secrecy, he would lose her if he didn't tell her the truth. At the same time, he wondered how little he could get away with revealing. 'Listen,' he began uncertainly, 'I've found... things in there that are precious, and I know there are more. I don't want to lose them.'

Nasim looked at him, her eyes full of horror. 'What precious things? You always said you hated money and that it was humanity's worst invention. Are these precious things valuable, like the gold you once said Nazi guards ripped from prisoners before burning them?' Now she was crying as she spoke. 'I thought I knew you. I thought you were a good man. Is it gold you're finding there?'

Faraz tried to wipe away her tears. 'Not that kind of gold,' he said sadly.

Still weeping, Nasim asked, 'What is it, then?'

'They're letters. Love letters, last letters of prisoners who aren't alive any more.' His voice broke. 'I'm trying to save them, Nasim.'

She looked at him in disbelief. Lost for words, she stared into his eyes, but at last she let him hold her. Blinking at him through her tears she said softly, 'Then why on earth didn't you tell me?'

'Remember your reaction to the drawings I found? I couldn't put your life in danger.'

‘What did you do with them?’

‘They’re safe. They’re published on the internet, so the regime cannot destroy them again.’

Nasim listened, a slight frown on her face, taking this in. ‘You should have told me. You could have trusted me. I want to read them.’

‘Fine. Just make sure you clean your computer. Delete all trace of every website you visit.’ Faraz went over to her computer and opened a page.

In a daze, Nasim sat down and started to read Xavar’s letters.

But Faraz didn’t give her Xavar’s latest letter. He knew it would upset her too much.

Chapter Fifteen

VOICES OF THE RESISTANCE

Two weeks passed in which Faraz discovered no more of Xavar's letters. Although he was constantly trying to work out where on the wing she might have concealed them, he was fast losing hope of finding anything.

One evening he was on his way home, his mind preoccupied as usual, when he heard shouts and, looking up, realised something was going on in the street. A female moral police officer, who had ordered a woman with too short a coat to go with her to the police van, was having the tables turned on her and getting a beating from the suspect instead. A knot of people had gathered and were applauding the suspect when male moral police jumped out of the van and tried to arrest her. The young woman resisted and people were trying to rescue her as the police started to drag her towards the van. A man stepped between her and the moral police, attempting to save her by appealing to them to let her go. The moral police officers, now surrounded by people, ordered the man to get back and not interfere. Then suddenly there was mayhem, the crowd pulling the young woman from one side and police pulling her from the other. By now, her scarf had fallen to her shoulders and she was trying to escape, while people shouted slogans against the regime.

Faraz watched as the moral police made a quick getaway before the angry crowd could beat them up, and the woman stumbled happily off into the dusk.

***

Faraz was sitting in the Art Café, waiting for Bahram, day-dreaming as he had often found himself doing since working at the interrogation centre, when Bahram threw himself into the seat opposite. His eyes were shining.

'You know, there are so many extraordinary responses online to Xavar's letters. People are thanking us for uploading them, and there are accounts from some of the other prisoners who were with her.'

'Really?'

'Yes. I specially wanted you to read these. I printed them out for you.' Bahram pushed some sheets of paper across the table.

'Hi, I'm twenty-two years old and it's now been a couple of years since I started tracking the writings of ex-prisoners. Before that, I was too emotional about prison and ex-prisoners to be able to read or hear anything about it. I was full of anger and hatred. Why? Well, my father was arrested, tortured and executed when my mother was pregnant with me. So, as you can imagine, I don't have any memories of my father. I look at photos of him and I don't recognise the man I see staring back at me. I look at his happy face in those pictures and imagine him feeling sad or being tortured. How would he have looked when he was thinking about freedom or about my mother?

Until a few years ago, the sight of fathers and daughters would leave a bitter taste in my mouth and I'd feel resentful and jealous of them. I love my mother, but she can't make up for my father's absence. The love between a daughter and father is not something you can replicate in other relationships. It's a unique bond. It's like the hunger that Xavar writes about and a satisfied stomach can't feel or understand it. Anyway, my father was another kind of Xavar, and he is buried in Khavaran.

Thank you so much for uploading her letters.'

'How many of these children are there whose parents were executed?' Faraz asked in amazement.

'Who knows? Read this one.' Bahram handed him another print-out.

'Thanks again for uploading Xavar's letters and sharing them with the world. As I wrote before in an earlier post, I spent time with Xavar briefly in that Joint Committee prison she speaks about. I loved her confidence and she seemed to enjoy being pregnant. Her calmness and kindness enhanced her beauty.

I'm looking forward to reading more of Xavar's letters. Lots of love, Pari.'

'Is this the same Pari who was with Xavar? The one Xavar wrote about?' cried Faraz excitedly.

'Yes. I wrote and asked her, and she replied saying that she's the one who was arrested because her brother and sister were revolutionaries. She spent a year in prison,' said Bahram.

Faraz looked anxiously at his friend. 'You are careful to remain anonymous on the internet, aren't you?'

'Don't worry.'

'Couldn't you ask Pari about Xavar and find out through her if she's still alive?' Faraz suggested.

'That was my first question, and she didn't know the answer. She wrote back saying that she'd searched for Xavar and couldn't find any trace of her. So she might still be alive. That's what we must hope for.'

They sat there, listening to the classical music and watching the fish in the tank, each lost in his own thoughts. Faraz was thinking that if all these people were reading Xavar's letters, perhaps one of the readers might be an 18-year-old girl called Baran. He so hoped she was. Or, if she hadn't already, that one day she would discover her mother's prison notebooks and might write and tell the world what had happened to Xavar.

Chapter Sixteen
THE COMING OF RAIN

As September arrived, Faraz was in the final days of his work on the conversion of the interrogation centre. His school term would start again in two weeks' time and he was desperate to find the rest of Xavar's letters before he had to leave. He simply couldn't accept that there were no more notebooks to be found, but every day he went to work and searched in vain. His uncle told him not to worry about finishing the job, and that he would ask someone else to do it.

Faraz was working in the final cell on the wing when, on an impulse, he left it and went back into cell 7, which he had completed weeks before. He stood in the middle of the cell in which he knew Xavar had spent some time, and imagined her sitting there, leaning against the wall with her eyes closed.

'Where did you hide your notebooks, Xavar?' he asked quietly, as if she could hear him. The cell had only one window, which was covered with a grille and so close to the ceiling that it was difficult to reach up to it. He had examined it weeks ago and so instead, this time, he got down on his knees and felt along the carpet inch by inch. There was no uneven surface that he could sense with his hands, nor was any part of the carpet loose where it was fixed to the floor. Again, he sat in the middle of the small cell and thought about where she could possibly have hidden a tiny, wrapped notebook without it being noticed; concealed it under the nose of the guards. He moved closer to the door and examined the carpet directly below the peephole, which would have been out of sight of the guards doing their rounds. Using his tools, he levered the carpet back and, on doing so, uncovered a small hollow in the floor, padded with a pair of socks to make the floor look even. His heart began to race as he retrieved what was clearly Xavar's notebook from underneath the socks before carefully replacing the carpet.

Removing the outer wrapping, he realised the notebook did not have a number on it, but he was sure it was Xavar's. He was puzzled as to why she hadn't numbered it and wondered whether this meant she had hidden many others that he hadn't accounted for. In contrast to the previous times he had found her letters, he didn't feel a need to rush home and read what she had written. It was as if he knew he had found her final words and he would not discover any more. A deep sadness washed over him. Would this notebook reveal her fate? He didn't want to know that she was going to be killed. He wanted to cling to the hope that Xavar was alive, just as he was, happy and safe.

But as he left the cell, Faraz came face to face with his uncle standing behind the door. How and when had he come on to the wing? Did Rohulah know what Faraz was up to? He pulled himself together and greeted his uncle nonchalantly, but the hair at the back of his neck stood on end when he heard what Rohulah had to say.

'Can I see what you've found this time?'

'I don't know what you're talking about.'

'Really? Don't you know that I've been in this world for the last twenty years? Did you think I hadn't noticed that you make sure you hear me whenever I come on to the wing? Every time I've come in, and your little piece of wood has told you that Uncle is coming, it has reminded me of something else: it's reminded me of prisoners who have devised thousands of different tricks to tell when the guards were on their way.'

Rohulah stopped talking and started to walk to and fro in a small arc of the long corridor before continuing his lecture - as if he, not Faraz, was the teacher.

'Don't you realise there are different ways of coming on to the wing? Have you forgotten that the first time you came here, I gave you a little tour of the balcony, which has a door to this wing?'

Rohulah was talking, but Faraz's mind was on the notebook in his pocket. He felt ready to die for it. He couldn't afford to give it up. There was no way he would abandon Xavar's writing into the hands of this monster. People all over the world were waiting for the rest of the letters she had written to her lover, and they were hanging on for her final words.

But he returned to his senses as his uncle came and stood in front of him, right up close. Rohulah had fallen silent. Though Faraz was above average height, he realised for the first time that his uncle was taller than him. They were staring into each other's eyes and Faraz sensed he had never felt as vulnerable as he did at this moment, with the fear of losing what he had so recently found. He could feel the presence of the notebook in his pocket, burning into his body.

'Do you think I didn't know what you were up to when you accepted this job, which your father wanted to kill me for offering? I knew you were never pro-government. And those who are not with us, are against us.'

Faraz felt a strange sensation rising inside him. As it reached his head he recognised it as hatred, and that he had never experienced it as strongly as he did now. He dropped his eyes, so his uncle wouldn't see. He must not make his situation worse than it was. Faraz was prepared to do anything to hang on to that notebook, but he was aware that he could in fact do nothing if Rohulah wished to take it from him. He knew his uncle carried a gun and could arrest him and get him searched by the other guards, who in reality were all around them, merely doing a different job from the one they usually did.

'Whatever you've found during the last few months, we have found more of them and they're nothing. They're no use to anyone. You can take this one home as well and show it to your father. Perhaps he forgives you and doesn't treat you the same way he treated me.'

Faraz raised his eyes and looked at Rohulah who was staring back at him with an expression he had not seen before. Was it victory? No, he had seen Rohulah's triumphant face when he came to offer this job and Faraz had accepted it. He felt confused and didn't know what to say or do. His uncle moved away from him, which made him more comfortable, but he still felt lost and humiliated. He was angry with himself for reacting like a schoolboy. Seconds passed, and he was still standing there, while his uncle resumed his pacing, a short distance away.

'Have you seen your grandmother? Did you give her my greetings?' Rohulah asked after a while, and Faraz felt better. So, his uncle was still homesick for the mother who had rejected her renegade son.

'I haven't seen her since I've been working here.'

Now Rohulah was nodding his head, watching him. For the first time in his life, Faraz felt as if he had been hauled up before the headmaster who was not happy with his results. If it wasn't for Xavar's notebook in his pocket, he would shout at his uncle to go to hell, but he stood there, like a good boy. After a long silence, Rohulah started to speak again.

'I might look to you like someone who doesn't care about his family, but that's not true. I missed your grandmother and I miss your father, too. That's why, despite his antagonism towards me, I sometimes go and see him. I wish my children had a relationship with you and Omid. I know your father blames me for the bad relations with him and your grandmother. But, as the old cliché says, it takes two to tango.'

Rohulah was silent again and Faraz thought, *so he's blaming both sides, is he?* What a fool his uncle was to think any two people who failed to dance together should share the blame. Couldn't he see that he alone had slaughtered Forood, and how his action had affected the whole family?

'They think it was for money that I joined the Islamic Guards,' Rohulah went on. 'But that's not true. Money came later. When I realised everyone was looting according to their power, I, too, had my share. Those at the top of the ladder took more than those lower down.

In fact, the first time I got my hands on some money that I hadn't worked for, I didn't take it from anyone. It was thrown at my feet, like a piece of meat to reward a dog after he has done his job well.'

He fell silent, but Faraz was gazing at him in disbelief. Was this real? Did he hear Rohulah say what he just said? *So, does he really know, then, that he's no more than a dog to his leader?*

'No,' resumed his uncle. 'At first it didn't occur to me I'd become rich by joining the Islamic Guards. I believed that Khomeini would bring a better life. Not just for a few but for everyone, including me. I believed that in a few years we would have no prostitution, and no one would be homeless or go to sleep hungry. You think I'm blind and don't see all those street children and beggars, or the women in the hands of pimps? I see the same things Nima or you see. The fact is that you can't do anything about them, and nor can I.'

Faraz felt his blood starting to boil. Unlike his uncle, neither he nor his father lived on money gained by torturing people in order to maintain the status quo. But he managed to stay cool.

'The revolution was a time when everyone took sides,' Rohulah continued, 'and some of us – perhaps like myself, your father and my mother – went to the extremes of our respective side. You might not believe it, but I saw parents who turned their children in for talking against Khomeini; sisters and brothers who reported on each other for being against the government. Like many others, I believed this was the path to heaven on earth and we all needed to sacrifice our lives.'

Faraz wanted to say, *but you sacrificed your son, not yourself*, but he kept quiet, trying to work out why Rohulah was telling him all this.

'I never knew that by supporting Khomeini, I'd lose my family.' Rohulah paused and, as if he had read Faraz's mind, said, 'I don't know what I'd have done if I'd known my family would reject me. But what I'm saying is, why couldn't we stay together as a family and agree to disagree with each other? Why is there no room for more than one opinion?'

Despite his efforts to stay calm, Faraz couldn't keep quiet any longer and said, 'Perhaps because it's more than just a matter of different opinions. It's the way people live their lives that forms their identity and leads them on to opposite paths. It would be like expecting people travelling on a completely different trajectory from each other to stand shoulder to shoulder.'

Rohulah cut him off. 'You might wonder why I stayed in my job, when I saw the corruption and poverty. But what would change if I left my positions? Nothing. Someone else would take them. You are working on this wing, but someone else would do it if you didn't.'

Faraz couldn't listen any more. The equating of his one small job with all the things Rohulah had done made him angry. He wanted an end to this conversation, but he didn't know how to cut his uncle off.

After a pause, Rohulah started lecturing him again. 'You were a child during the war with Iraq. A million people died of their own free will in defence of this country and a million more came back disabled. Do you think they were mad, or tired of being healthy and wanted to sacrifice themselves for nothing? No, they had a broader aim: to defend their country. I know your father was against going to war, but what if the Iraqis had invaded and occupied Iran? What would we have told our children then?'

Faraz thought, those people who went to war were set up to do so, as you set me up to work in your human slaughterhouse. He knew it was pointless to argue with his uncle and that Rohulah had a fixed idea about the world, but he couldn't hold back any longer and asked, 'Do you really think the regime would survive without the Islamic Guards? Don't you see that if the regime put down its arms for just a single day, it would be smashed to pieces?'

He watched his uncle's face take on a stony expression that he had never seen before. Rohulah was silent for a while and Faraz thought that, to his uncle, he was just another prisoner who hadn't yet been arrested.

'All governments have enemies within and without. You're a history teacher. You must know that the Islamic government would not survive without the Islamic Guards, of course. Israel, western nations and Russia are merely waiting for our government to fall to its knees to attack our country and cut it to pieces.'

As Rohulah was speaking, Faraz's only thought was how he could shut him up and leave this place for good. Then he realised his uncle had gone quiet, watching him.

'You look tired, Faraz. Go home and have a rest.'

'Sure. Goodbye,' Faraz said quickly, and had turned to leave when he heard his uncle say, 'If you speak to my mother, ask her if she would like me to go and see her.'

Faraz turned back and looked at him. 'I'll ask her.'

Rohulah nodded and continued his way down the long corridor.

As he hastily packed his belongings, nervous his uncle might change his mind and return, Faraz tried to work out which faction of the regime Rohulah was with: Khamenie's faction, or the so-called reformists? He found it hard to guess. Was it because his uncle was losing friends for some reason that he was now trying to regain his family? As Faraz walked away from the interrogation centre for the last time, he decided he didn't care. The only thing that mattered was the notebook in his pocket. He hadn't found Forood in there, but he had found Xavar and given her a voice.

***

JOINT COMMITTEE INTERROGATION CENTRE, WINTER 1984

Happy birthday to our little daughter, from you and me.

Love, Xavar.

She has your forehead and eyes, and my nose and lips. She's beautiful. I wish Mahvash was alive and could see her – she wanted very much to meet our Baran.

***

My love Azad, it has been a few days now since our little girl was born. You wouldn't believe it, but she's as lively as if she had not endured nine months in this place. She is hungry all the time and I don't have much milk to satisfy her, but she doesn't cry. All the other prisoners are interested in her and want to look at her. They know they shouldn't touch her because she couldn't stand too many hugs, but they sit beside her and watch her move her little fingers and laugh at her yawning.

I don't understand my feelings. I'm sad and yet I'm happy. I'm happy she's so full of life and so healthy, but at the same time I'm sad that the time I will have with her is going to be so brief. Looking at her, I feel strangely contented, but that feeling doesn't last long before I'm in agony that she'll have to grow up without her mother.

I was told by the guards that I'm going to have to give her up when my parents next visit. Yes, in a week's time I'll have to hand her over to my parents, and just thinking about it makes me cry. I have always looked forward to visiting hours, but now I wish my family weren't coming so soon. I'm not ready to lose her, and I don't want to die! I know that I can't look after her in here, but I wish I could keep her for a little while longer. It would mean I would live longer, too, and could give her all the love I possibly can, which is what we both need so much. She's part of me and it's very hard to let her go. I need time to prepare myself for this cruel separation, but they won't give me any time. I don't want

***

Eshg-e-man, I haven't been able to write for the past few days. I just needed to sit and watch our baby while she was still with me. Those days were my last with her, so every minute was invaluable. Then, six days ago, a guard took our child from my arms and gave her to my parents. At that moment, I was thrown into a state of mind I've never experienced before. I'm still in it. It was as if a hand reached into my chest and ripped out my heart. I was hypnotised by the sound of Baran crying as she was wrenched from the warmth of my body. Azizam, I don't know how to describe my feelings or what name I can give them. I feel as if I've been dropped down a deep well and I'm still at the bottom of it; no one can see or hear me, even though I can hear people walking above and can see their shadows passing overhead. I feel unutterably lonely, but I can't bring myself to speak to the other women. Some of them try to talk to me to keep me occupied and I watch their lips moving, but all I can hear is our baby, crying. I see her face and her tiny mouth waiting for milk. My painful breasts, full of milk, are craving for her. I feel as if I've lost a limb and the wound is unbearable.

When they met Baran, my parents seemed to be overjoyed and distraught at the same time. I think their tears were of both happiness at having a grandchild and sadness that her birth means they're about to lose me. Though we didn't talk about it, they must know I'll be executed now. I know this because for the last couple of visits they haven't even been able to pretend to be cheerful. They said you've asked me to name her and I told them the name I like is Baran. But, darling, see if this name makes sense to you when you meet our little girl. If it doesn't fit, choose another beautiful name for her. I like Baran because we both loved the rain and used to walk in it and breathe in its scent and kiss each other as we got wet. She's a rain child, so call her Rain, especially as my eyes are wet all the time these days. Since she was taken from my arms, I feel completely empty. When she was with me, she was asleep most of the time and woke up every couple of hours to feed. Every time I gave her my breast, she would first suck it with such urgency, and then after a few minutes the urgency would give way to a more relaxed sucking, with her eyes closed. She would soon tire but wouldn't let go of my breast. I'd stay in that position for a long time, looking into her face, my fingers caressing her head and watching her lips to see when she would start feeding again.

When she was with me, I was exhausted from lack of sleep. I never left her alone, keeping her beside me at all times whether she was awake or asleep. During the night, I would worry about falling asleep and suffocating her. During the day, my cellmates would tell me to sleep for a couple of hours while they looked after her. But knowing how soon I was going to lose her, I didn't want to miss a single minute of our time together.

Eshg-e-man, during those precious days, I wasn't even aware of my surroundings. I vaguely recall prisoners taking away my dirty clothes and Baran's nappies and bringing them back clean. I would thank them, but I don't think I understood fully what was happening around me. Now I realise I could not have coped without their help, as I was too exhausted from keeping our little girl fed and staying awake to watch her. These women helped me so much, but in a strange way I can't bear being with them any more. It's as if they've replaced my child, and I find it hard to engage with them, or with anyone else.

Now I exist in this cold place and I don't notice all these women. A single image sits in my mind's eye, the vision of our daughter clinging to me, and it makes me cry. During the few days that she was here, I felt different. Her dependency on me gave my life a new meaning. If her birth was the first shock, which we all experience, then this separation from me was the second, which she should never have had to endure. I imagine it must be very hard for her right now.

I wonder if you've seen her yet and how you feel. I'm not sure how much longer I'll be alive and whether I'll be allowed another visit from my parents. I would so love to see them and Baran just once more.

It feels strange that I don't know what you're doing. I can't imagine you at home or at work. I don't even know what your new home looks like. Whatever you do, wherever you live, I hope you're happy. I'm finding it increasingly hard to remember happier times. It seems that happiness isn't anything more than a word now. Worst of all, it's as if I've always been here and that the life that preceded it, and our relationship, is just a story; a love story that looks good written down, or in a film. But it did really happen, didn't it?

Living with a rope hanging over you or imagining the stones that are going to kill you, will make you go mad if you think about it. I prefer not to imagine such hideous things and instead to think about you and Baran, and yet thoughts of death

***

My love, they have taken me from the communal cell back to one of these small isolation cells. Cell number 7. One of this interrogation centre's many names is 'circle' and it seems as if my arrest will be coming full circle soon.

Azadam, since my trial I've been working on a stone and I've written your name on one side of it and Baran's on the other. I gave it to one of my cellmates who will send it to my parents. I've shown it to them during one of their visits. I've told them that it's for you and Baran. As I was finishing it, I thought about this stone that my hands have carved and what it means to me: a stone that I have sculpted, much like a stone that others will hurl at me to kill me. It's strange to think of the different uses for the same object, and for such different ends. The stones that will wound me could also be shaped and carved into things of beauty: necklaces, candleholders, vases. They could bring joy instead of great sadness.

I've discovered that the prisoner in the cell next to mine doesn't know how to use Morse code, so I've been teaching her, which has kept me busy. As I touch the cell walls to tap messages to my neighbour, I think about all the people over the years who must have touched them. How many prisoners have stared at them? How many hands have carved their names on to them? I can see the scars of time on these walls. There are holes and cracks everywhere. The walls don't talk, but I like to think they speak their own language through the words that are carved into them. The polish on the surface has almost disappeared and the walls are no longer smooth. I can read men's and women's names on the walls of the cell I'm in now, with different dates under them. I wonder how much longer these walls will witness torture.

Darling, why is it that after the people's uprising in 1978, this place wasn't raided and developed into something else, so that the new regime couldn't use it as an interrogation centre? Why didn't we transform it into a public place, such as a museum? If you live through another uprising, please ensure that people don't make the same mistake and leave the old prisons for the next regime to use as places of torture. At the same time, make sure that people do not destroy these prisons or compromise their identity by painting over the walls. I couldn't bear for history to be wiped out like this.

***

Faraz stopped reading and, as if reasoning with himself as much as with Xavar, he thought, I haven't destroyed your name. Your name is there and it's only a matter of removing the outer plaster to reveal Xavar engraved there, as it has been all these years.

***

Azizam, yesterday I was taken for interrogation. I didn't recognise the man's voice and so I knew it wasn't Ghulam. I was asked if I would like to confess my evildoing and finally collaborate with the state of god. He told me this was my last chance. As before, they wanted the names and addresses of people I used to know, as well as your whereabouts.

I said, 'I have nothing to say.'

'Fine. You'll receive half of your two hundred lashes now. And be ready early on Friday morning to be taken to execution by stoning, after you've had another hundred lashes for all your lies. You can tell the guards to call me if you change your mind and want to collaborate. I at least hope that the lashes and the pain you'll endure at your death will wash away some of your sins.'

I said nothing.

'Lie on the bed.'

I didn't move.

He pushed me on to the bed and fastened my hands to the frame while another person fastened my feet. Until then, I hadn't known that there was anyone else in the room and I wondered if it was Ghulam, but I couldn't say because he didn't speak at all.

My love, isn't stoning women to death a type of sadism? And since it's a collective action, exercised by men, it's a social, sadistic theatre of psychological and physical torture. I can't get rid of the image in my mind of one isolated man or woman buried half in the ground, braving the stones that are hurled at their head by a group of excited men shouting Allah o Akbar. My love, I imagine myself with blood running into my eyes, making it difficult to see what's happening and whether the stone-throwers are human beings. How easy it is to drain humanity from people via strict religion, laws or propaganda. I wonder how much longer this suppression will last.

Azadam, when I came back from the interrogation, as well as the pain in my back, I was very tired, as if a great weight rested on my shoulders. I lay down and couldn't stop thinking about Friday and what's going to happen to me. My mind was full of such harrowing thoughts. I was overwhelmed with physical and psychological pain and fell asleep. But when I woke up, I felt happy because of the dream I'd had.

In my dream, people were in the streets and demonstrating against the regime, while the Islamic Guards were shooting tear gas at them. People were burning anything they could find to counteract the effects of the tear gas. The scene was very similar to protests against the Cultural Revolution that took place over several days in front of Tehran University in 1980. In my dream, I was watching them happily from the window of a house, perhaps our house, and like my neighbours I was throwing down food and water to the demonstrators, who were mostly young. Then I realised they needed paper to burn to be able to open their eyes in the tear gas and so I dropped our 'archives' down to them. Do you know which newspapers I mean? The ones we bought every day and kept in the cupboard. The regime's newspapers with the names and sometimes pictures of the people who'd been executed. By the time I was arrested we had a big pile, but in my dream the cupboard was full of them. I threw them down to the young people, but instead of burning them they started to read them. Everyone in the whole street stood still and read the names of the previous generation who'd lost their lives fighting for freedom and equality. Then I saw Baran, our daughter, in the crowd, asking if anyone had seen her mother's name in the lists of executed prisoners. In my dream she was such a pretty young woman, with the same determination in her face that we both have. She was going from one group of people to the next, pleading with them to look for my name, and someone asked her in which year I'd been executed, and she turned in her red dress, which twisted around her body, and shouted back, '1984'.

My love, Baran's cry woke me up with a jolt. Please keep the newspapers for our Baran and if they publish my name, don't hesitate to let the next generation see it - or burn it, if it would ease their struggle! An uprising against this regime will happen. I know it will. It's no matter that I won't be around to witness it; I sense all the same that people will stand up again for their freedom and for what has been stolen from them in the name of god. I know that one day the regime will be forced to its knees by workers' strikes and the streets will be won by the people again, and I can see our daughter celebrating with everyone else. I can see this because I've learnt from history that all despotic regimes fall to their knees sooner or later. I hope that this time people will know what they want for the longer-term and not think only about overthrowing the regime. I hope they learn from our generation's mistakes.

My predicament has made me remember something I wanted to tell you. It'll be my final story. In 1974, one of my aunts went to see her daughter in France and when she came back and told us about the life there, she said, 'Whilst I was there, I could see what it means to live in 1974. And I realised that, here, we are living in 1947. How easy it is to travel back and forth in time through the simple act of crossing borders.' I would like to see her and tell her that since 1979 when the Islamic regime took power, to crush the revolution each year we have travelled back a century. So now we're living once again in the fourteenth century, which is why it's so acceptable to stone a woman to death. The same accusations - of not believing in god, or of having a relationship outside marriage - still stand. Originally, it was in the name of the Bible. Now it's happening in the name of the Koran.

My love, it's now Wednesday night and so I only have tomorrow left. Don't worry, I'm not scared of death. I only hate that it will take me away from you and our child.

***

Eshg-e-man, it's Thursday night and I realise now there'll be no final visit, no goodbyes. It's time to hide this notebook. I've already made a space for it, a little hole in the floor underneath the carpet that no one will find. I'll leave it there, knowing that part of me doesn't want you to read it and part of me wishes you could. I know how unlikely it is that you'll ever read these words, but I like to think that one day someone else might.

In the middle of last night, I woke to the sound of rain. I sat up and listened. It was the best music – the only music – I've heard these last few months. I felt such pleasure that it brought tears to my eyes. Listening to the drumming of the rain, I thought of you and our little Baran. Breathing in the smell of wet earth, I felt free for a few precious seconds. I was somewhere else, somewhere good. The sound of the rain spattering against the cell window took me to you and to our walks along the shore of the Caspian Sea. I could hear you saying, 'Listen: the sea is calling the river, she's giving him directions.' Oh, my love, did you hear me calling for you last night? What were you doing then? Were you asleep? Did you wake up to the sound of thunder and rain? Did you walk to the window, pull back the curtains, watch the rain and think of me? I'd better stop writing about this because I can't see the page any more. My eyes are misted with tears.

My love, you could think of me as the flame of a candle. But I don't want to be a solitary candle blown out by the wind; I want to be one flame in a big fire that cannot be put out even by a storm. I want to be a sea of fire, an uncontrollable burning forest. Yes, I long to be with others who are also isolated, so that we can be as one and confront power, any power, and usher in a just world.

My love, last night when the rain stopped I fell asleep again. I woke up early this morning with the feeling I had been with you and so I stayed awake, not wanting to lose that feeling.

Now I feel cold. I know it's winter, but this cold is different from the cold I used to feel when we walked in the snow or were buffeted by a cold wind. Here, it's as if they've already buried me in a grave. You should know that I'm not sorry - not for myself, at least. If I had to live again, I would travel the same route. I'm only sorry for our little girl, who couldn't choose her parents. What has she done to deserve a fate that's going to separate her forever from her mother?

I sense the rain has turned to snow. I'm sure I can smell it. I wish I could see it. I imagine watching the snow from the window of our living room. I imagine each snowflake that passes the covered window of the cell I'm in, as well as the snow falling where you are right now. Are you watching it? I wish I could join you and watch it with you as you put your hands around my shoulders and fill my heart. It must be dark now. If we were watching the snow together, we would see the way it contrasts with the blackness of the sky. I miss seeing snowflakes at night. They remind me of the stars.

It seems certain now that there'll be no last-minute reprieve. They really will take me away from you and my little girl and everyone else for ever. I'm going to have to abandon all these good women in this prison. I hope the news about me doesn't hurt you too much and you find respite from the pain of it in your love for our child. Remember, you must love her twice as much as other fathers to compensate for my absence. My love, don't tell her about me too soon. Let her grow up happy and tell her when she's strong enough to feel anger on my behalf, not sorrow. I know you'll do your best by her and so I can rest now, safe in the knowledge that my child – our child – is in good hands.

Before my execution they'll take my belongings and later they'll give them to my family, along with the name of the cemetery where I'll be buried. I guess they'll bury me in Khavaran: the graveyard for infidels. I'll leave my watch, but I won't stop it, because I don't want you to know what time they took me to be executed. I don't want you to feel sad at a particular time of day or night and be made to think about my death. I don't want you to live for ever more with that dismal anniversary. Although I'm sad I'm going to die, I'm not afraid of death. I'm not frightened – death will mean the end of pain for me. I just don't want to die so soon.

Azizam, now the time has come to hide these

final letters and face my fate, I don't like it. Death is staring me in the face now. How am I going to die? And does it matter how they kill me? Perhaps all I should hope for is the quickest, most painless death. But don't worry. Even if it's by stoning, I'll still struggle to keep my eyes open so I can see the men responsible. That way, I'll be visiting them every day and night for the rest of their lives. This isn't in revenge. No, my love, it's to stop them from continuing with this dreadful work. I want them to rethink their lives and to realise that they can't earn their living by torturing and killing people.

I wonder how our little Rain will be tomorrow. Will she feel the stones being hurled at my face? I'm afraid she'll carry for the rest of her life all the pain I'm about to go through. After all, she was inside me for so many months and I still feel I've lost part of me. She must feel the same. I only hope that she turns her scars to good use, to put an end to oppression and the killing of people.

I'm worried about how she'll feel tomorrow and whether you or my parents will understand her restlessness.

My love, whichever way they end my life, be with me. I'll be with you – and I'll be thinking of you both. Stay alive. Xavar.

Chapter Seventeen

THE SECRET LETTERS

Faraz had finished Xavar's notebook but stayed where he was on the sofa, unable to think or do anything. It was still dark when he heard his mother leave her bedroom. To avoid her, he turned off the light beside him and went upstairs to his room. He lay down beside Nasim. He was cold and wanted to cry. He had never felt like this before. He couldn't cope with the killing of Xavar. Or he needed time to adjust to it - for although it had happened twenty years before, the news had only just reached him. He knew that very many people had been executed, and were still being killed by the regime, but he felt as if he were losing a close friend.

***

Although there were still a few days before the school term restarted and Faraz could have gone to the interrogation centre and looked for more of Xavar's letters, or perhaps even for evidence of Forood, he went nowhere. After reading Xavar's last letter, he fell ill and couldn't get out of bed for several days, as if the pain in his mind was affecting his body. His parents and Nasim were concerned, but couldn't do much for him, except try to help him get stronger. Nasim sat beside him stroking his head and read to him whenever he asked her to.

'Bahram brought a birth certificate for me,' Nasim said one day when Faraz was starting to recover. 'And he gave me the address of a register office that will put last year's date on our marriage certificate.'

'Good. We have to marry next week, then. Where do you want to go for our honeymoon?'

'Anywhere, except prison.'

***

As Faraz started teaching again and engaged once more with his students, he slowly felt better. One day he went to see his grandmother.

'How good to see you. Are you all right? You seem to have lost weight.'

'I'm fine, Grandma. Sorry I couldn't come and see you these last few months.'

'Well, I was wondering why you hadn't been to visit since your birthday. It was unlike you, especially during the long summer holidays, when I usually see more of you. But you said you were working hard when you called. Now tell me, what were you doing? I've been wondering why your parents didn't want to talk about it. They really seemed not to be happy with you.'

Faraz looked at her as if searching for something and realised she had aged in the four months since he had last seen her. 'I don't want to tell you what my job was over the summer. At least not now,' he said. 'Not that I feel you won't trust me, but even talking about it upsets me. I need some time to get over it, but I'll tell you one day. I'd like to know what you think.'

'I'm sorry that whatever you did was distressing for you. You don't have to talk about it if it makes you upset.'

'However, I've brought you something. It's a special present.'

'What is it?' asked his grandmother curiously.

Faraz took out a small white-covered book from his inside jacket pocket and handed it to her. She took it and her eyes lit up as she read the title, 'The Secret Letters From X to A.' She examined the little book and said, 'Is it an illegal book?'

'It certainly is.'

'Who's it by?' she asked, excited.

'Xavar is the writer. But I don't want to tell you any more. You'll find out when you start reading it.'

'Thank you,' his grandmother said. 'Forood used to bring me opposition literature. He started bringing me books in plain white wrappers when the Shah was still in power. Later, I helped him distribute anti-Islamic regime literature. I still have some of the newspapers he gave me to read.'

They were silent for a while, each remembering moments they'd shared with Forood, the boy they had both loved.

'Can I ask you something, Grandma?'

'Sure. Go ahead.'

'Do you miss Rohulah?'

Faraz saw his grandmother look away from him towards Forood's picture on the wall. It was a while before she started to speak.

'Of course I've missed my boy, as I've missed Forood. I lost the son and the grandson that I loved most, both at the same time.'

Faraz was watching her, puzzled.

'I named him Rahim, one of the names of god. He changed his name to Rohulah when Khomeini came back from exile. I never liked him taking Khomeini's first name and I continued calling him Rahim, but still it didn't matter much. After all, he had taken another name of god. But that was the start of his being born again. I didn't realise at the time, that I was gradually losing my son Rahim. Then the day came that I woke up and discovered that Rohulah had sacrificed his own son for his foolish fantasies. Like so many people, I too needed to see the "state of god", to understand what all these so-called religions are about. As Forood so aptly put it, the story of god is the oldest fantasy and it has divided people the most.'

She was silent. Faraz couldn't ever remember calling his uncle Rahim or having heard anyone call him by that name. As if Rahim had died for everyone as he had for his mother, they always addressed him as Rohulah.

'My answer to your question is that, no, I don't miss Rohulah,' his grandmother continued. 'He is not my son. I lost my son when he let his own son be killed.'

After a few moments she added, 'Sometimes, I feel it was my fault that he became like that.'

'But he isn't the only one who did. You shouldn't feel responsible for how he turned out,' Faraz said quickly. He couldn't bear the thought that she blamed herself.

'I loved him so much, too much. He was born after ten children who died soon after birth or were stillborn.

So, to me, he was a god, not a child that god had sent me. I spoiled him. I gave him anything he wanted, if I could afford it, of course. I gave him the best share of the food. It didn't matter to me if I went hungry. Your grandfather was a bricklayer when we married, and we didn't have much to eat, but I made sure Rahim never went without. Later on, your grandfather was able to train as a mechanic, which improved our life a bit. I helped my family by knitting our winter clothes and sometimes I would knit for neighbours and they gave us things like rice in return.'

She fell silent, looking at Faraz's father's picture on the wall.

'Even when your father was born five years later, though I was very happy, the love I had for your uncle didn't change. It was as if he had made it possible for me to have another child as well.'

'Grandma, right or wrong, in every household there are favourite children. You did your best for your children. You know you did. And after losing so many of them, of course he was precious to you. You mustn't blame yourself for giving so much love to him. I'm just sorry that all that love seemed to get buried inside him and he wasn't able to give it back to Forood or to others.'

'I often wonder what else contributed to his upbringing, apart from poverty, of course. I can't help it, but I feel I'm a failure.'

'You're wrong, Grandma! *He* is responsible for who he is or what he does, not you.'

***

Faraz opened his in-box and saw an email from his brother, Omid. His first thought was that it must be another hate letter.

I'm sorry you haven't been well. I wanted to hear your voice, but Mother said you were asleep. People are sharing some letters on the internet, which it seems are from a woman who was held in that place where you were working. I wonder if you've read them, or know about the writer? Can you write to me about it?

Faraz read and re-read Omid's email. There was no swearing in it. *Why?* he wondered. Did Omid think that Faraz, a collaborator, had posted Xavar's letters on the net? Is that why he had written kindly to him? Faraz clicked on the reply and wrote a long email, as if he were writing to himself. He didn't send it, but he felt better. As if it was now his turn to torture his brother with passive aggression: silence.

Chapter Eighteen

THE MUSEUM OF WARNING, JANUARY 2003

Faraz's uncle called at the house to invite him to the opening of the Ebrat Museum.

'Since you worked there, I thought you might like to be present at the launch.'

'Oh. Yes. Thank you.'

'I'll pick you up, then, and we can go together. You should feel proud.'

Although he knew his family would be unhappy about it, Faraz didn't want to miss this final opportunity to get into the interrogation centre.

'Does it never occur to you that you've gone too far with this job?' Nima asked him.

Faraz said nothing.

'The President will inaugurate the museum and there'll be hundreds of cameras. This is history, my son, and your picture will be up there with the collaborators. Doesn't it bother you? You may be able to ignore the whitewash that's been carried out, but you can't hide your presence at the opening of this so-called museum.'

Faraz flushed, yet he said nothing.

'I'm sorry for speaking so directly but I always thought you were going there to look for signs of Forood. You said you never found anything. So I don't understand why you have to go back now, with all the cameras around, to mark this awful occasion.'

'I might see parts of the building that I wasn't allowed into before.' Faraz was conscious that his fixation on Xavar and her story had deflected him from his original purpose: the search for Forood.

'If they didn't let you see them then, they're hardly going to let you wander around now. You should give this more thought. Your interest in seeing inside this interrogation centre is morbid. You never liked your uncle. I don't understand why you work for him.'

'I don't work for him, Father,' said Faraz, stung.

***

Rohulah's driver stopped in front of the green gateway, which now had a large sign over it in Farsi, English and Arabic: Ebrat Museum of Iran. They had sat in silence all the way, but as his driver got out to open the door for him, Rohulah told Faraz to wait. He motioned the driver to stand away from the car and closed the door.

'Did you speak to your grandmother?'

'Yes.'

'What did she say? Would she like me to go and see her?'

'No,' Faraz said.

'What did she say, exactly?' Rohulah's face was taking on its stony look.

'She said, "Rohulah is not my son". She said, "I lost my son Rahim when I lost my grandson Forood."'

Faraz watched as his uncle's jaw quivered and the colour drained from his face. He could see how hard Rohulah was trying to control himself and not show any emotion. Faraz remembered the day he had found Xavar's final letter and Rohulah had been lying in wait for him outside the cell. He recalled his rambling self-justification. After a few moments, his uncle seemed to pull himself together and opened the door. As they walked towards the green entrance of the newly christened museum, he was the usual Rohulah.

The place had been transformed since Faraz's last day at work there. On either side of the door, on the walls, there were new pictures of the inside of the prison. They still had to step over the barrier to walk through, but in the courtyard, they could now see the luxurious car that had belonged to Nasiri, the head of the Shah's secret intelligence agency, SAVAK.

Once inside the building, Faraz saw that the walls were covered with pictures of some of those who had spent time as prisoners or guards during the Shah's regime.

He had no idea who the dignitaries were, who had gathered for the opening ceremony, but their way of talking and their clothes confirmed that they were all high officials, the wealthiest class in Iran. They had come to see the transformation of the place where all opposition to their despotism and greed had been stamped out.

Rohulah introduced Faraz to some of them, until they all had to stand to attention for the arrival of President Khatami, who shook hands with a few people. Faraz wondered what Khatami would say if someone somewhere asked him about the Islamic Republic's use of the interrogation centre in which they were standing, to torture critics of his own regime. No doubt he would deny that they ever tortured anyone, or indeed ever used this place. The Shah had said exactly the same, that there were no political prisoners. How ironic that Khatami propounded an expansion of international dialogue and that the United Nations had proclaimed 2001 the UN 'year of dialogue among civilisations', at his suggestion. Of course, Khatami proposed dialogue – so that the great powers could learn from each other how to squeeze people harder. Hundreds of dissidents, workers and political activists - as well as writers - were murdered, mostly during the 1990s. In December 1998, Faraz's parents had been shocked to hear that the bodies of Mohammad Mokhtari and Mohammad Jafar Pouyandeh had both been found, strangled. Nima and Ana particularly loved these two writers, who were also poets and translators. Yet they were only two out of many who were killed in the operation that became known as the 'Chain Murders'. Khatami was now in his second term. He had always said he would bring to trial those who had committed the Chain assassinations, but he never did. No one was ever arrested. In reality, Khatami worked as the lubricant for both factions of the regime, the hardliners and the reformists, in order to keep it going.

Now the President was shown around the museum in order to see for himself that all signs of its use by the Islamic Republic had been erased. Cameras documented the entire tour. The various functions that would have taken place in the prison were recreated using waxwork dummies and red paint. They passed a room that had been got up to represent the cell of the current leader, Khamenei, imprisoned during the monarchy. There was a picture of Khamenei in his youth on the wall, with information about his arrest and the time he spent in the interrogation centre. Then they saw a model of a man with bound hands and feet and blood pouring from his mouth. They continued past a replica of a man with his feet bleeding, and the President shook his head. Looking at the bleeding feet, Faraz wondered painfully whether Forood had endured this kind of torture, knowing only too well that it was what Xavar had gone through. He shivered involuntarily and at once became conscious of how his reaction might seem to those around him.

The cells used for solitary confinement displayed images of the leader of the Islamic regime, and the Islamists who fought to bring it into being. There was an image of a young interrogator, Arash, dragging a woman by her hair. The inscription said he had committed suicide at the age of 29. Near the cells there was a narrow corridor, labelled 'visiting area'. In the middle of this corridor a waxwork guard stood on duty with, on one side, the model of a prisoner and, on the other, a waxwork woman and child. The last room shown to visitors was the bathroom, with mannequins of prisoners standing in a queue. There was a disturbing audio-tape of shouting guards mixed with the sound of running water. Each prisoner, they were told, had three minutes to take a shower.

As Faraz had expected, the museum dealt only with the time of the monarchy, although even that was distorted. It focused exclusively on the Islamists presently in power, whereas in reality they had been in the minority of those held and tortured here during the Shah's time. The museum had airbrushed from history the incarceration of many other political prisoners who had suffered there, including Marxists and different Islamic groups. He thought of the name, Ebrat, that they had chosen for the museum, which served the concept behind all this theatrical propaganda. As in public executions or the theatre of suppression, the spectators were the primary reason for its existence: to spread fear. This so-called museum was a warning to its visitors, to frighten them about what would happen if they attempted to struggle for their rights.

Faraz tried to remain calm, always looking for a chance to escape to the parts of the building that were still hidden from public view. He wanted to see the wings he hadn't managed to get to, where male prisoners had been kept during the Islamic regime. Even at this late stage, he was anxious to find some trace of Forood, although it felt like hunting for a needle in a haystack.

When he became aware that his uncle was attending to some other people, Faraz slipped through a side door. He found himself in another corridor, but before he could go any further, a man had swiftly followed him and asked if he needed anything.

'Yes, I need to go to the toilet.'

'It's not this way. Come with me and I'll show you.'

As they re-entered the crowded hall, the man locked the door behind them.

Faraz trailed along the official itinerary, unnerved by his failed bid for freedom, but as he caught up with the presidential party he realised with a jolt that they had come to a place that was most personal to him: the very wing on which he had worked. Khatami reached cell number 7, but he walked past without bothering to look inside, as if to say he'd seen enough. Faraz felt his blood boil. It was in this cell that Xavar had spent the last few days before her execution. It was in this cell she had written her final letter. He wanted to shout loudly that if they pulled away the carpet they would find a secret hiding place, concealed by a pair of Xavar's socks. Then he thought, *No, those bloodsuckers don't deserve to know these things. They should continue to live their lives in a balloon of lies, until the day their balloon is burst by the people. Until that day, Xavar's socks should stay hidden as evidence-in-waiting.* Though Faraz managed to bite his tongue, and despite the fact he had failed to make it to any of the wings to look for Forood or for signs of other prisoners, he wasn't sorry to have come to their show tonight. He felt invigorated by his clear and present anger, which now gave him a new purpose in life: to find ways of fighting injustice, just as Xavar and Azad had done.

When the tour of the museum was over, the President stood near the small blue pond in the yard, now filled with chlorinated water in his honour, eating pastries with his men, apparently relaxed and untroubled. Faraz looked up and saw effigies of prisoners on the SS-emblazoned grilles, as if they had been crucified there. It was as if the grief of the presidential party had been merely for the cameras. In reality, they were celebrating the fact that all evidence of torture during their time in power had been removed, and that no one could claim that the place had continued to be an interrogation centre throughout twenty years of Islamist rule.

Looking into the President's face, Faraz thought, *you deleted part of what innocent people wrote on the walls of this building, but you can't delete their words from the internet, where they will spread beyond your control!*

Chapter Nineteen

FARAZ AND NASIM, FEBRUARY 2003

Since their marriage, Nasim and Faraz liked to spend time outside together and they often went for evening walks when Faraz came home from work. One evening, they went out to celebrate the anniversary of their first meeting, a romantic candlelit dinner at the Art Cafe, which had become Nasim's favourite restaurant, too. That evening they were very happy and returned home well after Nima and Ana were in bed.

But later that night, Faraz was woken by someone gently shaking his shoulder. It was his father looking down at him through the darkness, his finger to his lips indicating that he must be quiet.

'What is it?'

Nasim also woke up and immediately got out of bed and started to dress.

'Two cars full of Islamic Guards are sitting out there, just a few metres from our house. It seems they're waiting to arrest you when you leave in the morning. Here, I've packed a backpack. There's clothes, money and your passport, which I'm not even sure you can use. You'll have to get out on to the roof. Go quickly. Now.'

'I don't understand.' Faraz was still half-asleep. 'Why

do you think the guards are waiting to arrest *me*? And how did you even notice them?'

'Your uncle came to the house last night, while you were out. You were so late back, I thought I'd tell you in the morning. He said he was just passing and wanted to say hello to you, but it was so out of character that I felt there was something more to his visit. That's why I couldn't sleep. I was watching the road when the cars pulled up. I feel sure they're here for you,' said Nima anxiously.

'Why d'you think that? Did my uncle say something?'

'He asked me if you were going away.'

'What did you say?' asked Faraz.

'I said not that I knew of. But I felt sure he was warning us,' Nima said. 'He looked out over the garden for a long time while we sat in silence and then he said, "It would be good if Faraz went away to get some rest after all the work he's done at the museum." Then he shut up. I didn't know what to say. Before he left, he told us this country isn't safe for anyone any more.'

'So does this mean he's joined the reformists, the group of criminals who are losing power? Is that why he doesn't feel safe any longer?'

'I don't think he was talking about himself,' said Nima firmly. 'He was talking about you.'

'Father, Uncle Rohulah didn't save his own son, so why is he now trying to protect me?' argued Faraz.

'Times have changed, Faraz. Twenty years have passed since he let them kill Forood. He's rich now and doesn't need them. He's also getting old, so he might have realised that what he did was wrong and perhaps, by saving your life, he's trying to make amends for what happened to his son. After all, Forood was your age when they killed him. I don't know what's been going on, but if you think you're in any danger you have to escape now. Don't let them arrest you, or kill you and dump your body, like they did to Pouyandeh and the others.'

'Where's Mother?' asked Faraz, his head in turmoil.

'She's keeping an eye on the road and those vehicles,' his father told him. 'My boy, I don't know what you've done. But it seems they have something against you and your uncle was warning us. You must go now. You can come back if they don't knock on our door tomorrow. We'll soon find out if it's you they're waiting for.'

Nasim, who had been silent up to now, said quietly, 'I think your father's right. The cars must be for you. They're waiting because they don't want to cause a disturbance in the middle of the night and alert the neighbours.'

Faraz gripped Nasim's hands. 'I can't leave you here. They'll arrest you for being an accomplice and keep you hostage.' *Just as they did Xavar,* he thought to himself, but didn't say.

'Then the two of you must go together,' said Nima.

'How can you jump over the roofs? You're six months pregnant!' Faraz's voice was choked.

'I'll try to keep up. You must let me come. And I can hide in someone's house if I'm too slow, so don't worry. It's better that we at least try to escape,' pleaded Nasim.

He knew she was right, painfully aware that, like Xavar's, Nasim's wedding certificate was a fake. It could get her stoned to death for adultery.

'Before I go and fetch your mother to say goodbye,

will you at least tell me why they're after you?' Nima begged him.

'Search the internet for the name Xavar. You'll soon find out what I've done. I'm sorry I didn't tell you. I just didn't want you to worry about me. Xavar is the name of a woman who was imprisoned. What you will find online is the diary she kept during her imprisonment under the Islamic regime. I found it, bit by bit, in a series of different notebooks, hidden at the interrogation centre. Thanks to what we've done, everyone can read her now.'

His father was gazing at him, confused, fearful of losing his son to the Islamic Guards. 'Then, in that case, there's something else.'

'What, Father?'

'As your uncle was leaving, before he closed the door, he said, "Tell Faraz that the whole wing will be re-done soon." I asked him what did he mean by that, and why? And he replied, "Faraz knows what I mean. It's something between us." So what's that about?'

'The guards are outside. We must go. But I've only actually erased the writing from two of the cells. I preserved all the rest in that wing by covering the walls with plaster and paint, which could be taken off one day to expose the history they wanted to wipe out. It was simply too precious. I couldn't get rid of it! I'm sorry they've found out about it. They'll destroy it now.'

His father hugged him. 'I love you, my son.'

Ana entered the room and, seeing Nasim packing, too, asked, 'You're not going, are you?'

'I'm sorry, Mother, but we both have to go,' Faraz told her.

'Don't worry, I'll be fine,' Nasim said, hugging her.

'Why are they after you?' Ana's face was tight with fear and confusion.

Nima said, 'I'll explain afterwards. Our boy is a good boy, Ana. That's why they both need to go. Right now, while it's still dark.'

Ana flinched. 'How shall we know if you're all right?'

'I'd better not call you. They'll be able to trace us if I do. I'll get a message to Bahram and he'll call from a public phone and let you know. He won't use his real name, but you know his voice.'

'Okay, but they'll search for you tomorrow,' Nima warned.

'Don't worry. Payam's house isn't far away. We'll be there before daybreak and we'll stay a few days, until we find a safe way to get out of the country.' There was a catch in Faraz's voice. He felt like an exile already.

'Wear your black coats,' Ana said. 'So they can't see you in the dark.'

'I don't have one. Mine's red!' Nasim wailed.

'You can wear mine.' Ana rushed out of the room to fetch her new overcoat for Nasim.

Faraz lifted their rucksack and hugged his mother. 'Forgive me if I hurt you.'

'You haven't hurt me. Take care of each other,' Ana said, her voice shaky.

Faraz and Nasim followed Nima and Ana to the corridor and up the stairs that led to the roof.

'Don't forget to wipe the computer after you've read Xavar's notebooks. They'll search the house,' Faraz whispered as he kissed them both again.

He clutched his parents' hands for a moment. Then he opened the door.

Faraz and Nasim set out across the roof, turning just once to wave goodbye to Ana and Nima. As they jumped over to the next house, their neighbour woke up and turned on the light. Nima hissed at him to switch it off, and the neighbour asked, 'What's going on?'

It was as they reached the third roof that gun shots rang out and they heard the sound of a car starting. But Faraz and Nasim didn't look back. They dodged from one roof to the next and, since they knew the area so well, they took routes no cars would be able to follow.

The End

GLOSSARY

Xavar: East
Azad: Free
Azadam: My Azad
Nima: Just, fair
Nasim: Breeze
Omid: Hope
Faraz: Elevation, high
Bahram: has several meanings, including the planet Mars
Ebrat: Warning
Kashk: Whey
Ghulam: Slave
Rohulah: God's spirit
Eshg-e-man: My love
Azizam: Darling
Baran: Rain
Inshalah: God wants / wills
Jan: Dear
Peshmerga: Kurdish freedom fighter
Azadi: Freedom
Aziztarinam: My dearest
Mohr: is made of dried mud (from the Karbala), and some say its purpose is to show that worshippers approach god with humility, others that its significance is that it comes from the land where Muhammad prayed, and others again that it's simply because it is natural and

comes from the earth. There's no English translation, other than a 'praying stone'.

Mirzagasemi: An Iranian dish with aubergine and garlic.

Abgoosht: An Iranian dish made of meat, potato and beans.

Allah o Akbar: God is great

Payam: Message

Khavaran: A cemetery located in south-east Tehran. It was used as a graveyard for religious minorities, such as Christians and Bahais. Political prisoners executed during the 1980s were buried there and it is also a mass grave for prisoners executed in the 1988 mass-executions.

AFTERWORD

The writer of this novel spent six months of her eight years' imprisonment (1982-90) in the interrogation centre that is now known as the Ebrat Museum. All the events and places in this novel, such as the methods of torture, the prison buildings and the people who were incarcerated there, are based on her experience.

If you go to Iran, you can visit the Ebrat Museum, which was an interrogation centre for about twenty years during the Islamic regime.

The address is: Tehran, Imam Khomeini Square, Firdausi Street, Koshk Mesri Road, Rejaie Martyr Road, No, 18/1.

http://www.ebratmuseum.ir/Portal/Home/
https://www.facebook.com/EbratMuseumOfIran

AUTHOR'S NOTE

A few years ago, a friend of mine, the poet Hubert Moore, gave me a novel by John Berger, *From A to X: A Story in Letters*. He said to me: John Berger wrote letters to prison – can you write letters *from* prison? I told him that I'd think about it, and I couldn't get the idea out of my mind and so I embarked on this novel. Although my story is very different from John Berger's, I chose similar names for my main characters, using Iranian words.

ABOUT THE AUTHOR

Photograph: © Milan Svanderlik. London, UK.

Nasrin Parvaz became a civil rights activist when the Islamic regime took power in Iran. She was arrested, tortured and sentenced to death in 1982. Her sentence was commuted to ten years' imprisonment and she was actually released after eight years, in 1990. After her release, Nasrin resumed her activities and once again she found herself being followed by Islamic guards. She realised she could no longer stay in Iran and fled to England, where she claimed asylum in 1993. She was granted refugee status a year later, and has since lived in London.

Nasrin studied for a degree in Psychology and subsequently gained an MA in International Relations at Middlesex University. She then completed a Postgraduate Diploma in Applied Systemic Theory at one of the NHS Foundation Trusts, where she worked in a team of family therapists.

Nasrin has given talks on the violation of human rights in Iran, both in Farsi and in English, in several countries including Canada, Sweden, the UK and Italy. She talked at Leicester Secular Society (2018), Exiled Writers Ink, (2018), Bare Lit Festival (2016 and 2017), Southbank Centre (2015 and 2016), and for organisations such as Amnesty International, Cambridge PEN, the Medical Foundation, Saturday Forensic Forum (2013), Ledbury Poetry Festival and Eloquent Protest (2008). Nasrin's stories have been read at the Edinburgh International Book Festival.

NASRIN'S LITERARY AND ARTISTIC WORKS

- Nasrin's *One Woman's Struggle in Iran: A prison memoir* was published in Farsi in 2002, and in Italian in 2006 by Effedue Edizioni. It will now be published in English by Victorina Press.
- *Temptation* based on the true stories of a number of male prisoners who survived the 1988 massacre of Iranian prisoners was published in Farsi in 2008.
- Nasrin's poems and short stories are published in a number of different anthologies, such as: *Write to be Counted, Resistance Anthology, 2017; Over Land, Over Sea, Poems for those Seeking Refuge,* published by Five Leaves, in 2015. Her poems are published in *Live Encounters Magazine.*
- One of Nasrin's short stories, 'The Time of Assassinations', has been chosen as one of the highly-commended entries of the anthology *Words And Women: Four,* published by Unthank Books. Another of Nasrin's short stories, *A war against womanhood,* won the Women's World Award in 2003. In 2010, another short story was longlisted for the *Bristol Short Story Prize* and a third shortlisted for the *Asham Award.*
- Since 2005, together with poet Hubert Moore, Nasrin has translated some poems, prohibited in Iran, from

Farsi into English. They appear in the *Modern Poetry in Translation* series.

- Nasrin was the guest artist of Our Lives, in the 2018 Exhibition of Art by Foreign National Prisoners. Her paintings were accepted for inclusion in the exhibition's Calendar and for postcards.

ACKNOWLEDGEMENTS

I would like to thank Hubert Moore, writer Leslie Forbes, writer Jay Fejer, writer John Petherbridge, editor Ros Franey, playwright and Co-Artistic Director of Ice & Fire Theatre Sonja Linden, Gillian Balance and Sophia Brown for all their support.